Praise for *Table for One*

'A fast-paced, funny, touching, and nuanced story about smart young women who are all trying to figure out how to be themselves, while simultaneously struggling with the problems inherent to marriage, motherhood, singlehood, and purpose . . . In a culture that demands women be everything and nothing – all at the same time – Emma Gannon's novels shine a light on this moment, on this generation' ELIZABETH GILBERT

'It's a fabulous read: such a refreshing idea, deliciously unpredictable with a story that gripped me from the start. I found it uplifting and inspiring, and thought-provoking. Solo Power!' RUTH JONES

'I loved this . . . *Table for One* is a funny, warm yet galvanising read. It's a reminder about sublimating our needs to others, and taking care of ourselves' JENNIE GODFREY

'Joyful and affirming, the love – of life, friends, the unexpected, and oneself – just radiates from the pages. This is a dopamine hit of a book that'll also open your heart' CLAIRE DAVERLEY

'A reflection of online living and the tension between the externally perfect and inwardly fraught, hitting home how impossible it is to tell the story of a life behind a screen. It was lovely how these two women found and mirrored something back at one another' ABIGAIL BERGSTROM

'Reading *Table for One* was like slipping into a warm bath after a stressful week. It asks us to question what it is that we are working towards – and whether that is what we really want' CAL FLYN

'A sparkling revelation about the joy of choosing yourself, *Table for One* reminds us that the most important relationship we'll ever have is with ourselves. Emma Gannon has written a delicious celebration of solitude that left me hungry for more' FREYA BROMLEY

'Warm, generous, witty and so wise on the tension between societal pressures and ploughing our own furrow. This was a pleasure to dine with' LAUREN BRAVO

TABLE FOR ONE

EMMA GANNON is the *Sunday Times* bestselling author of eight books, including her latest non-fiction, *A Year of Nothing*, and *Olive*, her debut novel, which was nominated for the Dublin Literary Award. Emma also runs the popular newsletter, The Hyphen, hosts creativity retreats all over the world, and she is a judge for the 2025 Women's Prize for Non-Fiction.

When she isn't meeting friends or connecting with fellow book lovers, Emma can often be found exploring London or new cities, happiest in a café with a book in her hands – at her very own table for one.

emmagannon.co.uk
@emmagannonuk
thehyphen.substack.com

Also by Emma Gannon

FICTION
Olive

NON-FICTION
Ctrl Alt Delete
The Multi-Hyphen Method
Sabotage
Disconnected
The Success Myth
A Year of Nothing

TABLE FOR ONE

Emma Gannon

HarperCollins*Publishers*

HarperCollins*Publishers* Ltd
1 London Bridge Street
London SE1 9GF

www.harpercollins.co.uk

HarperCollins*Publishers*
Macken House, 39/40 Mayor Street Upper
Dublin 1, D01 C9W8, Ireland

First published by HarperCollins*Publishers* Ltd 2025

1

Copyright © Emma Gannon 2025

Emma Gannon asserts the moral right to
be identified as the author of this work.

A catalogue record for this book is available from the British Library.

ISBN: 978-0-00-838276-6 (HB)
ISBN: 978-0-00838269-8 (TPB)

This novel is entirely a work of fiction. The names, characters and
incidents portrayed in it are the work of the author's imagination.
Any resemblance to actual persons, living or dead, events or
localities is entirely coincidental.

Set in Berling LT Std by HarperCollins*Publishers* India

Printed and bound in the UK using 100%
Renewable Electricity at CPI Group (UK) Ltd

All rights reserved. No part of this publication may be reproduced,
stored in a retrieval system, or transmitted, in any form or by any means,
electronic, mechanical, photocopying, recording or otherwise,
without the prior written permission of the publishers.

Without limiting the author's and publisher's exclusive rights, any
unauthorised use of this publication to train generative artificial intelligence
(AI) technologies is expressly prohibited. HarperCollins also exercise their
rights under Article 4(3) of the Digital Single Market Directive 2019/790 and
expressly reserve this publication from the text and data mining exception.

This book contains FSC™ certified paper and other controlled
sources to ensure responsible forest management.

For more information visit: www.harpercollins.co.uk/green

to those who crave solitude

Part One

1

THEN

November 2021

Dom paused in front of the door of our new home to sweep me up into his arms and carry me across the threshold like a bride – although I was wriggling around so hard he couldn't keep me in his arms for long. I'd taken off my shoes, and he was somehow carrying those, too. It was just how I'd imagined it would be. *Click.* Picture perfect.

Two years ago now.

'We'll have to paint this,' he said, putting me down and gesturing at the smart but dull magnolia hallway wallpaper. 'Maybe some kind of sage green?'

'Like Scatterbox *brand colours*, you mean?' I swatted him away jokingly. 'Do you ever think about anything else?'

Scatterbox was the newish tech company we were building together and it was doing really well; it was the reason we could afford the move. (That and Dom's parents' little cash injection.)

He laughed. 'I just like that colour! And I want to go full Alan Titchmarsh. Prune the garden, paint everything, put up pictures, get a birdfeeder even . . . Thank god we're not in studentsville any more.'

I couldn't believe it either. Dom and I were finally moving into our dream house in Brockley in south London after three years in a dingy one-bed flat in a Homerton tower block. This little house was perfect for us. The previous owners had recently renovated, but then they got pregnant with their second child and wanted to move quickly. We got a good deal because they were in such a rush. We loved what they had done with it. It had grey stone herringbone bricks on the patio, a gorgeous navy-coloured kitchen, a garden big enough to have a few friends round for a barbecue, two spacious bedrooms and two good-sized bathrooms. No more going down in a shabby lift every time we wanted to get a parcel. No more hefting fold-out chairs from under the bed every time we wanted to have someone round for dinner at our tiny kitchen table. No more hostile flats either side, no more loud students or police sirens every five minutes. Now, our neighbours were young couples with kids roaming around on miniature bikes, on our very own street. It screamed 'early thirties', and we were proud. I posted a selfie of us on Instagram with our keys, with the key emoji.

'Think of all the thigh muscles I'm going to get now that I will go up *actual* stairs,' I said.

'There's so much *space*,' Dom replied, smiling, opening his arms wide and then folding me into his arms again.

There was a knock at the door, and a delivery driver handed over a long, flat parcel. When I ripped it open, a note fluttered out:

You know what they say: couples who plan together, stay together ;)
Happy housewarming, you two!
Pen x
PS – I've filled in a few already

Inside the parcel was a wall calendar with beautiful abstract paintings of seascapes and a page per month for the next three years. Some of the dates had already been scrawled on in black marker: *International Women's Day, Veganuary, Annual seaside trip, Pen's birthday! (V important day)*.

I laughed and showed it to Dom, who unearthed some old Blu Tack from a box in his man drawer and stuck it up on the kitchen wall. Our first piece of 'art' in our new home. It was perfect, and I felt that warm sensation in my belly of feeling understood by a close friend.

We couldn't face unpacking our kitchen boxes just yet, so we ordered a delicious eighteen-inch pepperoni pizza and ate it on the floor. The house was cold, and we hadn't figured out the heating system, but we didn't care. We had a cosy mattress on the floor in our bedroom, and we cuddled like penguins in our new linen sheets, our feet interlocking. We were just so happy to be together, embracing a new chapter after so many years as a couple. Everything was exactly as it should be.

The next morning, stretched out in the newly cleaned porcelain bath (we'd only had a drippy shower caked in limescale in the old flat), I checked my phone, and amidst all the nice texts from friends congratulating me on being a new home-owner, there was an email from a recruiter, via LinkedIn. It caught my eye. The subject line was: *How does New York sound to you?* Scatterbox was thriving, and therefore I usually had people emailing me to apply for jobs at my company, not the other way round. This message felt like a blast from the past; the first approach I'd had for ages from the world of my previous career, as a magazine writer.

From: Hassan <Hassan@Recruiters4you.co.uk>
To: Willow <willowjones@hotmail.com>

Hi there Willow,

We've been reading through a lot of the work that is available on your website, and we think you could be the ideal candidate for a new role fresh on the market, which we are looking to place quickly. Elaine Jefferson put a good word in for you.

We can't give too many details yet, but we can say that it is for a big New York-based publication, a globally iconic brand, and the salary would be very competitive. The relocation would be supported by the company (i.e. accommodation and visa sponsorship).

If you'd like to hear more, please do email or call me asap.

Regards,
Hassan

I was surprised to have received it. My weekly copywriting for the Scatterbox website was hardly in-depth investigative journalism. For a split second, I allowed my imagination to wander. *New York!* A 'globally iconic brand'. *The New Yorker? Forbes? The New York Times?*

I thought of the trip Carla and I had been on to New York to celebrate my twenty-seventh birthday. The huge breakfasts, the smell of pretzels on the sidewalk. Bagelsmith for hot coffee and eggs 'sunny side up'. Toasted bagels with lox and cream cheese. The good-looking bald man who worked there. The choice of different bagels: plain, everything, poppy seed, blueberry, cinnamon, sesame, cheddar. Roaming around Whole Foods, spotting an actor from *The (American) Office*. Evenings out at Carnegie Hall. Walks along the waterfront at Domino Park. Cocktails on rooftops. Ice cream in little tubs on the walk home with the orange sun low in the sky. One of my favourite cities in the world.

I burst the bubble quickly and shook the thoughts away. It was a silly daydream. It couldn't happen now. I already had the life I wanted, the one I'd worked for. I was a co-founder now. Everything was slotting into place.

I deleted the email. *Whoosh*. Into the little bin in the corner of my screen.

I had just moved into my dream house with Dom.

He wanted to paint the walls sage green.

We'd finally got our dream sofa from Loaf.

I'd bought a doormat on Etsy that said *welcome home*.

This was my path.

2

CUT TO NOW

Dom walks into the kitchen, suited and booted for an important investor meeting. I have made him scrambled eggs with a dash of butter and milk, just how he likes it. Usually, he is up and out by six a.m., but he lay in a little longer today.

'All right, Britney?' I say, nodding at his Bluetooth headset – although my aunt Carla would say it's actually Kylie Minogue who started the headset mic trend first. Dom's so busy building our company to the next level that he hardly takes it out these days.

'I'm knackered.' He sighs. No time to laugh. 'I was up 'til two a.m. talking to Australia.'

He is quickly eating forkfuls of egg out of the pan. No time for toast or even a plate. He catches a bit of rogue egg with his hand. He barely has time to chew and swallow.

It's crunch time at the moment; he's raising more investment for Scatterbox. It's been three years now since we clicked 'live' on the website, when we were cooped up in our tiny flat during the pandemic. Dom came up with the idea, and I came up with the name, slogans, and key messaging. We roped in a couple of Dom's uni friends too: Chad to do all the coding and Danny to set up our accounting software on Xero. I'd been a freelance journalist for a long time at that point and was itching for a new challenge. Dom had been furloughed from his trend forecast job at an agency and used his knowledge and spare time to find a gap in the market. He'd realized that online shopping had become a chore. The overwhelming number of choices was making people anxious, and being targeted by constant ads made any online searching feel like a battlefield. But consumers still needed that dopamine boost of discovering the perfect item and having it arrive after just a few clicks.

On the Scatterbox app, you insert your age, size, and hobbies, and we send you or a friend a box of stuff suited to you for a monthly fee. Books, clothes, activities, tickets. It's astonishing how well the algorithm matches people's tastes and interests. Your 'mystery' box is full of all the things you'll absolutely love. It's like your Discover Weekly playlist on Spotify on a good day, where all the songs are perfect for you. In our five-star website reviews, people say it's 'creepy in a good way'. Our current tag line is: *Scatterbox knows you better than you know yourself.* These days, we're inundated with brands wanting in on the action, ever since a pair of handwarmer gloves went viral, sending the company's share price rocketing.

Dom walks around the house, tense in his straight-legged black trousers and box-fresh leather shoes, like an Action

Man doll with limbs that don't bend properly. He smooths his gelled hair and checks it in the mirrored kitchen cabinet, and turns to leave. He has doused himself in aftershave. That scent was the first thing I noticed about him when we first met ten years ago – not on a dating app, despite the fact I had active profiles on five of them, but at the summer barbecue my friend Alice was hosting with her partner, Luke. It felt so chic and old-school – the Millennial equivalent of meeting at 'a dance', while everyone else was swiping and clicking. He was drinking a cold bottle of Corona, then walked right up to me and started a conversation about films he loved. He was confident, normal, open.

Today, though, he has heavy bags under his eyes, red cheeks, and I feel a rush of sympathy for him. He's been working so hard. For us.

'Shall I make you a coffee in a flask before you go?'

'Thanks but am already late,' he says, looking at his watch.

'What's the dress code for tonight again?'

'Smart. I'm going to change into a nicer suit at the office.'

'Maybe I'll wear my French Connection black dress?'

'Yeah, great. Sounds lovely.' He gives me a little peck on the cheek. Scatterbox is up for a marketing award tonight, and we're attending the ceremony in central London.

'Gotta run. See you later, Wizz.' His nickname for me. He ruffles my hair and gives me another kiss.

'Good luck in the meetings.'

Dom used to invite me to all the meetings, but I never really enjoyed them anyway, so now I leave him to it – he is the front-of-house businessman, and I like being behind the scenes, working from home and barely going into the office these days, even though I do have a desk there. Dom is good in the limelight; I am not. I'm chief copywriter, in charge of branding and pitch decks. Now that Scatterbox has become genuinely popular, it's changed our lives, and we're working towards being bought out. Life at home is good. We have everything we need: we've upped our interiors game, making our Brockley abode totally perfect, splashing out on Farrow & Ball. And, last year, we went on the holiday of a lifetime: a trip to Sorrento, where we drank limoncello, overlooking the beautiful blue coast.

If only my past self, desperately filling in dating profiles and writing a WordPress blog, knew this is how I'd end up, she'd be so relieved. House, boyfriend, job, success.

Tick, tick, tick, tick.

Relief, relief, relief.

Dom picks up another call on his Bluetooth, gives me a last wave, and leaves the house. The front door slams, and I go upstairs into our bedroom to get an outfit ready for tonight's awards ceremony. I go over to my wardrobe and open it; my hand brushes over the thick material of the silver dress that I wore to my thirtieth birthday party and the short lemon dress I wore to Dom's second cousin's wedding seven years ago. I finger the slinky gold body-con I bought for Pen's thirtieth, which now looks tiny on the hanger. I briefly consider a zebra-patterned tunic I wore to a work event in Amsterdam, but in the end, I pull out the black French Connection midi I had in mind: a baggy sheath.

I rummage around under the bed for a pair of shoes, find

a pair of old, black wedge espadrilles. And then something catches my eye: a box labelled *festival gear*. I know it contains nothing useful: glittery make-up, costume jewellery, ancient heels, mad hats. Nevertheless, I open the dusty lid and pull out a big multicoloured sequinned cape and smile. Pen and I bought matching ones for Bestival on the Isle of Wight and wore them at Glastonbury, too. They got splashed with camp stove noodles and G&T tinnies, and they picked up as much mud as our wellies. But we refused to take them off, our sequinned capes blew like flags in the wind as we sang on strangers' shoulders. All that laughter and wild abandon. Our voices hoarse from all the singing.

All of that feels so far away now. I run my fingers over the fabric of the cape, try on one of the hats and strike a pose in the mirror. I'm smiling, but there's a cold sore forming at the corner of my mouth, a little hollow ache in my chest. When Dom and I agreed we'd focus first on building our business, then on moving house, then hopefully on growing a family, I felt so ready to say goodbye to that chapter of my life. Who has time for festivals and fancy dress? I was excited to leave our old student digs behind – the hangovers, the slugs in the kitchen, the horrible leather sofas – and become a proper person who went out for cosy Sunday roasts in pubs instead of downing tequilas 'til dawn.

For a wild moment, I imagine turning up to the awards in a glittery cape, even though I know it would draw attention that I don't want and probably embarrass Dom. Nothing much in my wardrobe fits me now; I've put on weight since working with the team on these recent pitch decks, consuming pizza, red wine, cheese, and chocolate as we work long into the night. I don't exactly *mind* the little round belly that wasn't there before, but it's certainly a reminder that my otherwise perfect lifestyle is making me tired and bloated.

I dial Carla's number and cram my phone between my ear and neck while I replace the hat and cape in their box. My fifty-five-year-old aunt. She calls me her daughter-niece.

'Hi, darling.'

'What are you up to?' I ask.

'Just having a cup of tea. I'm . . . bath!' she says, in her usual jolly way.

The line crackles slightly.

'You're having a bath?'

'No, I'm in BATH!'

'Oh! What are you doing there?'

'Exploring. With my friend Marta. Do you remember Marta? She remembers you. Says you peed yourself at her house once. When you were little, obviously. We went to the Jane Austen Centre yesterday. She reminds me of you.'

'Who does?'

'JANE does! Remember when I bought you that big quill from Daunt years ago? You *loved* that. You kept getting ink on the kitchen table and thought I'd be angry, but I didn't care! I just loved to see you scribbling away.'

'How was it?' I ask.

'Charming but overpriced. We went on a tour around a room full of pictures, and the guide kept saying "although sources *say* it's Jane Austen, it might not be Jane", and I thought, I've just paid money to look at random pictures of women who might not even be Jane Austen!' She starts laughing. 'Anyway, what are you up to, sweetheart?'

'I'm about to try on some dresses for the awards thing tonight.'

'Oh yes! Start-Up of the Year. Congratulations!'

'We haven't won it yet! There are six of us shortlisted.'

'Wonderful!'

'I feel bloated.'

'Oh, you've no doubt reached the luteal phase of your monthly cycle.'

A very Carla comment. She is very into moons, patterns, and cycles.

'I'm sure you will get through it just fine. I'll rub my lucky gold Buddha for you and do a prayer when I light my candles tonight.'

'Award ceremonies are kind of weird though, aren't they? The other day, I used a loo in King's Cross that won "loo of the year" and thought it was a bit sad: the idea of grown adults dressing up in their finery and having a three-course meal to celebrate "Britain's best loos".'

Carla laughs. 'But this isn't best loos, darling. This is best start-up. Do you know anyone else who'll be there?'

'Alice and Luke are going.'

'Oh, lovely, lovely Alice! She'll look after you. I'm very proud of you, Willow. I saw an advert for Scatterbox yesterday in *Waitrose Food Magazine*! Marta also saw it and sent a pic of it to me. I couldn't believe it. Felt so proud.'

I feel a fizz of excitement. I wrote that copy, and now everyone who shops at Waitrose is reading it. 'Yes, it's all very exciting. Dom's leading the charge, really – he's super busy at the moment.'

'Sounds like you are, too, Willow. Scatterbox was half your idea, remember. Go and own it. And have FUN, you silly goose!'

I hang up and then pull the billowy black French Connection dress off its hanger and slip it on, looking critically at myself in the mirror. Who cares what I look like anyway. I realize that it's hard for women to undo decades of societal conditioning to do with their bodies, but I can't shift the feeling of discomfort. On paper, there's nothing to feel bad about.

I shake my thoughts away, put my normal clothes back on, and go downstairs to hoover the house.

That evening, I walk confidently towards the entrance of The Bloomsbury Ballroom, which is framed by a beautiful pair of doors made of wrought iron and stained glass. The ballroom is a 1920s Art Deco building in Bloomsbury Square designed for big parties, conferences, and corporate events. My bright red hair is tied up, showing little gold hoop earrings that Carla bought me for my birthday last year. I forgot to shave, and the stubble is rubbing against the material under my armpits, but even that can't dent my excitement.

I walk up the steps, and one of the straps on my espadrille shoe snaps – pings clean off. My sultry entrance has turned into a hobble. I can hardly walk.

'Noo! You OK?' Alice says, noticing me and coming over quickly. We arranged to meet in the lobby at six, and she is on time, as usual. Alice is always very punctual, the type of organized person who brings A4 sheets in plastic wallets to airports. On group holidays, while we'd all get drunk before the flight, she would make sure we all got to the gate on time. At uni, she was the only one who actually made sure our recycling was put in a separate bin, etc.

'Hi! I'm fine, I'm fine,' I say. 'One sec.' I get down on the floor and try to tie the strap in a knot. I'm sweating. I feel very hot suddenly. It's been a while since I've left the house.

Alice has a mass of curly hair and a nose-piercing and wears a crisp, perfectly ironed shirt with heeled suede boots. Her husband, Luke, is chatting to Dom a few yards away, and I can see that he is wearing an equally crisp shirt that matches Alice's. I realize that their company logo is stitched onto the shirts' pockets: a keyhole with a road stretching away behind it. Mystery Road is an online retailer for branded merchandise: they sell tote bags, pencil cases, and T-shirts for most of the top YouTubers and TikTokers in the country. Launching your debut merch collection with Mystery Road is like an Internet badge of having 'made it'. Even though they're probably our main rival for the Start-Up of the Year award, I love Alice and Luke. After all, Alice is one of my best friends; I've known her since university, and quickly introduced her to my other best friends, Pen and Lola. We've all been inseparable ever since. Alice has been there for me in such tricky situations and held my hair back one too many times after a big night out. The amount of times she's put me in a taxi and refused to accept payment. A truly good, loyal egg.

'All OK?' Dom says, coming over and putting a hand on my shoulder. 'Maybe you need to buy some new shoes, Wizz.'

I stand up, the strap finally tight again, and give Dom a kiss hello. But before I can chat to him about his day at work, a woman with a clipboard waves him and Luke over to get mic'd up for some promo video stuff. Off he goes.

'You must feel so thrilled about all of this! You guys have worked so hard,' Alice says.

'You too! But, you know, I think we could do with a holiday soon,' I say wryly, but it's true. It's showing on my dehydrated face and how achy my muscles are.

'Nights like this make it feel all worth it, though,' Alice says, as a man in a suit bearing a gold platter of drinks glides over to us.

'Ladies – care for some Champagne?'

'Yes, please,' I say, taking a glass.

'Not for me, thanks,' Alice says, smiling.

I feel guilty that I haven't already asked how she's coping. 'How are you doing?' I ask, my hand on her arm.

'I'm getting there. Still feel very flat a lot of the time,' she says. 'But we're going to try again. The doctor said it's totally normal for this to happen before a twelve-week scan, but still, it's been rough.'

'I bet. I'm so sorry. You're doing so well.' I put my arm around her, then distract her by asking about work.

Luke and Dom appear again, returning from the bar with more drinks.

'Where are your other founders tonight?' Luke asks Dom. 'Apart from Willow of course.'

'In New York, mate,' Dom says, sipping his pint. 'There's loads to do out there, so they can't make it tonight.'

Alice and Luke bump into an old friend and start chatting, and Dom is tapped on the shoulder by another woman with a clipboard, who beckons him to the corner for another photo op.

A tall man standing next to me tries to make polite conversation, noticing I'm a lemon. 'Are you nominated for something tonight?' he asks.

'Scatterbox. Start-Up of the Year,' I say, taking a sip of Champagne. 'Even though we're three years old now. Still technically a start-up, I guess.'

'No way! Me and my wife *love* Scatterbox. What is it that you do there?'

'I write all the copy,' I say proudly.

'Oh cool. Is that the endgame, or is the plan to eventually become, like, a "proper" writer?' He winks.

'Oh, well, I used to be—'

'Sorry, that's my colleague waving over there. I think I'm needed. Excuse me. Good luck!'

Why didn't I just say I was a Scatterbox co-founder?

Why am I annoyed that I didn't have time to tell him that I did actually used to write for magazines once upon a time?

Dom appears, and I hold hands with him on the way to our table, but it slips out whenever he greets someone he knows – and he seems to know practically everyone at the event. He really is good at this stuff. Mingling, handshaking, laughing, calling everyone 'mate'. For the second time today, I'm thankful I decided to stay behind the scenes. The occasional flash of limelight is fun – like tonight's event. But I haven't been invited to pose for a photo on the purple carpet, and that's fine by me.

We take our seats at a big, round table draped in a white tablecloth, with elaborate lilies in the centre. The menu is printed with the orange logo of Veep Cars, the official sponsor of the event. The lights overhead are multicoloured, flashing blue, red, purple, and there is loud background music playing, an aggressive club tune from the Nineties: 'Kernkraft 400' by Zombie Nation. The lights and music are incongruous with the elegant Art Deco setting, but it's working: there's a definite buzz of excitement filling the room.

The music reaches a loud crescendo, and our awards host appears. She's a blonde TV presenter with a pixie crop, whom I vaguely recognize from a daytime TV show, and she opens with a spiel about the importance of innovation and creativity in a thriving economy, blah blah blah. They start with the smaller categories: Best Business Podcast. Best Business Strategy. Best Business PR.

I try to focus, but it's taking forever to get through them, and my mind wanders as winner after winner gets up on stage to deliver a speech about not expecting to win, how grateful they are to their customers. Many of them thank their mum or their nan. I ask for a large white wine when a waitress in a black shirt comes to take our order. I drain it and order another.

I'm a bit tipsy now, tuning back in to the category before ours: Best Business Podcast. The winning company's chief marketing officer, a voluptuous woman in a gorgeous dark green trouser suit, goes to collect the award. She gives a surprisingly thoughtful speech about breaking the glass ceiling, overtaking all the 'stale males', and thanks her all-female team for their support. I clap politely, but my thoughts are whirling ahead: Start-Up of the Year is about to be announced. I feel a knot in my stomach. *Could we actually win?!* It's been years and years of hard work and late nights and arguments and . . .

'And the winner is . . .'
big pause
loud music
breathe in
'. . . Scatterbox!'

'No *way*,' Dom whispers, standing up immediately. He hugs Luke, then turns to me. 'I . . . did it!' Dom says, amazed, eyes wide like saucers.

'WE did it!' I say, squeezing Dom's shoulders and ushering him off towards the stage. 'Go, go!'

The room erupts into applause, and someone wolf-whistles. I stand up and clap loudly. My heart is bursting with pride for Dom and for everything he and I have achieved together since we scribbled our ideas in an old notebook three years ago.

A picture of Dom and our other two co-founders appears on the big screen. The host booms into the microphone: 'Scatterbox was founded by three friends who all met at Leeds University.'

I blink. I don't really mind that I've been missed out of the founders list, as I've been stepping back a bit more recently, but something makes me take a strong swig of wine.

'They have had a stellar year of innovation and expansion, underpinned by a strong brand voice that is allowing them to now go global. Here to accept the award is . . . co-founder Dominic Lewis himself! Please put your hands together . . .'

Dom is beaming as he walks up to the stage, takes the award, and poses with the blonde host while they have their photo taken. The crowd falls quiet when he says thank you into the mic and launches into his speech. He talks about spotting a gap in the market and the importance of doing the opposite of what everyone else is doing. He name-checks fellow founders Chad and Danny, who are working hard from the New York office, his dad, the new investor Callum, makes a joke about the constant late nights, and concludes by saying how he couldn't do it without – I breathe in – the amazing loyal customers who buy the product.

He walks back to the table, still beaming, the trophy clutched tightly in his hand.

I feel a hot prickle of shame creep up my neck. What was I expecting? I just churn out content to fill the website and newsletter. He's the one driving the strategy and finding new markets for our products. And the investors are the ones taking all the financial risk. He's had his moment; I'm happy for him. *I am.* I plaster on a smile and blow him a kiss.

'Well done, pal!' Luke says, shaking his hand when Dom sits back down. 'And well done to you, too, Willow!'

'The brains behind many of the good ideas we've had,'

Dom says, ruffling my hair. 'Look, it's weirdly heavy.' He passes the silver statue to Alice to have a feel.

'You can use it as a doorstop,' Luke jokes. 'Like Gwyneth Paltrow does with her Oscar.'

'Congratulations.' A beautiful, olive-skinned woman in a short white dress squeezes Dom's shoulder as she walks past.

I excuse myself and go the bathroom. I don't know what is wrong with me. I should be throwing my arms around Dom, celebrating with him for getting us this far. Instead, I feel flat, drained, shaky. My feet hurt, and I've drunk way too much, too quickly.

I dilly-dally in front of the mirror, wondering what to do. I put on lipstick and pat concealer under my eyes where the skin has gone a bit blotchy. I wash my hands slowly with the posh lemon-scented handwash. I overhear two girls giggling at the sinks, combing their hair, commenting on how fit the Scatterbox founder is.

The woman next to me, also washing her hands, smiles at me in the mirror.

'You're Dom's girlfriend, right?'

'Yes, hi – I'm Willow.'

'I'm Kate. I work at Veep Cars? We're the ones sponsoring tonight.'

'Oh yes, lovely to meet you,' I say politely, grabbing some paper towel to dry my hands.

'You're coming to the after-party, right? We've hired another venue just ten minutes down the road.'

'Oh, maybe,' I say, stifling a yawn. 'It's been a long night.'

'It'll be fun. Dom said he's coming.'

I go back into the main room just as Dom is being whisked away to do some talking-to-camera pieces and get introduced to all sorts of important businessy people. Alice and Luke keep me company by the bar.

'Congratulations again, Willow,' says Luke. 'If we had to be beaten, I'm glad it's by the two of you.'

'Thanks, Luke.'

'I think we're gonna head soon – it's nearly midnight, and we're knackered.' Alice yawns and looks at her watch. 'By the way, Pen wants to do a sleepover at her flat – are you free next Friday? She's got a rare night off.'

Pen is a midwife at Chelsea and Westminster Hospital, and her schedule is usually insane.

'Oh.' I check my diary in my head. 'Sorry, it's mine and Dom's curry night.'

'Can't you change it for one night? I know she really wants you there.'

'Let me check with Dom.'

She is looking at me strangely, but she tries to cover it up, turning her face into a smile.

'OK. Are you going to be all right here on your own?'

'I think so. Dom doesn't seem ready to leave yet.' I nod towards the crowd, where he is hugging two men I don't recognize and high-fiving someone else. I laugh nervously.

'Maybe you can slip off if you're tired? Surely he won't mind.'

'Oh no, no, I'll wait.'

Alice and Luke give me a hug goodbye and make an exit.

I spend an hour killing time by the bar until Dom comes over.

'Are you up for this after-party then?' Dom slurs at me, holding a fresh pint of beer. 'It looks fun.'

'My feet kinda hurt,' I say.

'Just for a few minutes? Show our faces?'

'Do we have to?'

'Willow – it's *our big night.*' He holds my shoulders. 'We won!'

I let my face soften. 'You're right. You're right.' I shake my head. 'Sorry. Yes. Let's go.'

'That's my girl,' he says, giving me a big kiss on the cheek.

It's a short taxi ride, seven minutes, to the after-party at Berners Tavern. There are press photographers outside, a handful of semi-celebrities and influencers milling about, wearing oversized beige outfits and smoking cigarettes. Inside, tequila shots on trays, bar staff in posh bow-ties, cocktails balanced on tables with edible flowers floating on top, and a loud hum of laughter all around.

'One sec – I just need to go and say hi to Callum. He's just arrived. I'll be *right* back.'

I am offered a pastel-coloured cocktail and down it in one.

I see Dom coming out of a bathroom with Callum, our new investor, both of them touching their noses a bit too much. I don't want to get involved. Even if it's not my scene, I'm aware that doing recreational drugs is some sort of bonding session between businessmen, and Dom is doing what he needs to do for our company.

There is nowhere to sit down, my feet are killing me, and the purple cocktail is making my head swim. I zone out completely, wandering the bar for over an hour, avoiding people's eyes – not that anyone wants to talk to me – until finally – *finally* – Dom taps me on the shoulder and asks if I want to go home.

I am so relieved when we finally climb into the back of an Uber, which thankfully arrived quickly, sitting on the warm seats with Magic Radio playing as we drive past Big Ben all lit up. I rest my head on the window and look down at my phone. 3.04 a.m. All I want is a peppermint tea and to snuggle up in bed next to Dom.

I try and hold his hand, but he wriggles it away, tapping away on his phone, texting Callum.

We climb into bed. I drink some water, and Dom starts kissing my neck. He smells of booze and fags, and I know he'll be too drunk for foreplay, but I don't mind. He reaches over for a red Durex. I stopped taking the pill a while ago as it made me hormonal and unhappy all the time.

'Let's just see what happens,' I say, waving the wrapper away. 'A baby wouldn't be the worst thing . . . ?' I whisper. I realize I'm pretty drunk, too.

'No, no, not yet,' he says, tearing at the wrapper with his teeth.

'Why? We're ready.'

'Things are too hectic right now.'

'I think we should try soon though.'

'*Soon*,' he says, kissing me on the forehead.

The mood has been killed, the condom discarded, the moment deflated.

I realize his eyes are glassy; he's too drunk to be having this conversation. But I hang onto this response, always the response: *soon*.

Soon.

Soon.

Soon.

He passes out, naked. I lean over him to turn the lamp off. He's snoring within minutes.

I stare at the ceiling, wired and numb. I feel a longing that I can't name; there's somewhere else I want to go, but then I can't think where I'd go without Dom. I shake away the thoughts.

This is the *plan*, Willow. Build the company, move to a bigger house, have a baby, grow a family. *This is what people do. This is what you want.*

I slip out of bed to go to the bathroom, padding quietly across the carpet, down the hallway with the sage-green walls. I pause near the door, my eye snagging on something lying by the foot of the bed. My old festival cape, its sequins glinting in the darkness.

3

THEN

April 2021

Two and a half years ago, Dom and I were at a smart restaurant on the Strand, having afternoon tea with his parents. I've never really liked afternoon tea, but it was what we always did when we saw them. His parents loved it, and I played along. It was so formal. The delicate 'finger' sandwiches, the endless pots of blended loose tea that went cold, the home-made (dry) scones, the obsession with jam, the old-fashioned teacups and doilies. The over-the-top environment of it all.

Carla would roll her eyes at this. Too pretentious. 'Just make a ham sandwich and chill out,' she would say.

The atmosphere always felt fraught in these high-tea places, the way you had to sit really still and upright and wait your turn to pick something off the ridiculous tiered stand like you were with the Queen. Today was no exception. We were sitting opposite Dom's parents, Florence and Bill.

Florence wore a peach-coloured cardigan and lots of large gold bangles, and was piling jam and cream onto a scone. Dom and I were squished on top of a sunken sofa, and his parents were on sunken chairs. The table was too low down, making it all a bit awkward to reach for things. I felt like I was in a kid's doll's house, playing pretend grown-ups, always worried I'd knock something over and ruin the whole thing.

'How was the journey?' Dom asked his parents, filling up our water glasses.

'It was fine! There were some people in first class who weren't meant to be in first class, which was disappointing. You pay all this money and then people try and cheat the system!' Florence said.

'We should have reported them,' Bill said, blowing his nose.

'How's the flat? Have you done it up yet?' Florence asked.

'No, Mum. Because it's a rental, we don't want to spend heaps of time doing it up – it's not our forever place,' Dom said. 'Don't worry – we'll find somewhere soon.'

'You should look into mortgage rates, Dominic – you two should be thinking about home ownership at your age.'

'Renting really is just pissing money down the drain,' Bill added.

Florence, gently dabbing the corners of her mouth with a thick napkin, continued: 'We owned our first property at twenty-three, didn't we, Bill? Bythorn Terrace, it was called. It had three bedrooms and a little garden. Do you remember it?' Bill was a bit deaf. She slapped his arm. 'Bill?'

'Oh, I remember it. Great little doer-upper that was.'

He laughed to himself. 'We got on the property ladder nice and early. I think we paid nineteen grand for it. I know it's different for your generation, but let us help you, for god's sake. It's hard to watch you flail around.'

'We'd like to do it on our own, if we can,' Dom said. 'We've only just launched Scatterbox. It's doing well already, and we have high hopes, and as the company grows, so will our savings—'

'Yes but when will that be?' Florence asked.

'Companies take years, sometimes decades, to grow, Dominic. Come on now. It's not likely to be soon, is it?' Bill said. 'Let us help you. Just a loan, if you prefer?'

Dom gulped down some water loudly. 'Well, we're both working very hard to hopefully make it happen. It's already growing quickly, and we have a lot of interest—'

'Have you even started looking? For houses? Even for inspiration? You should have a proper house, with a spare room, really. Come on. It would be nice for us to come visit and not stay in a hotel,' Florence said. 'My friend's daughter, Sarah, said she sets up alerts on a website called . . . Moveright, is it? And you get to put in your criteria.'

'Mum, we know what *Rightmove* is,' Dom said, sounding more clipped now.

She sighed. 'Well, we're just trying to help.'

'I know, Mum, but do we need to have Question Time right here, right now? Willow and I know what we're doing.' He looked at me, and I nodded back at him.

'Well, I'm sorry to scare you, darlings,' she said, straightening out her blouse, 'but you might need to feel a little more rushed. I read in the *Daily Mail* that women's fertility drops off a cliff even earlier than we thought. It's not thirty-five – it's actually thirty-two, and, Willow, that's how old you are now. You'll be a geriatric mother if you leave it any longer. Well, actually, darling, I think you already are. I'd already had three children by the time I was your age.'

I suddenly felt really hot. I was already so aware of the passing of time. I didn't need to be told.

'Mum, please,' Dom said, keeping his voice down.

'You've been together for so long now. Why wait?' Florence asked.

There was a pause in the conversation. Dom and I had visibly had enough now, both leaning back in our chairs.

'Sorry, I am not trying to grill you, pumpkins, but you're my only son and, Willow, you are like a daughter to us – we *love* you, and I just wanted to know whether a wedding of some sort might be on the horizon, so that I can fantasize about one day wearing a hat or imagine being a grandmother. Give us something to be excited about,' she said, suddenly looking as though she was about to cry. 'Willow, perhaps the idea of having a child is hard for you since your own mother – well—'

Bill put his hand on her arm to silence her. I was flabbergasted at how two people could make everything about them so easily. In that moment, I despised them, but I was also grateful for the pressure: I secretly did want Dom to hurry up. I wanted to begin these big life milestones. I did want to move out of our tiny flat and into a house. I also wanted Dom to propose, but I knew he wouldn't until we had our own place. He'd always liked doing things in the right order, which was something I loved about him. It made me feel safe, secure. Like he wasn't going to just up and leave. Unlike my own mother, as Florence felt the need to point out.

Dom was silent, and I could see him wrestling with his pride. Eventually, he gave in at the sight of Florence blotting her crocodile tears away with her napkin, then rummaging around in her handbag, looking for her lip balm.

'Mum.' Dom sighed. 'Yes. You can lend us the deposit for a house. Thank you. We'd love that.'

I breathed in and out deeply. I was happy with that: it meant security, stability. A future with Dom. The next rung up the ladder.

Florence looked happy; Bill looked happy; even Dom looked happy.

I looked down at my belly, bloated with scones and smoked salmon, and for a moment I imagined a soft round bump.

'Feeling full, darling?' Florence asked.

'Yes,' I replied. 'Yes, just a bit full.'

'Let's have some more fizz to celebrate your beautiful future together,' she said, snapping her fingers at the passing waiter. 'So much to look forward to.'

4

NOW

'Do you guys have any New Year's resolutions?' Pen asks me and Dom as the three of us sit in our local pub. She takes a huge bite of jackfruit burger and gets vegan mayonnaise all over her chin. She is wearing two black jumpers on top of each other, smelling of L'Occitane body oil. She is tiny and often wears many knitted layers to keep warm. Her thin wrists are decorated with various beaded bracelets she's threaded herself, and she has two black arrows tattooed on her left wrist. She tried to persuade me to get matching ones, but it was just after we launched Scatterbox and I was worried that our investors would think it was unprofessional or that Dom would think it was tacky.

I met Pen and one of my other best friends, Lola, at primary school, and we've basically been inseparable ever since. Lola was always a safe space for me, one of those friends who rarely changes from her default personality: chipper, smiley and supportive. My relationship with Pen was more fiery, more intense, more like sisters. I watched her grow from an eight-year-old tomboy into a teenage goth who bunked off school, first to go to Korn/Slipknot gigs, then to join climate change marches. We all continued on to the same sixth form together – St Raymond's School for Girls, a prestigious grammar school – where we spent two years doing our A-levels. Pen's parents managed to get her in, in the hope that it would get her back on track and rein in her rebelliousness. And Carla thought it would be a good idea to get my grades up a bit – everything had dropped off a cliff after my mum left. Carla was (and still is) anti-private school, but St Raymond's was free; you just had to pass all the entrance tests. It definitely did the job in giving us some confidence. The tag line was 'where girls come first', which always made us snigger.

During our free periods at Raymond's, Pen, Lola and I would go and buy fizzy laces and milk bottle sweets from the off licence near school and share badly rolled cigarettes (Golden Virginia tobacco Pen stole from her brother) behind the bike sheds. Lola was quite into boys from an early age and would drift off to flirt with the sixth-form lads from the college down the road. Pen and I would stay behind and chat in our little bubble, oblivious to it all.

Those years cemented everything I already knew: that Pen gets me like no one else.

Now she works as an NHS midwife, proving wrong every exasperated teacher who said she would 'make nothing of her life' by delivering hundreds of babies and volunteering for charities in her spare time. It's usually impossible to get her on a Sunday because her shift patterns don't match the working week, but today, we're sat in a corner booth of the pub, by a window overlooking the road. Young mums and dads wearing papooses keep walking past.

'I don't really believe in New Year's resolutions,' Dom responds, taking a sip of his pint. 'Just a way to sell us new stuff, isn't it? One big marketing technique for Peloton, basically.'

'Er, didn't you recently win a *marketing* award?' Pen laughs, with her signature husky voice.

Dom looks a bit annoyed.

'New Year's is literally the *only* time in the year I feel a sense of hope. Then real life comes crushing down again.' Pen sighs. 'My New Year's vibe for this year is: Say Yes to Everything.'

'Even mansplainers who order rare steak on a first date?' I joke.

'Even them,' Pen replies solemnly.

Pen had such horrible dating experiences that, last January, she filtered for men with 'feminist' and 'vegan' in their bio for the rest of the year. As a result, she's had zero good dates lately as it's been such slim pickings. Most of the time, though, she says she likes being single and actually enjoys turning a bad date into a no-strings one-night stand. She lives by the rule that no experience is wasted – even a bad date makes a great anecdote.

'Are the dating apps still terrible?' Dom asks.

'They're dire. They don't want honesty, just for you to play the game. But, like, a really shit game. No one is their true self on there. It's all marketing bollocks. Everyone calls themselves a "foodie" just because they've eaten from a street-food cart once.' She folds her arms. 'You two are lucky. It can really suck being single. Especially on Sundays.'

Dom looks across the pub at a dog that is barking loudly; he seems distracted from the conversation.

'What about you, Willow? Any resolutions or wishes for the New Year?' Pen asks me.

'Well,' I say, stealing one of her chips, 'I really want to start writing again. Just for me.'

'Oh, that's a great idea,' Pen says, offering me her ketchup. 'I used to *love* reading your old blogs. It was like you were writing your reader a little letter.'

Before I met Dom, when I lived with Pen and was scratching around trying to get into journalism, I used to blog about the highs and lows of being single. One week, I would explore the bone-aching loneliness of a weekend in an empty flat, and the next I'd describe the joy of taking a spontaneous road trip to the seaside with my best friend.

Which reminds me. 'Actually, Pen, there is something else I've been thinking about. I want to drive again.'

'Oh my god, I remember when you passed your test when we were eighteen!' Pen says. 'You were so angry at Lola for passing her test before you, hahaha.' Pen has never learned to drive because she thinks it's so bad for the planet – but that didn't stop her treating me as her personal chauffeur when we were teenagers. 'What was that Tracy Chapman song we couldn't stop listening to?'

'"Fast Car"!' we say in unison.

'But I've got a car,' Dom chips in. 'I can drive you places. You don't need to.'

'I know, but I just miss it. The feeling of the open road . . . the wind in your hair, like a puppy hanging out the window, the fluffy dice . . .'

Pen throws her head back and laughs. 'Remember when you were little and used to make collages of retro cars? You had a thing for Minis, didn't you?'

'Minis are weirdly expensive,' Dom mutters.

'Oh, come on, Eeyore – Scatterbox will earn you millions soon,' Pen teases. 'Anyway, we're not talking about *realistic* things right now – we're talking about New Year's hopes and dreams!' Pen says. 'Let Willow DREAM. You're meant to open your heart to the impossible. Ask the universe to guide you!' She takes her final bite of jackfruit and wipes her last chip through the ketchup. 'I think you should do it, Willow – the logistics will fall into place. If you miss being behind the wheel, you should get back there. YOLO, right?' Pen gets up to go to the toilet and places her boney hands briefly on my shoulder as she walks past.

I notice that 'Driver's Seat' by Sniff 'n' the Tears is playing on the pub jukebox.

Dom looks at her as she walks off, then says, 'Sorry, I didn't mean to be grumpy. Of course you can do whatever you like. But I think I'll leave you girls to it,' he says, putting some cash down, enough to cover the whole bill.

'What?' I say.

'I'm just a bit stressed with work – got some stuff I need to tie up back at home.' He downs the dregs of his pint and grabs his jumper from the back of the chair.

'Can I help you get through the to-do list?' I say, touching his leg. 'I hate that it all falls to you at the moment. I'm sure Pen won't mind if we leave early.'

'No, no, it's fine. I just need to get my head down and get it all off my plate. You girls stay.' He kisses my head and quickly leaves.

'Lovely Aesop hand soap in there,' Pen says, coming back from the loo, reaching her hand out so that I can smell it. 'You know they're totally cruelty-free? They don't even use beeswax in their products.' I can tell she's about to go on one of her mini-lectures when she notices the empty chair. 'Wait, has Dom left? Where'd he go?'

Pen sits back down and fiddles with a paper straw. It's very rare for her hands to stay still. It used to get her into loads of trouble at school. Now her hands bring new life into the world.

'He's gone home to send emails. It's such a busy time for us at the moment,' I say. 'He said to say sorry for his grumpiness.'

'Fair enough. Is it because I said YOLO?' Pen says, grinning. 'I know he thinks only idiots and hippies say that.'

She's right, and it makes me smile, too. Dom can be an old fogey at times. He has always mocked Pen's love of recycled clothes and 'tree-hugging' personality. 'No, it wasn't anything you said. It's just crazy at the moment. His PA emailed me the other day about—'

'WAIT. STOP. NO.' Pen puts both her hands on the table. 'His *PA* emails you?'

'Yes! Well, sometimes! She books in our date nights.'

'You're *killing* me.'

'I don't mind it,' I say. 'It's kind of sexy?'

'You two are *deranged*. Good job Scatterbox is doing well, because it is the Camilla Parker-Bowles of your relationship.'

'Pen, we're fine – things are good.' I laugh it off, shaking my head. I know single people want to believe that couples are all secretly having a terrible time, but this evening, I'll go home to Dom, and we'll eat comfort food and snuggle up in front of a crime drama on the sofa. And what could be better than that?

'OK, weirdo. Please can we go to the seaside together soon? Blow some cobwebs away and set some witchy New Year's intentions like we used to?' she asks. 'We missed it last January, and I'm *sure* that's why I had such a shit year.'

'Yes, definitely,' I say. 'That would be lovely. I'll just check dates when I get home.'

'Shall I email Dom's PA then?' Pen says, nudging me.

I laugh and go to the bar to get in another round of Bloody Marys, making mine a Virgin Mary at the last minute. I'll stay and chat with Pen for another hour or so, but I feel bad for Dom, and I want to be sober enough when I get home that I can help with work if he needs me to.

On the way home, I pick up some good pork from the local butcher on our road and plan to cook Dom our favourite comfort dinner, a simple recipe I used to make in our twenties when we still lived in student digs: sausage pasta with caramelized red onion, rigatoni, chopped tomatoes, broccoli, and the secret ingredient – a can of Heinz cream of tomato soup. Dom hasn't been cooking at all and has just been living off strawberry Huel lately, and I've been spending a lot of time alone in the kitchen. I don't really mind, because it means I can put on a podcast and retreat into my own world for a bit.

Tonight, I'm listening to a podcast about creative writing and accidentally drinking half a bottle of red wine, while also splashing some into the mixture.

I lay the table beautifully, with tall candles and striped napkins, but when we sit down to eat, Dom doesn't comment on any of the effort I've made and just starts wolfing down his food.

'Hungry then?' I say, pouring us both more red.

'I've got to get back upstairs onto my emails – things are kicking off.' He looks genuinely apologetic.

I sigh and put down my fork. 'More emails? Really? Things seem to always be kicking off. Can't you have one night off? Or at least let me help so you don't have to do everything?'

'We're so close to bagging this new investment, Wizz. Callum is emailing me at all hours. I just need to be across everything. And I know you would be brilliant at helping, but for now they just want to hear from me. Things are going mad after our award win. *The Times* want to do a profile on me!' He pauses at my look. 'I mean, on us . . . on Scatterbox. Obviously.'

He picks up his phone to check a notification, and I mirror him without thinking, picking up my phone and clicking onto Instagram. I am met with a Reel of someone's new 3D baby scan.

Hearing me sigh loudly, he puts his phone down.

'I feel like all the technology is moving on faster than I am,' I say, putting my phone down with some force. 'By the time we have a baby, you'll be able to scan your own belly whenever you want at home via a sofa plug-in.'

'Not a bad business idea.'

'Dom!'

'What?'

'Be serious, please. I am thirty-five.'

He puts down his fork. 'People have kids much later now. None of your mates even have kids yet.'

'Alice is desperately trying. Lola said Fred wants to be married first. Pen doesn't want children. But I do, Dom. We're in a good position to try now.'

'I just need to get this meeting over the line—'

'And then the next meeting, and the next meeting – until we die?'

'No, *this* meeting—' He puts his phone down with a bit too much force.

'Why is everything about work and the business? Why is this our life? Scatterbox was meant to be a fun idea, a fun side project! Now look at us! Is this actually a *life*?' I'm gesturing with my fork and a dot of tomato sauce spatters on the wall. I feel like a frustrated teenager again. 'If I'd known the business was going to take over our lives, I wouldn't have suggested it in the first place.'

He calms slightly; his shoulders drop. He comes round to my side of the table and puts his hands on my shoulders.

'I just need to sort out this next phase. As *soon* as we've secured the new investment, things will go back to normal.'

'Promise?'

'Yes.'

'OK.'

'Sorry.' He squeezes my shoulder, then puts his dish in the sink and goes upstairs to his beloved laptop.

Sorry.

Soon.

Soon.

Promise.

While I wash up the pans and contemplate the huge pile of ironing I keep putting off, Carla calls me.

'Hello, my *award-winning* girl!' she says. I can hear the sea in the background, her boots grinding against hard sand and her two little dachshund dogs, Bubble and Squeak, by her side. She'll be on one of her brisk evening walks on the local beach in Eastbourne.

'Why are you out walking so late – it's dark!' I say.

'I'm big enough and ugly enough to defend myself. I love a stroll in the dark. Anyway, B&S scare everyone off – their barks are stupidly loud for such tiny dogs. Plus, I can't really sit still any more. Menopausal nonsense probably. How are things? Congratulations! How does it feel?'

'It felt good for maybe five minutes? Wish I was in Eastbourne with you right now to be honest.'

'Come and stay then! Get a bit of sea air! Things a bit stressful still? It's a hard life being a successful entrepreneur, darling!'

'Yeah.' I sigh, my whole body drooping. 'The award's made

everything worse. Dom's working even *more*. Hopefully it's just a phase, but it's kind of exhausting. He's turned into a zombie. Barely eats, barely sleeps.' I sigh.

I don't want to elaborate further. I don't want to tell her the sick feeling in my stomach, the late nights in the office, Dom's distant behaviour, my sneaking feeling that I've become his support staff rather than his business partner. Otherwise, my feelings will be too real.

'How are *you*?' I ask, changing the subject.

'All good, darling. It's been beautiful here, one of those cold but blue-sky January days, and I spent it repainting the She-Shed and listening to Enya. You've got all this to look forward to when you're older.'

Carla is a classic Gen X fifty-something who did hard drugs in the Nineties and now lives a more wholesome life by the sea. A few of her friends had their lives ruined by addiction in their twenties, and she decided to change her lifestyle and became more spiritual. She learned how to read palms and now does tarot readings for the locals in what she calls the She-Shed. She also hosts the local book club there, so it's lined with bookshelves and hung with wind chimes and seashells, which she strings together with all sorts of different coloured bunting. It's one of my favourite places in the world. She's never had a partner, never really dated, was never that interested, loves living alone with her two dogs. She's iconic, basically.

Carla took me in when I was six years old. My mum got pregnant with me at eighteen while she was travelling the world, and I'm not sure she even knows who my dad is. My mum was a free spirit, a travelling nomad, and none of that changed as she got older. She decided to have me, figuring she'd just strap me to her back and keep on travelling, but Carla convinced her that babies need stability and suggested she move home, where Carla would help her adjust to a settled, stable life – teach her to be an adult, I guess. But Mum was prone to depression, and it worsened. One day, when I was six, she just packed up and left.

When I was eight, she came back. We thought it would be for good, but she left again, and we haven't seen her since. Carla took over straight away, and eventually legally adopted me. Even though I don't *call* her 'Mum', Carla is absolutely a mother to me. The best one. My number one.

'Sure you're OK, hon? You really do sound a bit flat,' she says, blowing out slowly. I can tell she might be having a puff on a secret rollie.

'I don't know. I feel like I need to hurry up and live the rest of my life. I want Dom to either propose or for me to get pregnant – we've been together for so long now. It's like I'm waiting for something to happen, but I don't know what. He's hardly ever home, and even when he is home, his eyes are glazed over or on his phone or laptop.'

'Oh, darling. I understand, I do. There is so much pressure put on women and their biological clocks and so much scaremongering. I don't think you need to panic. What is Dom saying?'

'He's focused on the company. He keeps saying "soon".'

'Maybe he means it,' she says.

'I'm older than Jesus was when he died. Jesus had already

started a spiritual, political, and intellectual revolution by now.'

'Sweetheart, I don't think you need to be as productive as Jesus. He fed five thousand. You don't need to do that.'

'I just think it's dangerous to keep saying "one day". Don't you think? Do you ever feel like your real life doesn't match up with all the plans you had when you were younger?'

'Well, I was never much of a planner, really. I'm happy with my life. I've got the sea, I've got the dogs, and most importantly, I've got you.' She breathes out smoke again.

'You certainly didn't plan for me to infiltrate your life,' I say.

'I wouldn't have it any other way.'

'Do you really mean that?'

'Absolutely. God gives us many gifts, Willow. Please will you come visit soon? Bring Pen. I miss her energy. Remember when the two of you plastered seaweed all over the Shell forecourt to protest against oil spills? She's a firecracker, that girl. How is she?'

'She's fine,' I say, smiling at the memory. We were only fourteen. It took us weeks to gather enough seaweed, and we stank for about a month afterwards.

'Gotta run. I love you.'

'You too. Try and go easy with Dom for a bit and see what happens. Sometimes when we stop pushing, that's when things start to take shape.'

5

THEN

July 2018

It was the evening of my thirtieth birthday party, and Lola, Pen, Alice, and I were getting ready together in a hotel room above a Northeast London bar called Zetter. I'd often walked past it and had fallen in love with its quirky, mismatched interiors, complete with a faux stuffed kangaroo wearing boxing gloves in one corner of the restaurant. When Carla told me she would hire a private dining room for my birthday present, it was my first choice by far.

    Pairs of sheer tights, hair straighteners and make-up bags were strewn all over the bed, spilling out mascara wands and shimmering eye-shadow.

    Lola had finished her make-up and was flicking through a magazine, scoffing out loud at a quote from one of the Kardashians (Khloé? Kylie?) about how they get scared when they throw an event because they worry no one will show up. I didn't confess to Lola how much this comforted me. Even *they* – these public women with millions of followers – worried that no one would come to their party and that they would be stood there like a lonesome lemon.

I had padded out my guest list more than I should, inviting people I would probably list as 'acquaintances' rather than real friends. I didn't want to admit that in the course of getting a boyfriend, settling down and bringing in a decent income through freelance journalism, I had become pretty anti-social. I felt it would look odd if I had less than thirty guests for turning thirty, so I invited people who were really quite new friends, as well as a few I used to be close to but hadn't spoken to for years. I was worried now that even though they said 'yes' on the invite, they could easily bail at the last minute.

'Who fucking *cares* if no one else comes? We'll have fun even if it's just us four,' Pen said, putting on some lip gloss in the mirror. She was right. It was already fun getting ready with the girls, just like old times.

I wore a textured silver dress, billowing and bold, with matching silver shoes, and led the way downstairs. I was nervous, but the dress buoyed me up. A way to enter into a new decade, as a human-sized light bulb reflecting off every shiny surface.

We went into the rented side room, which was laid out like a chic, intimate dinner party, with little round tables and tapered candles. Pen said it looked like a miniature wedding. A wedding for myself, perhaps.

Despite my nerves, everyone showed up: thirty friends

collected from the last few years of my life during school, university, internships, different jobs. They spilled into the cosy room, bearing warm hugs and thoughtful gifts. Alice and Lola presented me with a photo collage of our early twenties, mostly of the four of us wearing skinny jeans and doing duck-pout selfies with way too much lip gloss. Dom brought me a huge bunch of sunflowers, and Lola tied one into each of our hairstyles. We all ate our three courses: pea soup, fish and dauphinoise potatoes, and then chocolate brownies. I was sitting between Pen and Carla, with Dom opposite, and I felt so grateful for these wonderful people in my life.

Pen started a game of 'funny stories about Willow', and she and Carla were soon one-upping each other. There was the time I accidentally mooned our PE teacher because the shorts Carla bought me (four sizes too big) fell down, and the time I reversed Carla's car into a red postbox. Carla was drinking strong G&Ts, and everyone leaned in when she spoke; her natural warmth meant she commanded any table.

Carla paid the bill, and Pen turned up the music. The waiters kept topping up my wine glass with Cava, and soon I was dancing around the tables to Bananarama's 'Cruel Summer', linking arms with Pen and Lola. My lower back got sweaty from all the dancing and group hugging, and when I finally sat down, Pen gave me her present: a vintage fountain pen and a beautiful vegan-leather notebook with thick, cream lined paper. There was space for my own writing in the front, and in the back, everyone at the party had written meaningful notes about my friendship with them.

We'll always have each other. Welcome to your thirties: where girls come first. Happy bday. Pen x

As per the Ronan Keating song, 'Life is a Rollercoaster' – I'll ride the rollercoaster with you! Lola xoxo

Keep on writing! Keep on being you! Love you, Alice

All the Cava made me cry at the gift, but they were happy tears, and I hugged Pen long and hard.

At around midnight, the staff politely asked us to wrap it up. Someone was playing and singing Jon Bon Jovi very loudly, and they had a noise curfew for the sake of their hotel guests.

'So, Pen has booked a karaoke booth down the road!' Alice said, putting her arm around my waist. 'Let's get your things. We can continue wailing the lyrics of "Livin' on a Prayer".'

Dom was already holding my bag. 'Hey, she's a bit wasted – I don't think karaoke is a good idea,' he said.

'Oh, come on, it's her *birthday*, Dom,' Pen said tipsily, wagging a finger at him. 'She doesn't need you telling her what to do.'

'I'm not,' Dom protested, stroking my hair. 'It's up to her, of course.'

'Willow – what do *you* want to do?' Lola asked, crouching down like I was a child.

I nestled into Dom's chest.

'Karaoke,' I said, hiccupping.

'Really, Willow?' Dom said.

'Um, well . . . maybe, actually, bed.'

Pen had her hand on her hip.

As I went up the creaky hotel stairs with Dom, I caught a glimpse of my three best friends looking disappointed, gathering their coats and bags. I hoped they'd go anyway – carry on our long-standing karaoke tradition rather than allow it to crumble away into nothingness. Alice always sang Madonna's 'Lucky Star', Lola tried (and usually failed) to do an Eminem rap ('Without Me'), and Pen and I loved duetting on the classic tune we'd sung together since school: En Vogue's 'Don't Let Go', which we always knew was way too ambitious with too many high notes.

I knew Dom was right, that I was too drunk to keep partying, but as I climbed out of my shiny silver dress and into the sheets of our hotel bed, I suddenly felt so sad. It felt like an ending of sorts, and it caught me by surprise. How is it possible to feel so lonely when you're with someone else in a luxurious super-king bed?

6

NOW

I'm standing in front of the bathroom mirror, applying make-up for a rare office day at Scatterbox: mascara, concealer, eyebrow gel. It's been ages since I've torn myself away from my comfortable WFH setup (tracksuit bottoms, sheet mask on face, vast mug of Yorkshire Tea, the occasional daytime nap, Netflix on in the background), and I'm actually excited to go into the office for once. Dom has a big meeting with Callum, and I'm being wheeled in to talk through our messaging strategy before he signs off on new financing this afternoon. Nice to be invited and feel involved.

Just as I put the lid back on my mascara, the light glows on my phone. A new email to my personal email address. I open the app, guiltily ignoring the week-old messages from the girls' WhatsApp group suggesting dates for our seaside weekend, and click on the new email.

From: Elaine <elaine@jefferson.com>
To: Willow <willow@scatterbox.com>

Dearest Willow,
    Long time no speak, dear one!
    Questions for you:
    Are you still doing any freelance writing?
    Are you still based in London?
    Are you free today?
    Excuse typos, sent from iPhone, or I might have had some WINE

I'm surprised to hear from Elaine; it's been *years* since *The D-Low Magazine* days. I close the email app and open LinkedIn to check what she's up to now. It opens automatically on my own profile – which I log in to sometimes, usually after a few drinks, to remind myself that I once had another life.

A little green dot shows she's online now. *Intense* is how I'd describe Elaine. Loud. Always biting her nails or twiddling her hair or chewing a pen. She gave me my first job because she found my cover letter amusing. I wrote to *The D-Low,* a popular new women's magazine, saying that their covers were so light and frothy you'd never guess that the writing inside was so sharp it could bite. I said that if she didn't expect their readers to judge books by their covers, she shouldn't judge me by my cover letter . . . so would she invite me for an interview? (Elaine told me later that she thought I'd tortured the metaphor, but she liked my chutzpah.)

Back in 2013, magazines were still doing well, and I loved everything about working there. I had friends in the office, free snacks, an eccentric boss who liked me; I used to go for after-work drinks, go to press events, go to screenings, fill my brain with things that made me feel curious and alive. We used to sit around a big table every morning and discuss the news stories of the day and spend hours discussing the latest trends and our personal problems. The picture editor would pull up images from Getty, and we would sit around gossiping about the last celebrity trends and call it 'work'.

I loved being a writer in that office. I eventually went freelance, but it was such a formative time. Dom used to teasingly remind me that I didn't exactly save the world with my journalism (one memorable headline was: 'Are Shepherds Hot?') – but I enjoyed my time there. I used to travel all over the UK, reporting on local events, connecting with people, readers, ideas. People used to read my articles and send me the occasional nice tweet.

I open Elaine's message again and stare at it for a few moments, my thumb hovering. Surely there's no harm in finding out a bit more?

From: Willow <willow@scatterbox.com>
To: Elaine <elaine@jefferson.com>

Hey Elaine, how are you? Long time no speak. It's nice to hear from you. I am intrigued . . . W x

From: Elaine <elaine@jefferson.com>
To: Willow <willow@scatterbox.com>

Meet me at The Club for coffee this morning? Working on a very exciting new project and would love to speak to you about it. Sorry to be so cryptic. Top secret!
  Excuse typos, sent from iPhone, or I might have had some WINE

I shouldn't really skive off work this morning, especially as I need to prep, but the Callum meeting isn't 'til three p.m. My fingers tap out a reply before I really know what they're doing.

From: Willow <willow@scatterbox.com>
To: Elaine <elaine@jefferson.com>

Sure! What time? See you there. W x

From: Elaine <elaine@jefferson.com>
To: Willow <willow@scatterbox.com>

FABULOUS. 11.30am? Won't take long.
  Excuse typos, sent from iPhone, or I might have had some WINE

I immediately feel guilty, like I'm cheating on Scatterbox, on Dom – after all, I told Dom I'd be in the office all day, but I'll still be there in time for the meeting with Callum. And it feels so good to hear from Elaine. I'm relieved to still be in her orbit. A part of me that still exists in the ether – a side of myself that has been kept away stashed in a box. A creative way of processing the world that is wholly mine and that I closed off so me and Dom could form our mini team, our partnership for the future.

That guy's voice at the awards ricochets in my head: *is the plan to eventually become, like, a 'proper' writer?*

The butterflies in my tummy flutter nervously as I approach the ostentatiously discreet entrance of The Club and remember that I am about to enter The Worst Place on Earth.

As I push open the big heavy door with no sign on it, the stagnant energy hits me, ironic for a place that gathers 'creatives'. The bar/diner/art gallery at the front is where all the most ego-led media people hang out – those who want to be seen. It's rare to catch them working; they mostly pose for social media in clothes from the kind of designer brands that don't have logos and instead rely on others with a keen eye to notice how exclusive they are. Cheap-looking plastic raincoats that are actually Moschino. Ugly shoes that are actually Balmain. The plainest-looking T-shirt that is actually from The Row.

It's in places like this that I understand what people mean when they say: 'I couldn't live in London.' They are imagining *this* London: a club where membership costs as much as a mortgage, on a street full of self-important city people rushing past, taxis belching pollution, and rickshaws blaring music in the small, winding streets.

Even Carla is rude about London, and she knows it's not really like this. I always remind her of the good bits that I love: the giant sprawling parks (Holland Park and the actual peacocks!), the big green marshes, the River Lea, the Serpentine, the pedalo boats, the massive trees, the museums, the cafés, the arthouse cinemas, the fountains . . . The fresh, open-air London, full of life and possibility, not this bleak, desperate, coked-up version.

A young, fresh-faced woman at reception with her hair slicked back and long almond-shaped nails asks me to sign my name as a guest without looking at me. She just waves me upstairs while continuing to look down. 'Elaine is on floor two.'

'Thank you.'

She doesn't reply and carries on chewing her gum, typing away. I'm just a nobody to her. To everyone here, probably. *Who cares about a random business award, when I'm not making anything I'm proud of.*

I climb the wooden stairs, and I spot Elaine immediately. The same straw-like hair, the same neon pink lipstick, the same glasses perched on her head. She's sitting on a dark-green vintage-style sofa with a cup of coffee on a saucer in front of her, scrolling on her phone with a pink thumbnail to match her lipstick.

She looks up as I walk in.

'Willow, doll! How are you?' She stands up. She smells expensive, her jumper freshly laundered. She hugs me, and I feel like a child. Her New York accent carries, the sound always turned up to the max.

A guy sat on a nearby table adjusts his headphones, picks up his laptop and moves into a different room, frowning at the volume of her voice.

'It's good to see you! How are you? It's been so long,' I say, taking off my coat. I look behind me, anxious that someone I know will see me. Like who? Scatterbox colleagues?

'It really has, hasn't it? Hopefully I don't look too different,' she says, pawing at her face. 'I've had my fair share of Botox since. Ha. I'm good! Although, just came from a meeting in the depths of East London. Jesus Christ, you could play a game of "hobo or hipster". Literally, these people. Can't tell if they're genuinely homeless or running an award-winning creative agency . . . the *size* of their beards . . . Anyway – how are you? How's that sexy husband of yours?'

'Well, he's not my husband yet,' I say, 'but yeah, he's good, thanks.'

'Really! You've been together for *years*, haven't you? Since the *D-Low* days?'

I change the subject. 'How's work? Everything looks very busy from LinkedIn?'

'Oh yes! I've been posting like a little maniac, haven't I? It's all systems go at the moment – I've got lots to talk to you about. Lots of newness. I love this weather, the turn of spring! Gives you hope, doesn't it, when the world is going to absolute shit.' She downs her coffee, and I'm pretty sure it's not her first of the day. Her eyeballs look wired and massive. She beckons a passing waiter. 'Excuse me! Can we order some more drinks? Another latte for me – what would you like?'

'Just a water is good. Thank you.'

'She'll have wine. A large of glass of Gavi,' Elaine says.

I try to protest, but she does a *shh* motion with her hands.

'You look like you need it, doll. So, what's new with you?'

'Oh, well, you know, I helped set up that algorithm gifting company, Scatterbox? I mean, Dom runs the company, really, but I did a lot of the founding stuff, and now I do all the copywriting. I've got an investor meeting this afternoon as it happens—'

'Well, that all sounds very busy and *important*.' Elaine wiggles her eyebrows at me, and I blush. 'Why are you here with me if it's all going so well?'

'Well . . .' I pause. Why *am* I here? 'I guess I'm curious. I'm not doing any real writing there, and I've been thinking about doing more of it.'

Even though we haven't seen each other for years, she still seems fond of me. I remember when Elaine and the other higher-ups used to think I was young. I was the *twenty-four-year-old Millennial in the room*. We would be in an important meeting with clients, and she would spotlight me: 'Willow will know the answer to that! What do you think about Snapchat, Willow? Can you teach me how to put a filter on my face? Should we be looking into 3D printing?' I wonder if Elaine realizes I'm an Old Millennial now ('geriatric' according to Florence) – the kind who uses anti-wrinkle cream and when she 'gets low', she can't get back up again.

'Let me get right to it, I've got something new cooking, and I need some writers on board. I'm launching a new print and online mag for Gen Z readers. *Much* younger than me obviously – I'm an old dog now, ha! Hopefully you can help bridge the gap. We're calling it . . . *Z Life*. We've got some big cheese investor who knows nothing about publishing and is pummelling loads of cash into everything. Magazine budgets are making a comeback, honey! Now, look, you're super talented, Willow, and from the sounds of it, you're underused at Scatterbox.' She takes a big glug of my Gavi. 'We're doing this series called "Opposites Attract". So, we have a Tory interviewing a Lefty, a vegetarian interviewing a big meat eater. I thought of you for our piece: *Millennial monogamist interviews a Gen Z singleton*. We can pay you a couple of grand for the article. What do you think?'

I take a sip of Elaine's water. 'It sounds really interesting,' I say, needing some time to think.

There's that fluttery feeling in my stomach again, but my mind is pretty sure it's a bad idea: *Scatterbox is your priority, Willow. It needs all your attention. You shouldn't really be talking to Elaine.*

'You don't need to decide now. I can follow up with more information?' she says, reading my uncertainty.

'That would be good. Thanks. Let me have a think about it.'

'You're a great writer, Willow. And we work well together. It could be the perfect opportunity to break back into the world of journalism. *Z Life* is going to have a big launch. *Do* think about it.'

She orders the bill, air-kisses me goodbye and disappears into another room, talking loudly into her AirPods.

* * *

I wander into the street, blinking at the bright sunlight after the dark and seedy atmosphere of The Club. I am suddenly ravenous, tummy rumbling, and decide to get lunch at a small vegan restaurant nearby, which instantly reminds me of Pen. I can go over my notes for the investor meeting there, too.

'Table for one, please,' I say, my forehead forming sweat-beads.

'Sure thing!' A kind-looking waitress says and takes me to a small table by the wall, then explains the long-winded menu to me, lots of dishes involving hummus and baba ghanoush. I feel awkward making eye contact with her for so long while she talks about the various specials and soups.

I look around and realize I am the only one here on my own. The restaurant is packed with couples playing footsy, enthusiastic friends showing each other things on their phones, work colleagues having wine, kids drawing on the tablecloth with crayons. It's busy and noisy, and I suddenly feel super self-conscious.

Come on, Willow, you used to love eating in restaurants on your own! So why does this feel so awkward and hard?

The last time I was properly on my own at a restaurant was on a trip to the BFI shortly before I met Dom. I had been stood up by a guy from one of the apps and bravely decided to continue the date by myself. I surprised myself by having a great time. I loved the film (*Frances Ha*), walked along the waterfront, browsed in Foyles, and then found a fantastic dumpling spot, where I nestled into a corner and eavesdropped on the conversations around me. It was the best date I'd had in months.

A week later, I met Dom, and after that, of course, my nights were full of him. Joined at the hip.

There's a couple sitting right next to me, holding hands across the table, and he is stroking her wrist, which has a tattoo of a dove on it. The woman glances at me and smiles. Suddenly, I don't know what to do with my hands. I don't know where to look or where to focus, without looking weird and staring everyone else out. I feel silly. My chest feels constricted.

The waitress slowly takes away the glass and cutlery on the other side of the table. 'Here's the specials menu. Can I get you a drink in the meantime?' She grabs the pen behind her ear.

I feel like everyone is looking at me. I am about to take the plunge and order the charred aubergine and pitta when my phone suddenly pings with a message from Dom.

Where are you?? Callum's here early. Wants to move strategy meeting forward by a few hours . . .

Shit. It's at least thirty minutes to Farringdon.

I smile awkwardly at the waitress and mumble something about having to leave, then race to the nearest bus stop, heart pounding.

Soon enough I arrive, slightly sweaty, at the Scatterbox office, which is at the top of three flights of stairs in an old Fifties brutalist building in Farringdon. It's a big, open-plan office with a pool table, beers in the fridge, bean bags, a gaming room – oh, and Pete the office parrot. The decor was Dom's idea, wanting to inspire the next generation of tech employees. I trot into the room, panting, and a dart flies past my head, nearly grazing my ear.

'Sorry!' a young French tech guy called Guillaume says, putting his hands up in a *sorry-not-sorry* gesture. Another Gen Z engineer called Tom codes frantically.

Dom's PA, Lisa, spots me and marches over with a clipboard in hand, big brown glasses sliding down her nose. 'Hey! Good to see you, Willow. Change of plan. Dom took Callum out for lunch and will take him through the documents, says he'll cover your messaging presentation and see you at home. Sorry, you literally just missed them.'

Shit shit shit! I've been preparing for this for weeks. 'How come the meeting got moved? I wasn't across any of the emails?'

'Callum's flight changed.' Lisa shrugs. 'But don't worry about it. I'm sure Dom will do a great job.' She brandished the clipboard towards me. 'Since you're here, do you mind signing off on some of these office supplies? It would really help me out.'

'Oh – um – I'd rather wait 'til Dom is back. I'm a bit out of the loop at the moment. I can give him a nudge when I see him.'

'OK, thanks.' She smiles and shrugs and then turns on her heel and is off to tick another task off her to-do list.

I go and sit down, cheeks flaming. I've never felt more useless in my own company.

I work on my laptop in one of our glass meeting rooms for an hour. I see a group of young lads standing around watching a TikTok on someone's phone and two of the girls laughing, flirting, flicking their hair. I wish they'd turn the loud music down. I wish the girls wouldn't wear crop tops in the office and shorts with their arse cheeks out. I don't recognize any of the songs being played.

I suddenly think of Elaine and the office she ran at *The D-Low*. It wasn't perfect by any stretch, and we worked late a lot, but we never played obnoxiously loud music, and we always made each other tea. We respected each other and each other's space. We made an effort to even make the office smell nice, with room sprays and scented candles. I catch sight of myself in the laptop reflection, and see I'm frowning. The dreaded two lines, the '11s'. I Google *forehead patches for wrinkles* and turn my laptop away so that no one can see.

My Scatterbox inbox is weirdly quiet: nothing from Dom this morning to warn me the meeting was moving, nothing from Lisa. I haven't been cc'd on the agendas for company meetings lately either; the last email about Scatterbox was from seven days ago. I refresh and refresh; nothing new comes in.

Then I think of Elaine, her idea for me, her mentorship, the way she always encouraged me to take on new assignments back at *The D-Low*. I check LinkedIn, and see a new message from her:

SO good to see you. Have a think. Please let me know soon! I'm commissioning all the launch bits over the next few weeks. Fee is £2,500. £1 a word.

I feel suddenly very curious about this 'Opposites Attract' piece – and the extra money would be nice.

I start Googling out of curiosity.

```
solo travel gen z women
single self-love influencers
single gen z instagram
solo influencer sex-positive
singledom influencer community
```

One name keeps coming up again and again. At the top of every search. Naz Chopra. 'The Poster Girl for Single Life' says *Vogue*. 'The Indulgent Life of Naz Chopra' says *Vanity Fair*.

I type her Instagram handle into my browser on my laptop. Her handle is @singlenaz, and she is verified, with 2.2m followers. Her bio reads: *SINGLE / HOT / SOLO DATE EXPERT / FREE SPIRIT / SELF-LOVE FOREVER*.

I move around to the other side of the glass meeting room so that no one behind me can see my screen. I put on my headphones and click 'play' on a clip that Naz just shared on Instagram of her appearing on a recent daytime TV show. She is sitting in a big squishy armchair in a big television studio. She is petite and has a slight Brummie tone to her voice. She has shoulder-length black hair, red lips, a septum piercing, bejewelled headband. She looks barely old enough to drive, yet she has so much confidence that it is radiating out of her.

She is promoting her new book, *Woman: An Island*, which is propped up on the coffee table in front. It's a glossy hardback, with gold foiling that reflects the light and an endorsement on the cover from *Sex and the City* author Candace Bushnell. Naz's name is in large font across the book and again along the bottom of the screen in big promotional capital letters, along with her Instagram handle: @singlenaz. She is good at self-promotion, beginning most sentences with 'as I mentioned in my book . . .' I turn the volume up.

Naz's voice is crisp and clear. 'I believe everything in life is a choice. Every single morning, from the second we open our eyes, we have decided whether we are going to have a good day or a bad day. It's *all* in our minds.'

She taps her temple while she speaks these last words, and her face lights up. She glows on screen. There is a dewiness to her skin, the studio lights reflecting off a creamy highlighter substance on her cheeks. She flicks her shiny black hair over her shoulder and continues.

'Every day, we get to choose to be the loves of our own life – there is a fork in the road, and we pick a path through the wilderness of the forest. You either choose the one that leads to the good wolf or the one that leads to the bad wolf.' She holds her hands out like a clam to indicate the two paths.

I recognize the host – it's the same woman who presented the awards ceremony, with the blonde pixie crop. She's holding a pen and waving it around, trying to get some authority on the conversation. 'If you like making good choices in the mornings, how do you start your day?'

The cameras pan from one woman to the other. They're both wearing so much make-up that I can see the foundation colours hovering on the surface of their skin.

'Well, I am single, so I get to make *all* the rules. No phone in the bedroom. No looking at it until I've done my stretches, done my morning pages, and set my intentions for the day. I can't let anyone's stale energy flow into my mornings. Open your windows, let the light in, set affirmations. Go where the vibrations are the most inviting.'

'Vibrations?'

'Yes – we are all just vibes and energy and stardust.'

I roll my eyes. Vibrations, affirmations, journalling . . . If I did write the piece, Naz would be the perfect Gen Z subject. Self-obsessed, full of spirituality 'lite' catchphrases, and stubbornly locked into her own world view: unable to see beyond her own narrow horizons and understand what's so wonderful about relationships. They involve compromise, of course, but also partnership, safety, and mutual respect.

The thought makes me feel another twinge of guilt for letting Dom down today, and I resolve to cook him something delicious tonight to apologize.

'You're in your early twenties, yes?' the blonde host asks.

Naz Chopra nods, her shiny hair swinging.

'Your generation seem to value freedom and independence. You include recent stats in your book that say a large percentage of Gen Z are currently single. Why do you think that is?'

'Men are gross, firstly!' She looks playfully to the camera. 'I'm *joking*. But, you know, we don't *need* them. I could have a baby on my own, if I wanted to. I would need some sperm, but I don't need *a man*. My older sisters moan about their useless husbands, but they got married at a young age because it was the "done thing". I prefer navigating life alone – it's a total joy, in fact. I don't have to compromise on anything in my life. I love being celibate, too.' She leans forward to pick up a glass of water and sips it, hands still, no nervousness in sight.

'In advocating for single living, you seem quite anti-men?'

'Well, I think men need to do the work on themselves the most, to be honest, yes. But of course, I want to include all people in this discussion, regardless of sexual orientation – whether you're straight, bi, gay, whatever. The point is: being single shouldn't come with such a stigma in this day and age.'

What can she know? She's practically a child . . .

The host splutters her words out in response: 'But isn't a relationship, and marriage in particular, *supposed* to be hard? I'm sure many of our viewers would say that's what relationships are . . . a sacrifice. They take work; they aren't always easy.'

'Yes.' Naz sighs. 'But we're brainwashed into thinking it's normal to be forever tied to someone annoying and clingy – gender non-specific – and always justifying their rubbish actions. I want no part in it. Independence is a much more attractive idea to most young people. Google searches for *solo female travel* grew by 15 per cent this year – why do you think that is? We'd rather be alone than with someone mediocre.'

The blonde host looks a bit defensive, uncrossing then

crossing her legs again, and I wonder if she is one of the married women Naz is talking about. 'What do you find is the most challenging thing about single life?'

'That people don't believe me,' she says seriously. 'People always say: "Oh, but wait until you meet the right person! Oh, but you're so young! You'll change your mind!" It's infuriating. Why can't we believe women when they say what they want?'

She really is strikingly beautiful: huge eyes, glowing skin, very straight teeth. I'm sure they are the teeth of Invisalign braces – aka the teeth an Instagram advert probably bought for her.

She continues enthusiastically: 'We are all here on this giant spinning piece of rock in space, and yet we lose ourselves in an instant for someone else! We lose ourselves to mortgages and taxes and boring miserable relationships, and we worry about little face wrinkles and little rolls on our bellies, and we forget what we *really* want from our lives. We forget to be *selfish*—'

There's a knock at the door, and Guillaume pokes his head into the meeting room. My Naz bubble bursts.

I snap shut the laptop guiltily, and the video stops. It's as if he can sense that I'm cheating on Scatterbox.

'OK if I use this room in five? I'm interviewing the new hires, and this has the best soundproofing.'

I didn't know we were hiring newbies, but I smile and say yes, of course.

'Tell Dom I'm working from home the rest of the day, OK?' I say casually to Guillaume as I gather up my things.

It didn't seem like Dom wanted me here when he comes

back, anyway. He's probably annoyed at me for missing the meeting, and I don't blame him. My one chance to demonstrate publicly how hard I've worked on Scatterbox, and I blow it by going to The Club of all places. I start biting my nails nervously.

I go home via the Italian deli and load up on antipasti, good wine, and a leg of lamb studded with garlic cloves. When I get home, I drop my keys on the side, take off my shoes, put my slippers on and tie back my hair. As I go towards the kitchen, I spot a pile of Dom's shirts in a washing basket on the floor – clearly a prompt that he's running low on shirts. I sigh and get out the ironing board. At least I can somehow make it up to him.

Once the ironing is all folded in a neat pile, I Google a lamb recipe on BBC Food, and an advert for Naz Chopra's book pops up. *Woman: An Island*, again. I'm not surprised I'm being targeted with ads after my earlier online search, and I can't resist clicking through to Amazon to have a look. It has nearly a thousand reviews, even though it was published only last week. This hardback book with an extremely simple cover costs £22.99!

I quickly check Twitter and see her latest post from five minutes ago.

> @singlenaz: it is your BIRTHRIGHT to grow on this Earth. you, me, a sunflower, a blade of glass. we are all the same. what's stopping you from facing the sun and growing taller?? what, or who, is blocking your sunlight?
>   9k likes, 33k reposts

Are you serious? I 'like' it, and then 'unlike' it. I suddenly feel irritated, like some itchy chemical has been left on my skin. What's wrong with being in love, sharing a life with someone, and yes, sometimes sacrificing your own happiness for someone else? It doesn't mean anyone is blocking your sunlight. What's so good about being single, anyway? Why tout it as a romantic lifestyle choice?

I click back onto the recipe page and start assembling the ingredients I need. Then I put on Radio 2 and spend the rest of the afternoon marinating and slow cooking the leg of lamb, humming along to Lenny Kravitz. My leg is twitching; I wonder what Dom's going to say when he comes home, but if we're going to have a row about pulling our weight at work, at least it can be over a meal I've slaved over.

My belly rumbles, my hunger making itself known – or maybe it's also nerves.

7

THEN

August 2016

You look hot, Lola said on WhatsApp, in response to a mirror selfie I shared in the group, showing off my dress and doing the peace sign ironically.

SMOKIN, Alice typed.

Thanks, gals, I replied, putting on some lip gloss in front of the mirror and feeling in that moment like I could, in fact, scrub up quite well when I put my mind to it. My face was sun-kissed from a recent city break to Seville with Dom and his family, and I didn't need any foundation or blusher. I was glowing.

Seven and a half years ago, Dom and I were attending our third wedding of 2016, a summer full of people we barely knew getting married. This particular wedding started at eleven a.m., which we can all agree is too early to start. It was Dom's second cousin getting married at a nondescript manor house in Surrey, a wedding venue that looked like all the others. The bride wore a meringue that felt very retro Eighties, and the groom was pissed from breakfast beers before the wedding even started. Everyone knew he'd be in bed, face-planking the sheets by nine p.m.

The day dragged on for so long that I kept having to take 'loo breaks' in which I sat in a toilet cubicle, doing some breathing exercises while listening to random women compliment each other on their outfits in a clearly fake way. Alice had told me about box-breathing, and so I did what she'd taught me: *breathe in for four, hold for four, breathe out for four, hold for four.*

The day felt endless, like I would age five years by the time the wedding finished and gain wrinkles for life. I couldn't stop yawning. I needed a little breather, but there was nothing left to scroll through on my phone. I couldn't do any more small talk. No more weather chat. No more work chat. No more uncles cornering me, asking me pointless questions. Weddings were much more fun when you got to spend them with friends, not your other half's parents and extended family.

When I came out of the loo, Dom handed me a drink.

'Let's just drink to get through it – I'm bored, too.'

'*So bored,*' I whispered.

'We have no option but to get wasted,' he said, holding me by the shoulders.

We looked over, and a random assortment of Dom's cousins were in a line, doing a dance and singing all the moves to the *Rocky Horror* 'Time Warp' song. Everyone else was sitting in their chairs at circular tables, watching the strange 'Time Warp' dance, tapping their feet as though they were watching some kind of interpretative dance. The tone on the dance floor suddenly changed when the DJ decided to play 'Puppy Love' and invited all the 'loved-up couples' back onto the dance floor. No one was having fun. Even the groom was clearly going through the motions, hoping the day would end soon.

'I know what we could do to pass the time,' Dom said, grabbing my hand. He pulled me back towards the toilets, twirling me around and then pushing me inside a room next to the men's – a baby changing facility.

I felt a thrill of excitement between my legs, the spontaneity, Dom taking the lead, looking tall and broad and handsome in a suit. He locked the door. He pushed me against the wall and kissed my neck in a way that made me feel eighteen again. I was wearing a short, lemon-coloured dress, and it had already risen up by him rubbing his hands all over me. I tried to stay quiet, breathing heavily into his neck, standing in front of the sink, putting my hands on it for support, trying not to break it. He pulled down my lace underwear, and I turned around, standing on tiptoes, while he pushed into me easily and smoothly, in our own familiar way. We caught each other's eyes in the mirror and held our breath while someone tried the door handle. Thankfully, securely locked. Thankfully, we didn't have to face one of his cousins mid-act.

Afterwards, I smoothed my dress down, redid my lipstick, and Dom checked his phone. I felt smug, that feeling of knowing in that moment that your relationship is exciting and intimate and fresh. That feeling of *nobody knowing what we just did.*

'We'll have to make this a regular tradition at weddings,' he said, tucking his shirt in, buckling his belt.

'Even our own?' I said, pushing a strand of sweaty hair behind his ear.

'Hope so.' He kissed me again, opened the door tentatively, and we sneaked out, back to the dance floor – back to the land of interpretative dance.

I sat back down at the white-clothed table, and Dom handed me a vodka tonic, then went off to jump up and down with some guy neither of us knew. I imagined our wedding day and smiled to myself. It would be so much better than this painfully dull snooze fest. We were more exciting than this. We'd just had sex in the bathroom. Nothing about our life would ever be bland and conventional.

8

NOW

From: Lisa <lisa@scatterbox.com>
To: Willow <willow@scatterbox.com>

I've booked a table for you and Dom at Zetter, tomorrow, 8 p.m. Dom says to meet at 7 p.m. for a drink beforehand. Would you like me to book you a taxi from home to take you there?

Thanks!
Lisa

Everything has been strangely calm since I missed the Scatterbox meeting. Dom was vague about it when he got home, saying it was probably for the best since Callum mostly wanted to talk through business strategy with him anyway and then go for pints. He thanked me for ironing his shirts, and he ate his lamb slowly, appearing to savour it, slowly adding lots of salt and pepper, instead of wolfing down his food and racing upstairs to do yet more emails. We even had sex when we got into bed – rare these days, with Dom in the office so much – and as I snuggled into his armpit afterwards, he kissed the top of my head and said, 'We did good, didn't we?' Sleepily, I agreed.

Tonight, he's taking me out for dinner at Zetter, and I've persuaded Alice to come clothes shopping with me in her lunch break. I thought about asking Pen, but I know she'll tease me about Lisa booking our restaurant and judge my outfit choices. Too plain, apparently. Pen thinks I should always wear bright blues and flashy greens to offset my red hair, but the awards night made me realize what I actually need are some plain, high-quality staples that fit me properly and don't break on the way into a fancy party. If I find something I can also wear for my date with Dom tonight, that will be a nice bonus.

Inside the fitting rooms at John Lewis, I hang up my items: a black dress with a quirky big collar, a white shirt, a denim dress, some black twenty-denier tights. My thick red hair is clipped into a bun on top of my head, and my little gold earrings shine and reflect in the mirror. My face looks pale, and my freckles are prominent – I should have worn make-up to try on clothes – and my body is fleshy and purple in the harsh lights. I don't exactly get a thrill from these outfits when I see them in the mirror, but they're flattering, and I look like a thirty-five-year-old professional who wants to be taken seriously. I know Dom will like them, too.

I change back into my holey old jeans and pull aside

the curtain. The woman working in the fitting room has a soothing Australian accent and long black braids. She's humming to herself, then sees me and smiles, while moving things along the clothes rail.

'How did it go in there?' she asks.

'I think I'll take them all,' I say, clutching an armful of clothes.

'Awesome!'

Alice is just outside the fitting-room door, looking at the accessories rail. 'Willow, look, an old-school bumbag – didn't you and Pen wear these to festivals all the time?'

'That bumbag is a popular one, you know. It's unisex, and it's gone viral on TikTok! Selling out fast,' the Australian says chirpily.

'Ooh, they're on sale. Think I'll get two – one for Dom. He'll love it,' I say.

'Aw, is that your boyfriend? You know what they say: couples who dress together, stay together.' She chuckles to herself and hums again.

Alice and I leave to go and pay. A minute later, I turn back on myself, realizing I forgot the tights. There is another woman inside the fitting room, so I have to wait. When the woman comes out, wearing a gorgeous dress, she twirls in front of the full-length communal mirror. I instantly recognize her.

It's only Naz bloody Chopra.

The single guru author woman.

And she is even more annoyingly beautiful in real life. The same dark green jewelled headband sits on top of her shiny dark hair. The same red lips. She is trying on a bright pink and orange patterned dress from the designer section which shows off her waist and boobs. She's paired it with leopard-print boots, and everything clashes gloriously with the tattoos of the moon, sun, and stars that cover her chest and arms.

I wonder what it must be like being that radiant, like a fluorescent light bulb. I wonder why the universe picks only a few people with that level of sparkle – like they have a spotlight on them at all times. Have they been 'chosen'? They aren't the type of people who get normal jobs and do normal things and follow the normal codes of society.

I step just out of sight, backing into the bras and nude pants, feeling weird watching her try on clothes, even if she is outside the fitting room now.

Naz turns to chat to the nice Australian woman who is still sorting the clothes rail. 'Was that woman just in here buying a *matching bumbag* for her boyfriend?' Naz snorts. 'Jesus, what happened to feminism! I'm sure she can do better than that.'

The Australian woman is looking awkward now; she knows that I'm standing right here. She smiles and coughs, continues putting clothes onto hangers, trying to do her job.

I step forward awkwardly. 'Hey, I left some tights in the fitting room, can I grab them?'

'Oh, hi! Yeah sure.' Naz grimaces slightly and goes behind her curtain and out again. 'Here you go,' she says, handing them to me.

I know you, but you don't know me.

As I turn to leave, I look back, and Naz smiles at me. A warm, knowing look. I don't know what to make of it. It's like she's exposed something inside me, and I feel a burning sensation in my chest.

Alice has gone off to try some new lipstick at the Charlotte Tilbury counter, and I stay just out of eye line from the fitting rooms. I wouldn't say I'm hiding exactly, but I'm curious to see what Naz does next. When she comes out, she puts her big sunglasses on and walks over to the designer section. She picks up a jumper I looked at earlier (£400!) and drapes it over her arm in a confident way. I watch her through the clothes rails as she moseys around the shop, snaking her way around mannequins and display tables and jewellery stands. She touches everything lightly, brushing her hands over the material, rubbing fabrics between her finger and thumb. A young girl, perhaps thirteen, recognizes Naz and tugs at her mum's sleeve, and Naz waves and smiles at the young girl and her mother. She turns my way, and I dart behind a mannequin (pointless, way thinner than me) and use this as my prompt to find Alice and leave. I don't mention it to Alice; I'm embarrassed by what I overheard Naz say, and don't know how I feel about it all yet.

Alice heads bravely off for yet more appointments at her family-planning clinic, and I walk down Oxford Street to meet Lola for a quick lunch. As I catch sight of my pale reflection in a shop window, I wonder what it would be like to be Naz Chopra for the day. The glossy hair, the great skin, the money, the attention, the freedom, the recognition, the ease, the inner confidence.

I get a text from Lola saying she is still in Benefit getting her eyebrows done, so I pop in on my way past. She has thick black dye on each brow.

'Hello!' she says. 'Don't be alarmed!'

'Looking good, slug-brow.'

'I always ask them to do them much darker so they last longer. Do I look ridiculous?'

'Only a bit,' I say. 'But you pull it off.'

'Otherwise, it's an absolute rip-off. £25 to dye my eyebrows every few months.' She looks in a handheld mirror and I can see bits of fake tan in between her fingers as she holds it. 'It's called "pink tax".'

Lola probably spends the most time on her appearance out of all of us: dyed blonde hair with dark roots poking out; whitened teeth; smooth skin due to baby Botox; and expensive moisturizers advertised by Victoria Beckham on Instagram. She's always trying new products that have been sent to her by various wedding brands as part of her job. Lola founded a wedding events planning agency called Wedded2u and is constantly on her phone chatting to freaked-out brides.

Once she's done, and her eyebrows have calmed down, we wander over to Pret and sit by the window with two decaf lattes and avocado and chicken sandwiches.

'Sorry, one sec,' Lola says, firing off an email. '*Nightmare* client.' Part of the wedding planner payment 'package' is that they can call or WhatsApp her at any time. A rookie mistake, she is realizing now.

She puts her phone down and takes a sharp breath in. 'Women really are *hysterical* just before their weddings.

Sorry. I'm not meant to say that word, am I? Bit nineteenth century of me.'

'Busy time?' I ask, taking a big bite of my sandwich.

'Very. And Fred's super busy at work too at the moment so I just feel like everything's a bit all over the place. The client I was just emailing is a completely *mad* woman saying that she keeps "having vivid dreams" that the caterers won't show up. Then she had another "dream" that the band had cancelled. I'm surprised she hasn't yet had a "bad dream" that I'm standing over her about to beat her with my clipboard. She rings me up and has a go at me. About her dreams! Little does she realize that SHE is the nightmare.'

'Yikes.'

'Honestly,' Lola continues, shaking her head, 'these women are perfectly sane when you meet them a year before the wedding – softly spoken and pleasant, with sweet, pretty names like Amy or Annabel or whatever. Then, slowly, as they spend more and more on Daddy's credit card, they become more and more *deranged*. One woman demanded that we changed the mirrors in the studio because she didn't like the way she looked in her dress. And a new client I've just taken on wants me to find a watercolour artist who can *paint* the entire day of her wedding and then have all the paintings individually framed for guests. She wants me to find someone who can *paint* two-hundred-and-fifty guests, for twelve straight hours, without breaks! The narcissism, honestly. Sometimes, I unplug myself from the matrix for one moment and . . . ANYWAY. How have *you* been? Distract me from my misery,' she says, putting her phone in her pocket, taking a deep breath and scratching her head.

I hesitate. Somehow, I'm not ready to talk about the opportunity to write for Elaine. Or my run-in with Naz. It's been a week now since she made the offer – perhaps she's given it to someone else by now.

I stick to news of Dom and Scatterbox, instead. 'Well, everything has been going great guns since the award. But Dom's been pulling a ton of late nights, and apart from a couple of cosy evenings in, he's being a little quiet and distant.'

'Ooh.' Lola puts down her sandwich. 'Do you think he might be about to propose? In my professional experience, this is *classic* male behaviour right before a proposal. They act all quiet and secretive, while they fish around for the ring and get their head around it.'

I feel a jolt of excitement. I sit forward in my seat. Could that be it? 'Well, Lisa has booked us in for dinner at Zetter tonight. And it's not even our monthly date night.'

'Oh my god! Yes! Lisa is probably in on it. Maybe she's helping him with the ring, too. Seriously. I know this shit. I can sniff it out. Men act so, so weird right before they propose. They go super quiet and awkward. And they often ask for help from other women they know.'

'Do you think?'

'Yes! And I mean, you've been together for *so long*! It totally makes sense,' she says. 'Ah, I do love a wedding that I don't have to plan.' She sighs, sipping her coffee, then pauses. 'You aren't going to make me plan it, are you?'

'Never. I just hope you're right. I'd love to get excited about something,' I say, holding out my hand, imagining a ring on the finger. 'I'm ready. *Really* ready.'

She touches my hand. 'I'm sure he's just been thinking about the perfect way to do it.' Another email pings into her phone. 'Gotta go. Keep me posted on your hot date with Dom. Text me about it the minute you get home!' She kisses me on the cheek and gives another little 'ooh' of excitement before skipping out of the door, black eyebrows and all.

I spend the afternoon writing and uploading new content to the Scatterbox homepage, and as soon as six p.m. hits, I go upstairs to get ready for my date night with Dom. I pick up my phone to FaceTime Pen and see that it's been nearly two weeks since we last spoke. To be fair, I have been slightly avoiding her lately – I'm just too tired at the moment to say yes to her spontaneous plans. She's always keen to book supper clubs or last-minute rooftop cinema outings, and she's been bugging me about doing one of our seaside trips – and as the only single one in the group, she doesn't always get why her friends can't always just take off at a moment's notice. I don't want to hurt her feelings by admitting that, right now, I'd rather have a quiet night in with Dom than go out somewhere fun (and exhausting) with my best friend.

She doesn't pick up, so I send a quick text asking how she is, throw my phone onto the bed and get changed into my new black dress with the big white collar. I know it will look smart: understated but stylish, and I can glam it up with some bigger gold hoop earrings, black heels, and dark lipstick.

At the last minute, I scoop the bumbags I bought earlier into my tote bag. I know I shouldn't get my hopes up, but if Dom *does* present me with a ring tonight, it would be quite witty to return the favour by giving him a retro bumbag that matches mine. A nod to some fun things we could do this summer? Maybe a festival together? A vow to inject a little bit more fun into life? It's the little things, right?

Meanwhile, my phone pings on the bed.

Pen: Sozzz am bit busy rn. You OK?

I'm glad she's busy – I know that being single sometimes gets her down, so that's one less thing I need to feel guilty about. I send her a thumbs-up emoji followed by the heart emoji.

When my taxi arrives, Dom is already waiting outside the entrance to Zetter hotel bar, looking handsome, scrolling through his phone, frowning slightly with concentration. He looks up, sees me, smiles and waves, opens the taxi door and holds the umbrella over us both as we step inside. Fond memories swirl through my mind: coming down the stairs, feeling beautiful in my sparkling silver dress, dancing with thirty of my friends, eating canapés and drinking Champagne, and singing along to the playlist Pen made at the top of our lungs. Dom and I walk inside and a young friendly waiter gets us seated on a squishy sofa in the corner of the cocktail bar.

'Ooh, I like your collar,' the waiter says, winking at me. 'I'm Barney, and I'll be your server this evening.'

'Thank you,' I reply. It's nice having a compliment, I get a flash of confidence.

I look at Dom, who's looking down at his phone again.

'I'll leave the menus here,' Barney says, smiling at me. 'I'll be back in a jiffy.'

'Doesn't feel like five years ago that I had my party here,' I say, making conversation.

'I know, crazy,' Dom says, finally putting his phone into his trouser pocket.

There's a man playing the piano softly in the corner of the bar, which is mood-lit, enclosed by long curtains, and full of wooden tables and vintage furniture. Dom smells nice. He's wearing a new aftershave, and his hair smells of citrus fruit shampoo. I feel happy to be with him; we're finally out of the house together, away from the mundane routine we'd got into ever since we moved into the Brockley house. The endless conversations about work and meetings and ironing and Scatterbox. I stroke his leg with my foot under the table; then Barney comes back to take our drinks order and puts down some water and nibbles, a bowl of nuts and olives.

'We'll have a carafe of the Malbec, please,' I say.

'Actually – I'm going to have a non-alcoholic beer,' Dom says, looking at Barney and closing the menu. 'I've got to be up early tomorrow.'

'Oh! OK, just a glass of the Malbec for me in that case,' I say to Barney, smiling and handing over my menu.

'Coming right up, lovebirds.' Barney smiles at us and spins away.

'I thought I'd order what we normally have,' I say.

Dom adjusts his shirt collar slightly. 'It's all good. I just don't fancy drinking tonight.'

He's nervous! I think, remembering what Lola said.

He takes a sip of tap water from the glasses in front of us.

'You look nice,' I say.

'So do you,' he says.

His phone vibrates in his pocket. He checks it quickly, presses it back down. I watch the tall man in a navy blazer who's playing the piano, and I zone out as I listen to the music. I study Dom's face as he reads the menu. He looks older, suddenly – some crow's feet around the eyes. I feel a squeeze of love for him in my chest, tinged with nostalgia and sadness. The laughing boy I met at a barbecue in our mid-twenties has grown up into a handsome man, and he has specks of grey hair coming through around the sides, above his ears. We've been through so much over the decade we've been together: different jobs, different houses, grandparents' funerals, illness, growth, different versions of ourselves. I have faith that despite a few bumps in the road lately, we will keep growing together. Lola once described two people being in love as 'two separate houses that have been knocked through'. We are entering into our next chapter, where we need to give the interiors of the houses we've built together a little refresh.

He puts down the menu. 'Willow, there's actually something I need to ask you.'

There's a pause. He's definitely nervous.

'Yes?' I say, smiling.

He rubs his hands together, sweaty palms. 'It's very full on at the moment, I know, and—'

I sit forward on the sofa.

'—and I think there's something we need to discuss.'

'OK . . .'

'Look, I am needed on a really important business trip. That was just Chad confirming some details.'

My cheeks go bright red. I realize I am holding my breath. Not the conversation I was expecting.

'It could be for quite a significant period of time. There's stuff we needed to confirm. I had to get the financing signed off when Callum was over last week. That's why I'm telling you this now, and it might seem quite rushed and out of the blue.'

'What do you mean?'

It's like a bubble that's growing larger and larger in the air, and it's about to burst. That awful, gradual realization of something bad happening that I can't stop. The realization that I wasn't needed in the meeting because he was plotting something else entirely.

'Willow, look, there's no easy way to say this. I'm moving to New York. First for this trip and then for I don't know how long. I want to work out there and grow the business. It's a really great opportunity. Chad and Callum want me to go over there and get a new team set up and—'

'*Callum?*'

'Yes.'

'*New York?*'

'Yes.'

I take a sip of water at the wrong time. It goes down the wrong way. I splutter. I wipe my mouth.

'I know, I know it's a lot. But I'm needed there. For this business. For my own career growth.'

'Are you expecting me to come with you? Am I needed there, too? Is this what you're saying?'

'Well, that's also partly what I wanted to talk to you about . . . I really want to go. And . . . I want to go alone.' He rubs his sweaty hands on top of his trousers. 'We're restructuring the team – and—'

'And what?'

'These new investors, Willow, they are being ruthless about our overheads . . . and it makes sense to cut down on senior roles. We did sort of make up your role, and let's be honest – there hasn't really been much for you to do since the launch. I really need to step up my game, and I can't really be held back.'

My mouth drops open. 'You're . . . *firing* me?!'

'No! No. Of course not. Think of it like a buyout? Look. I'm really so sorry. About all of it. I know this is a lot to take in. But there's no easy way to say it. I can't sit and pretend this life is working for me any longer,' he says, sipping some water shakily.

'Wait. *Scatterbox* not working out . . . or *us* not working out?'

Barney comes back with our drinks on a silver tray, piercing the conversation with an awkward pause.

'Zero per cent beer for you, my man, and the wine for the lady . . .' Barney says.

'Yeah yeah, we've got it, thanks,' Dom says rudely.

Barney backs away slowly.

I can't bring myself to smile politely at Barney. I am blinking a lot, confused.

I'm being *fired* and *dumped* in one foul swoop?

Can this really be happening? Is this a joke?

'Can I get you anything else? We do a Happy Hour that finishes at—'

'*No thanks*,' Dom says under his breath.

Barney mutters something and leaves.

'Look, let's be honest, we're kind of coasting along. I don't want to coast any more, Willow. You're burned out. You're unhappy. So am I. We need to start afresh. Did you really think things were going well, with us, at the moment? We've hardly been together. Hardly spoken . . .'

My stomach is churning now, and I feel sick. I feel *sick*. I think of the stupid bumbag in my tote, wrapped up in stupid tissue paper.

How could I have got this so wrong?

'I – I don't think you know what you're saying,' I stutter.

'This is a big opportunity. I need to take it. Travel is very good for creativity—'

'But . . . you love our home? Don't you? Why would you want to leave? You painted every single wall, fixed every leak, pruned the hedges, hung up frames . . .' I am trying so hard not to cry. If I start crying, I won't be able to stop. He doesn't usually make rash decisions. I thought he hated the whole YOLO vibe.

'We've had an amazing time together. But we're at a fork

in the road now. I feel like I need to live my life in a different way. Time is moving quickly – we're not getting any younger, and this is an exciting time for the company. When else will I get a chance to work and see the world and be so flexible with my life? This will be good for you, too, in the long run. Willow, I'm really sorry. I'm just not able to go to the next stage. I'm not sure if I even want a family.'

I don't know who this person is. He is speaking so matter-of-factly, all the love and joy drained from his face. He is speaking in the past tense. He isn't looking at me; he's looking through me.

'Can't we discuss this? Work something out?'

I stare at his face and see that something has changed: he is no longer the Dom I met years ago. He is done. No longer the man who wants to marry me. The warmth has gone; replaced with a cold, selfish distance. The wall is up. He is on a solo mission; I can see it now. I am clearly no longer the person he remembers either.

I bite my lip, still trying not to cry. 'What about our plan? You kept saying "soon"!'

He won't look me in the eye. 'Sorry. I know. I *know*. Things have changed. *I've* changed. This is really hard for me, too,' he says.

'How long have you been feeling like this?' I ask.

'A while,' he says, looking a bit sad himself now.

I search his face for proper answers but can't find what I'm looking for. I have a frog in my throat now, and it isn't going to budge.

'Do we have to discuss it here?' I whisper, tearing up now.

This bar has such fond memories, and it's fast becoming a place I'll never want to come back to.

'I really am so sorry. You could live in the house still, if you like. I can move out and give you space.'

'I can't believe this is happening,' I say. 'I need you, though. I need you, Dom—' I put my hand around his wrist.

He wriggles free. 'Willow, no.'

I'm embarrassed by my desperation, and I can't stop myself any longer. My tears start to fall, spilling down my cheeks.

'What do we do now?' I sob.

He puts his face in his hands, as if he can't look at me.

Then, he does look at me, and he seems sympathetic all of a sudden. 'You should go home; I'll book you a cab. I'll go to my parents'. I really am sorry I had to tell you like this. I wanted it to happen in a different way, but then tonight I got all these confirmation emails . . .'

I leave the bar, and he doesn't come after me, which makes my stomach sink. Why isn't he following me? Why did he pick this bar that I love to do it?

Then he reappears, checking I'm OK, asking if he can book me a cab. I tell him to leave me alone, and I walk outside in the pouring rain. Everything feels heavy. My arms and legs and my sodden black dress with its stupid fucking collar. I step through all the puddles in the road. I don't have an umbrella. I trudge through the streets, soaking my shoes. I walk past the place we went to with his parents a few years ago for afternoon tea; the cocktail bar where we celebrated securing the Scatterbox offices; a steak restaurant I took him to for his twenty-eighth birthday.

Ten years obliterated in a ten-minute conversation.

I give up walking, a blister forming in my shoe, pinching at my skin. I lean against a brick wall, catching my breath. A woman with two young kids stops to ask me if I'm OK. I nod and plaster on a smile to hide my pain. She can't stay; it's raining, and her kids are getting soaked. I just allow the rain to pour down onto me and stand there in my heavy, wet clothes. Then I flag down a cab, and the driver looks at me in his rear-view mirror, spots that I'm crying – but he doesn't ask me any questions, just kindly hands me a tissue and a mint.

When I get home, I'm still in total shock. Sat at the kitchen table, drenched, my phone pings with a notification. It's a preview of a message from Lola full of diamond emojis and question marks. I leave her message unread. I can't bear it.

I spot Dom's leftover plate in the sink, a plate he has not bothered to wash up even though it would take two seconds, and I throw it on the floor, smashing it to pieces, debris going everywhere. I don't clean it up. Instead, I crawl upstairs and crash into bed, desperate for the oblivion of sleep.

Part Two

9

NOW

'I think we need to get her in the shower.' I hear Carla's concerned voice. She's obviously used the spare key. I can't move. I don't know what day it is.

'Is she asleep?' I hear Lola whispering back.

Their light footsteps patter around me. They are approaching my bed. I have a pillow stained with light brown coffee covering my face so that I can barely see anything. Why are they tiptoeing around my bedroom like a little pair of mice? Lola actually does look quite like a mouse, very small features, cute pointy ears, and rosy cheeks. Carla is heavy-footed in her flat-form Birkenstock sandals that make the floorboards creak.

'Is she . . . breathing?' Carla whispers, lowering her head to the bed.

'Maybe we should run a bath—' Lola whispers back.

'—and then we can lift her into it?'

'I'm going to crack a window.'

'Good idea.'
'You know what, I'm going to get some Febreze . . .'

When Carla and Lola find me, I am naked under a mound of laundry and Dom's dirty clothes, my red, greasy hair splayed out messily on the pillow. I don't actually know how long I've been lying like this. There is a pile of banana skins next to the bed, because all I have been eating are bananas. I ate them slowly; it felt primitive.

I upturned the laundry basket onto myself in a moment of desperation, wanting to feel close to Dom. I am burying myself inside a cave of Dom and his past unwashed aromas, and I don't want to come out from this pit. It's not my finest hour, I'm aware. But I enjoy breathing in the scent of his deodorant. That musty energizing male scent mixed in with old stale T-shirt material. A familiar smell I woke up to every morning for the last decade of my life.

I have absolutely no idea who I am without him – without being in a couple, next to him, in response to him, within the giant context of him.

Who am I?

Carla gently takes a hold of my ankle and gives it a wiggle. I feel her weight pressing on the end of the bed. Bubble and Squeak are here too, I smell them before I see them. Carla places one of the dogs on the bed and she starts licking my toes. The other barks loudly.

'Willow, darling. Come on. We're here for you. It's OK.'
A pause.
She wiggles my dirty foot again. 'Willow.'

'Not coming out,' I say, my voice muffled under the pillow.

'You can't fester in here forever, sweetheart.'

'Maybe I can. I can become half-woman, half-mattress. Maybe Channel 4 can make a documentary about me.'

'I'm going to get a wet flannel and put it on your face if you don't come out from under there,' Carla says, something she used to threaten to do when I was a teenager and was refusing to get up and go to school.

I take the pillow off me and look at her and cry. An animalistic cry, more like a guttural roar. Carla and Lola get into the bed with me and lie there for bit, stroking my greasy hair. We lie in silence, the three of us. Bubble and Squeak nestle at my feet. I know I smell bad and that Dom's crusty clothes smell bad, too. Tears pour from my eyes and drip into my ears. I feel like a stock image of a woman crying. The results of searching *heartbroken girl in bed* on Shuttershock.

Carla and Lola move me gently out of the laundry/bed situation, linking their arms with mine, and we walk slowly down the stairs together to the sofa, as though I'm an elderly person and need a walking stick. I am in an old grey dressing gown, naked and vulnerable underneath, and Lola slides a large polka-dot mug of warm tea into my hands. She has brought with her a pile of magazines, three packets of bagels, and a long strip of Penguin chocolate bars. She tells me a joke from the back of one of the bars, but it fails to land. In our teen years, we'd come home from a boozy night out and eat two bagels each and mainline three Penguin bars before passing out, spooning. The items sit silently on the table, and I appreciate the small act of love, even though I can hardly speak.

'Sweetheart,' Carla says softly. 'It's quite cold – shall we turn the heating up?' She is rubbing her hands on her knees, getting up from the sofa. 'Where is the heating unit?' She looks at me, and I have a blank expression. 'Actually, don't worry. I'll figure it out.'

I walk past the hallway mirror and catch my reflection – my face is withdrawn and colourless. Even my freckles are pale; my skin looks like porridge. In the kitchen, the shared calendar Pen gave us as a housewarming gift is stuck on the day Dom left: a time warp where linear time doesn't exist. Days roll past, but they blur into one. He hasn't messaged me since he packed up most of his stuff and moved back to his parents' house. I texted Florence multiple times as it felt easier to try and get information from her, but she just keeps saying vague things like I need to 'give him some time'.

I keep texting her, but she's no longer replying.

The house feels echoey and odd and so different without him here. The flowers in the kitchen are dead. A light bulb is broken in the hallway, and I don't know how to change it. Things are no longer as they were.

Downstairs, Lola is firing up *Bridget Jones's Diary*, putting the DVD in the PS4 (which fortunately Dom forgot to take). We sit and slowly eat the chocolate and bagels together. Carla cleans the kitchen, wearing Marigolds and spraying every surface with a luminous pink spray.

'When did he leave?' Lola asks.

'About a week ago. He packed up a load of stuff himself,

which was so awkward, and then a removal van came to get more things.' I cannot believe how quickly it happened. We had that chat at the bar, then he went to his parents', and then practically all his stuff is gone a week later. 'It makes me think he's been planning this for ages?'

'Oh, sweetheart, I'm so sorry,' Carla says.

'Why didn't you tell us straight away?' Lola says. 'We would have come straight over.'

'I don't know,' I say. 'I guess I had to let it sink in.' I don't think I can bear to face Pen, not yet. She'll see inside my soul and know that I can't face life without Dom, and she'll try and give me tough love to shake him off. I don't think she ever really liked him that much, and I'm not ready to hear that. I'm not ready for pep talks about being 'strong'. I'm not ready for her tough sister love.

Lola rubs my back. 'Pen and Alice both send tons of love. I know they'll want to see you as soon as you feel ready – but you just choose your moment, OK?'

I nod.

'And what's the deal with work and everything?' Lola says. 'Is there anything we can do to help?'

'Well, I'm leaving Scatterbox. Dom's organizing an "exit fee" for me.' My eyes fill with tears again.

'Wow. Are you OK with that?' Lola asks.

'I think so? I feel so, so sad about what's happening, but in terms of the job, it's a relief to not have to go back there.'

'Makes sense to have a clean break from that place,' Carla says, eating a digestive biscuit.

'But it's doing so well?' Lola says.

I shrug. *So?*

'I'm sure you'll get a good payout,' Lola says.

'We don't have to think about that, now,' Carla adds gently.

I put my head on Carla's shoulder, and she flinches slightly.

'I say this with love, Willow, darling, but you need to wash your hair now.'

'Huh?' I say, a mouth full of bagel.

'Smells very bad, my love.' She says it so tenderly, with her hand on my shoulder.

'I'm going to run you a bath,' Lola says, getting up from the sofa.

The gesture of running a bath for someone – putting in the bath bubbles, testing the temperature, and lighting some candles – is a very intense kind of love language. I feel it deeply. It also highlights how much my relationship with Dom has evaporated over time; I can't remember the last time he made me feel physically loved or taken care of.

When I walk into the bathroom, Lola is crouching down, blonde hair tied back, sleeves rolled up, cupping some lavender salts in her manicured hands.

I sit on the bathroom floor. 'Thank you,' I croak.

'Nearly ready,' Lola says, testing the bath water once more with her hand doing a figure of eight and sprinkling in a few more bath salts.

I strip off, and she helps me in slowly. I am slightly embarrassed by my unruly bush, but it's nothing she hasn't seen before, and I sink down into the suds. She turns the Roberts radio on the shelf to BBC Radio 2.

'Right, now, try to relax. Settle your nervous system. We'll be downstairs. Take your time.' She gives me a sympathetic smile and shuts the door slowly, before turning back in. 'Would you like me to wash your hair?'

I could cry, I nod.

Lola lathers up my hair and gives me a head massage, while 'Breakdown' by Tom Petty and The Heartbreakers plays on the radio.

She finishes massaging. She rinses. She leaves. I do feel better, being in water. I let the foamy bubbles roll over my stomach. I try to block out the intrusive thoughts I have about dunking my head under and staying there.

I want everything to go back to the way things were. I miss him making his disgusting Huel and lumpy protein shakes. I miss the sight of our two sides of the bed: mine with three books piled neatly, a pair of tortoiseshell glasses and a marble face roller; his with empty mugs, an overflowing wallet, two watches, and a big gross pile of loose silver change. I miss a full fridge with meals for us to enjoy together. I miss being part of a two.

I sink further into the soapy suds, and the tears come again.

10

THEN

July 2015

For my twenty-seventh birthday, Carla took me on a surprise trip to New York. She told me to pack clothes for hot weather, and when we arrived at Heathrow, she passed me a gift bag. I unwrapped a yellow mug that said *I ♡ NYC*. I had no idea this was the plan; I'd pictured a package holiday to Lanzarote or Tenerife, not New York. It had been on my bucket list for years.

When we arrived, it was sticky and humid with highs of 30°C. Not even the smell of hot rubbish lining the streets in bin bags could put me off. I was finally in the city that never sleeps! We stayed in a tiny little hotel room in Williamsburg, which was basically just a small double bed surrounded by four walls. We dumped our bags and went to explore, fending off any jetlag. We got the subway to Manhattan, got off at 14th Street–Union Square, the 'Oxford Circus' of New York, and walked for an hour, up towards Central Park, in pretty much a straight line.

We walked past so many exciting and iconic sights from the movies: yellow taxis, pizza shops selling by the slice, tall buildings that make you feel dizzy if you look up for too long, huge department store windows, bagel shops, vintage stores, signs for psychics, the New York Public Library, endless coffee shops. Everyone was wearing leggings or cycling shorts and holding a big iced coffee, and most people had a small dog. We walked past a little shop selling second-hand typewriters, and I lingered outside for a while, looking in the window. There was a bright red one, the sunlight shining off the metal, the price tag ($325), and a sign that read: *Rare find. Bright red Silver Reed Silverette typewriter, made in 1980, fully functional, with new ribbon and original hard case.* It immediately made me feel warm and fuzzy.

'That's exactly like the one I got you!' Carla said, noticing me looking at it.

'It is, just in a different colour,' I said, smiling. 'That was the best gift anyone ever gave me. I hope you didn't pay that much for it?'

'So what if I did? You know, I think you had a past life here, in this city,' Carla said. 'I think you used to be a little old lady with a typewriter overlooking Central Park. I think you're attracted to the energy here because you're chasing down a former self.'

'That is *such* a you thing to say,' I laughed. 'Come on.'

We walked into Central Park, saw an old man playing 'Despacito' on a mandolin who smiled at us, and gazed at lots of turtles swimming in the ponds. We found a patch of shade under a tree, and Carla took off her sandals, rubbing her feet.

'Did you ever come to New York with my mum?' I asked, picking a blade of grass.

'No, she didn't like big cities,' Carla said. 'She craved only peace and quiet. She used to try and find car-free islands. She loved being where no one else wanted to go. I don't think she would like it here.'

'Do you like it here?'

'Well, I like it, mainly because you like it, and it's nice seeing you happy.' She smiled.

'It's strange to not know where she is, isn't it?'

'I know, sweetheart. It is strange. I do know that she would be really proud of you.'

'Would she? Then why isn't she here?'

'You know why. It's complicated.'

That was always Carla's line. And it's true: depression and mental health are complicated.

'She's been a stranger to me for such a long time,' I said.

'I know,' Carla said softly. 'But we can always talk about her, as little or as often as you like.'

I changed the subject. 'I've been invited to a networking event tonight in Manhattan – Elaine used to live here and she's sent me an email about it, said she'd put my name down. I wonder if I should go.'

'Well, do you want to?'

'I think so, yes. More contacts are never a bad thing. Elaine's always telling me that.'

'Then you should go!'

'Are you sure you don't mind? We're meant to be on this special trip together.'

'Not at all – I will run a bath and do my crosswords. We've got heaps of time, the whole week! Go and have fun.'

The women's networking event was hosted in a small Italian bistro with a back room. I'd got the subway on my own and navigated a few blocks as dusk fell over the city, gazing at brownstones and bar queues and neon restaurant signs. When I arrived, a very tall woman in a rainbow dress came over and introduced herself loudly.

'Willow, so nice to meet you – I'm Nina, and this is Kimberley and Jemima. We are all freelancers for the *New York Post* and *The Washington Post*. So happy you're enjoying New York!'

'Nice to meet you. Thanks for having me.'

'*Love* your accent,' Kimberley said. 'I'm a fan of Kate Middleton. Don't you just love her?'

'I guess,' I said, taking a drink from a passing waiter.

Nina then spoke loudly again, telling us at length about how important her husband was and describing in detail his new role as chairman of their local golf club, telling us how they'd just moved to some new Hamptons area – I didn't catch the name, but she kept saying it was the 'Cotswolds' of New York.

'So, you work with Elaine Jefferson?' Kimberley asked me, once she could get a word in edgeways. 'That's cool – I used to work with her, too, when she lived in New York.'

'Yeah, she's great. I've worked with her for a few years now in London at *The D-Low*. I'm just visiting on holiday with my aunt at the moment. I love how Elaine is always sending me random opportunities.' I laughed.

'If she likes you, she'll always give you a leg-up. You know, I've always wanted to come to England. I want to visit Edinburgh.' She pronounced it *Edin-bor-ough*.

'It's lovely there.' I didn't say it's actually in Scotland.

Then she got out her phone and started Googling flights to Edinburgh, turning her back to me, and I stood there in silence. I suddenly felt homesick and didn't want to be in the restaurant any more. The room was spinning slightly; I took it all in, the clashing voices, the women with YSL bags and big fake smiles and loud laughs, talking over each other.

Somehow it wasn't the night I'd expected. Feeling a headache coming on, and social anxiety churning in my gut, I made up an excuse to leave.

'You're back early?' Carla said, when I opened the hotel room door with my keycard. She was already in bed at nine p.m., wearing her cotton pyjamas and watching TV.

I dumped my bag and sighed. 'It was fine; I just wasn't in the mood.'

'Oh, honey, come here. Look, I'm watching *Sex and the City*. Get into your jimjams, and I'll order us room service. I was just about to order something anyway. They've got chickpea burgers.' She put her cheap reading glasses on and opened the big leather menu.

My whole body suddenly melted into a happy place. I got

into the warm bed beside Carla, underneath the crisp white hotel sheets, and felt comforted beyond belief at the smell of her cocoa butter moisturizer and the sound of her ordering us burgers and salty French fries.

Ambition and networking could wait. Instead I'd watch fictional characters staying up until dawn in the Big Apple while I lay there under a cosy duvet with the one person who always understood me and was always there. Next to Carla, I was always home.

11

NOW

It's the last day of me living in what was once Dom's and my dream home. All my clothes and cookbooks and kitchen equipment are already in boxes. The sight of the empty kitchen makes me want to cry. The dismantling of a future that no longer exists. A shared house that used to be so warm – with the heating on blast, kettle always on, Dom's pants drying on the clotheshorse – is now a shell of itself and freezing cold. It's any old house now, stripped of all personality. The house was put in Dom's name, via Scatterbox earnings (also in Dom's name) – and now I'm being told, in no uncertain terms by his lawyers, to step back. As we're not married, it's unlikely I'll be able to get anything once it sells. I don't have the energy to think about any of it right now. It's all too bleak.

'Dom's probably feeling right at home in New York already,' I say, sighing.

New York was my dream.

'Come on, sweetheart -- let's try and be as quick as we can. We need to get you out of this house,' Carla says.

'Bad energy here.' Lola shivers. 'It's definitely time to go.'

We get down on our hands and knees to put my remaining bits into huge blue IKEA bags. We do a supermarket sweep and start loading everything into Carla's trusty RAV4. Clothes, cutlery, pots and pans, picture frames, photo albums, magnets on the fridge from holidays, shared books, my box of ancient festival gear. All the remnants of a home.

Next, I go into our shared office space: the tiny little spare room next to our main bedroom. I clear out the cupboards and find lever-arch files of boring admin, council tax documents, bills, NatWest statements.

I come across a wooden box of ticket stubs and old DVDs and feel the lump lodge back in my throat. When Dom and I first started dating, we used to meet at the same diner in Shoreditch every week and then go to the cinema. Before the movie, we'd peel back the layers of each other over a burger.

If Pen were here, I know she'd tell me to chuck them in the bin without a second thought, but I can't quite bear to do it. Instead, I put them into a box marked *Admin – keep* and decide to deal with them another time.

Once I've finished my rummage through overflowing drawers, I pull out a box from a cupboard in the spare room. I'd completely forgotten this was here. It's heavy and dusty, and when I open the lid, more dust flies out, going up my nose. I cough and sneeze and feel momentarily sick, remembering that dust is basically dead skin cells and old bits of hair.

I open the box, and there it is: my old typewriter, the one Carla gave me. Still looking shiny and new, electric blue, a classic Silver Reed from the Eighties.

Carla pops her head around the door frame and sees me staring at it.

'Oh! You used to *love* writing on that,' she says. 'You used to write me letters to practise your typing. Do you remember?'

It feels like yesterday that Carla gave it to me for my birthday when I was a teenager and I spent long full days in my bedroom, tapping away. I remember Carla bringing me up food and glasses of squash, because I was so obsessed with it. Once, I copied out the full length of *Matilda*, word by word, to practise my typing speed.

'I forgot all about this,' I say, stroking the keys. 'Yeah, I used to love it.'

'Why did you put it away for so long?' she asks, kneeling down next to me.

'I don't know,' I say.

Perhaps there's a lot of myself that I put away?

Inside the typewriter box is a handwritten note from Carla, which she gave me along with the gift:

Dearest Willow,

Happy birthday, sweet one.

The thing about writing is that it's not just some random pastime: it's a way of owning your own narrative. It's very important for women to do this. Every time you type something, you are taking back power. You get to be the author of your own life. The amazing thing about typewriters is that you can physically see the act of magic happening! Ink and paper. It's not ephemeral and digital and gone tomorrow. Each key being pressed so deliberately, the letters printed onto the page, making the right choices, slowly. Remember this. Write your life!

C xxx

I think about Naz, the article, Elaine, my old writing career. I know now isn't really the time, but my fingers itch to look at her feed. I sit down on the spare-room bed and open Naz's Instagram page.

I immediately wish I hadn't. She's just been on a #*presstrip* to Sri Lanka, and the photo reel is full of spectacular sunsets over white-sand beaches and fresh seafood platters that make my mouth water. I scroll back and see that, in the last month, she's also gone on a tantra retreat in Tulum – courtesy of the 'female pleasure' company she's currently working with – plus a wine tasting tour in Italy and a music festival in Barcelona. I see she's just posted something new and scroll back up – it's her smiling with a copy of her book in front of the Notting Hill independent bookshop Lutyens & Rubinstein, wearing a big Rejina Pyo dress that's been #*gifted*.

I turn my phone to airplane mode and bring one of the heavy boxes out to Carla's car. I stand there for a moment, in the cold, under the grey London skies, holding a relationship's worth of rubbish in my arms, wondering if my life will always look like this.

Once I've chucked out the contents of the spare room

and Carla's hoovered the floor, we're done. The rest will go into storage whilst we decide what do with it; a job for when I have the strength. Lola puts some Post-it notes on cardboard boxes. We're sweaty and tired, so we decide to go to The Nag's Head down the road for one last pint, before I leave this neighbourhood forever.

This is it, I think to myself.

Lola grabs three pints from the bar and three packets of salt and vinegar crisps. I look at them both from across the table, slumped in my seat, unsure how to thank them enough for their help today. Fairy godmothers, the pair of them.

'So, first job,' Lola says, holding out her hand, 'is blocking Dom on all social channels. Following him in New York is just rubbing salt into the wound, you don't need that in your life, Willow.'

'I can't,' I say, clutching the phone tightly.

'You can and you will.' Lola forcibly grabs the phone and demands the passcode so that she can get to work.

Next, Carla puts a notebook and a pen on the table.

'Here. It will make the heartbreak and the reality of the situation easier, if you look the remaining admin in the eye,' Carla says, handing me the pen.

'I'll do it later,' I say, pushing it away.

'It's best to get it out of your head. Putting things down on paper is the answer. Trust me. When in need, pick up a pen. You know this. Come on.'

She puts the blue biro in my hand and gives me a reassuring nod, like she's a wizard handing me a wand.

- *Cancel joint Hello Fresh subscription*
- *Put a forwarding out-of-office on shared email address*
- *Then delete shared email address from phone*
- *Bin Two Together railcard*
- *Tell mutual friends (Bill and Laura, Christian and Kemi) that we can no longer come to their weddings as a couple*
- *Tell accountant/move money out of the shared bank account*
- *Work out who owns what: TV, furniture, bedding, IKEA lamps, soup spoons, artwork*
- *Message Dom's parents to say thank you and goodbye?*
- *Cancel next year's holiday hotel booking on Booking.com*
- *Put photo albums of us together in a box or bin?*
- *Get new job*
- *Get new home*
- *FML*

As I write the last one, tears prick again, but Carla rubs my arm and says, 'I know you think your life is over. But you have so much to give this world. I promise you this is really just the beginning.'

I swallow. I'm so grateful for her support and for Lola's, too. I wonder about the others. I know Alice has another appointment with her doctor, but I haven't heard from Pen in the last week or so – not since she sent me a few sympathetic messages when she heard Dom and I had broken up.

'Do you know how Pen is?' I ask. 'I thought she might be here.'

Lola looks a bit awkward. 'Pen's actually on a weekend

away at the seaside. I messaged her earlier. She told me to give you a big hug for her.'

'With who?'

'A guy.'

'A *guy*?'

'Called Mike.'

'Really?'

Pen has not been on a good date in years.

'I know,' Lola says, raising her eyebrows slightly.

'Who is he?'

She shrugs. 'Haven't got any intel yet.'

I instantly feel even sorrier for myself. 'She could have texted me,' I grumble.

'I know. I'm sorry. I'm sure she will. She seems a little . . . distracted.'

'It's not like her,' I say, looking at my phone. My empty phone with no new messages on it.

Carla is sitting in the chair that Dom normally sits in. His chair, his local pub. His brand of beer (Neck Oil) would usually be in front of him in a pint glass.

'Dom's in New York now. He has a flat in the East Village.' I sigh. 'Sorry, *apartment*,' I say mockingly. 'I couldn't resist a quick look on Instagram.'

'Oh no, Willow. Social media is the curse. It stops people from healing.'

'I don't want to disconnect yet. I want to keep tabs on him. I want to follow his movements. I want to know what he's doing, who he's with . . . which neighbourhood of New York he's in.'

'I don't think that's wise. I think that needs to be nipped in the bud now,' Lola says matter-of-factly.

I feel like they're ganging up on me.

A part of me does want to tune into his every move like it's a Netflix horror show. I want to see who he meets, what he eats, where he sleeps, the girls he's tagged in photos with. I want to screenshot his Instagram Stories and zoom in. I want to live his New York life alongside him, in the same way I want to pick at a painful scab. I am sad and confused and jealous and feel sick constantly, like I've eaten a dodgy prawn. New York, too. New York, a city I've dreamed about for so long. A city where I have such fond memories with Carla.

'However you feel, I *promise* you it will pass. It always passes. I know how much you cared for Dom; I know it was something special, but when people leave our life, we have to accept it,' Carla says, looking out of the window. 'It's just the way the Earth is moving – you are being pulled in a new direction. You can't fight it. I'm so sorry.' She rubs my back. 'It is the way, the *tao*.'

I stare into space. I am a floating brain and body. I am not Willow. I don't know who she is without a partner. I am a shell, a carcass, a picture that needs colouring in. The pub speakers are playing a song that reminds me of Pen.

'Fast Car'.

I text her, but the text doesn't deliver. Only one tick.

12

THEN

January 2015

Nine years ago, we were sitting in our favourite spot on Eastbourne beach. The sun was low in the sky, and the sea was calm. Pen had brought a small stainless-steel bonfire; we had no idea if this was allowed or not, but we'd done it every year for the past four years without anyone saying anything or telling us off.

Each year, we would write down a wish, something we wanted for ourselves, and we would put the pieces of paper in the fire to burn. I always thought you were meant to burn the things you wanted to let go of, but Pen's way was slightly different. She said we had to write down our 'intentions' and then throw them in the fire to seal them – by doing so, you were sharing them with the 'fire gods' and watching them burn to show you were serious.

We sat on tartan blankets, and I opened up the

overflowing picnic basket, pulling out plastic glasses, white wine, baguettes, cheese, and mini sausages. Pen was wearing a cape, and we found it hysterical.

'Capes are IN FASHION,' Pen said, rolling her eyes at us.

'I'm sorry,' Alice said, taking small breaths between laughing. 'It's just that this intention-setting business is witchy enough as it is, and now you're in an actual cape.'

'You really look the part, babe,' Lola said, wearing a light pink hoodie and tying her hair in a bun.

'Oh, shh, and write down your intentions please,' Pen said, chucking biros and little scraps of paper at us. 'And take this seriously. Otherwise the fire gods will reject your ideas.'

'Oh please,' Lola said.

'Remember that your intention can't include a timestamp on it. That is not how the universe works. You can set a broad intention, but you can't expect it to happen by a specific date. You have to remain open. Don't be too greedy – the universe doesn't like greedy.'

'Really? Oh.' Alice crossed something out on her piece of paper.

'I don't make the rules,' Pen said, chewing at the end of her biro.

I looked out to sea, and we went quiet for a moment, each of us taking our time to write down what we wanted to say to ourselves. The clouds were moving quickly across the sky, and I looked for a sign. What did I want? Everything was good. I lived in London with Pen. I had great friends. I had a job at a grown-up magazine. I was falling in love with Dom.

I bit my lip, my pen hovered over the paper. Eventually I wrote down: *please help me find what is still missing.*

After we put our intentions into the fire, Alice lay down with her head on my lap. 'Do you ever feel like you're in a freeze-frame moment of your life?' she said. 'Like, you're very aware that you're inside something that will be a really significant memory one day?'

'Yeah, this definitely feels like one,' Lola said. Her toes were stretched out, legs fake tanned, nails polished a soft pink, sandals discarded to the side. The waves curled into themselves like ribbons of butter under the inky sky. 'Like, right now. The four of us, with so much of our future ahead of us.'

'People say it won't always be like this,' Pen said.

'Nah, we'll always stick together,' Lola said.

'We'll be fine.' Alice was pouring out white wine into plastic beakers. 'We just need to always be honest with each other.'

'You losers can't get rid of me that easily,' Pen said, lighting up a Camel Blue.

'Especially in that cape,' Lola said.

'All you need is a broom,' Alice added, cheekily.

I laughed and gazed into the bonfire, the flames flickering around all our paper promises, and reflecting back in the pupils of my eyes.

13

NOW

The morning after the move, I wake up at Carla's in Eastbourne, in 'my room'. It is so familiar to me, which I am grateful for. The large window in front of the bed with a distant view of the sea. The plants lined up on the windowsill. The pale pink walls. The floral bedding. The blue rug with stitched-on waves. I spent my entire childhood here. Carla could have turned it into a spare room, but it has remained untouched.

There are still Polaroid pictures of me, Lola, Alice, and Pen stuck on the walls by the white desk in the corner. Photos with friends I'm no longer in touch with, old work colleagues who moved away. Band tickets, film posters, Post-it notes from school. The healing crystals from Carla that Dom used to tease me about and the inspirational quotes that I was obsessed with as a teenager, ripped from *Just Seventeen*. A framed picture of me and Pen one hot summer in Spain sits on the desk, a selfie of us sweating our tits off in 40°C heat, smiling and clutching two cold beers. I put it face down in a drawer.

I sit down and lift the typewriter box onto the desk, blow more dust and cobwebs off it, and open the lid.

I tear out a page from an A4 jotter, and line it up, twisting the platen knob slowly on the side. I think back to a conversation I had with Ms Gower, my English teacher. She gave us writing prompts during our classes to help us process our feelings and develop our writing skills. Years after I left school, she kept emailing me to ask if I'd written anything, encouraging me gently from afar. I tried to reach out to her a few years ago, but she must have changed her email address or changed her name; maybe she got married, moved away, disappeared.

I search for her name in my emails and reread one from fifteen years ago.

> Dear Willow,
>
> One prompt I love is writing down what you remember, any old memory – start there, beginning with 'I remember'. When we start writing down anything we remember, our brain goes into 'word association' mode, so you can start writing about a beautiful horse you see in a field one day and then end up writing about your grandma who used to ride horses as a young woman.
>
> Keep writing!
>
> Feel free to send me anything. I'd be happy to read it.
>
> All the best,
>
> Ms Gower

I feel a sadness in my stomach, I never did send her anything. I never did give the writing prompt a go – I was too busy partying. I stretch out my fingers, look out of the window, and decide to type memories of Dom, the keys making a loud clacking sound as I go:

I remember
    Our first date. You booked us tickets to see some *Planet of the Apes* film. Pen was right: I hated the movie and closed my eyes for most of it. It's such a stupid film really, but I loved being sat next to you: your hand on my knee, the roomy seats, the snacks, the cosiness, the comfort, the popcorn smells. The beginning of everything.

I remember
    I went on a night out with the girls in Soho, and I had a terrible time, and I couldn't stop crying in the toilets, and you drove all the way into central London to come and get me. I couldn't stand that feeling of being alone in the bathroom. You were there, on the other end of the phone. You were so understanding back then.

I remember
    When my laptop broke just before a big magazine deadline at *The D-Low*. You bought me a new one. You put it on our bed, with a ribbon around it, a bag from the Apple Store. Ever since Mum left, I

never believed in relying on a 'safety net', but you felt like mine.

I remember

When Carla and I met you at the airport. I was eight. We had a banner. We thought that you'd come home this time to settle and want to be with me at home, be a family. It didn't take long for you to start leaving the house with the door left wide open and disappearing again.

I remember

One night you came home late. Carla was looking after me. I was in bed, and I wasn't asleep, but my eyes were closed. You were swaying in the doorway, wired. You turned the bright main bedroom light on and just stared at me across the room, your daughter, asleep in her bed surrounded by her soft toys. It was like you wanted to make yourself connect, like you wanted so desperately to want to stay but you couldn't. You turned off the light eventually and closed the door behind you.

I put the lid back onto the typewriter. I take the paper out and scrunch it into a ball and chuck it in the bin next to the desk.

Carla pokes her head around the door. 'Can I hear you typing?'

'Meh,' I say, pointing at the bin. 'It's no good.'

'Impossible,' Carla says. 'So nice to see you on that old thing again. It's a beautiful day, and I'm out in the garden. Join me?'

Carla's bungalow has a good-sized garden that she takes great care of by pruning and weeding. Her She-Shed is down at one end, painted the same creamy white as the clouds in the sky. Flowerbeds in a wavy design with tall verbena sprouting everywhere. You can see a sliver of sea from the front window of the shed, a pale blue horizon that, today, seems to wink in the sun. The smell of faint sea air always feels welcoming.

While Carla does some weeding in her enormous straw hat, I get on the old exercise bike in the She-Shed, determined that one good thing to come from leaving Scatterbox will be getting my energy levels back and getting rid of the extra roll of flesh that's appeared in the last year or so. I work up a good sweat, then collapse on a towel in the garden under an apple tree and check my phone.

I've got another email from Elaine. It's been a few weeks since we met, and she's slightly running out of patience. I don't even know if she'll still want me to write the piece, now that I'm no longer exactly a 'smug married', even though she doesn't know that. I mark it as *unread*.

Lola calls me, and I sit up and lean against the tree trunk. The bark digs into my back, but it's not wholly unpleasant.

'How are things?'

'I feel fourteen again.'

I remember that feeling of swooping around the Brockley

house with Dom, marvelling at how much space we had. Carla's bungalow is the opposite. It's small and cosy and crammed with stuff. Her living room has two large yellow sofas, lots of blankets, a wood burner, and big thick curtains that enable you to shut the world out. She always has something delicious cooking, and the house is covered with ornaments picked up from her travels, back when she was a working artist, selling her pottery and ceramics. Second-hand books everywhere. Little Buddha statues, hamsa hands, Indian elephants, Maneki-neko figures and large candles crowd surfaces and shelves. Because of the dogs, there's also dachshund memorabilia everywhere: stitched onto cushions, printed onto postcards, embossed into fridge magnets. Her bathrooms are cliché seaside dweller with beach-themed decor. One has a wicker basket in the shape of a crab; the other has a sign hanging above the sink saying *beach hut*. She loves colour, loves art, and her spare room is a giant walk-in wardrobe with a huge chest of drawers for her collection of handmade beads and vintage costume jewellery.

Her technicolour house is so full of life, and it feels jarring to be back here wearing a black T-shirt and grey tracksuit – to feel so at home, yet so adrift, too.

'Oh, love,' says Lola. 'I'm calling because we want to take you for lunch in London. Pen and Alice are coming. Get the train in on Saturday morning, and I'll book Lina Stores. Our treat. Something to look forward to and get you through the week?'

'Thank you, that sounds great.' I feel my shoulders relax slightly. The idea of people and life and street-style and tall buildings and red buses again. You aren't judged closely in

London – you can only be anonymous. 'Are you sure Pen will come? She's not replying to any of my messages.'

'Yes, yes! It was her idea. And any time you want to come and stay, just let me know, OK?'

'That would be lovely. And how are you?'

'I'm good! The bridezillas are being a bit calmer, and Fred and I are in Devon right now for a few days. It's really lovely here.'

'Lucky you.' I wish I was doing something like that with Dom.

'See you this weekend, OK? Can't wait. Look after yourself, will you?'

I hang up and return to Elaine's email. I know I have to give her an answer soon. It's not fair to keep her hanging.

I go inside and get my iPad and look up Naz's website bio again. By now, I pretty much know it by heart:

Naz Chopra is a lifestyle blogger and 'single life' influencer, best known for her popular blog, *How To Be Your Own Life Partner*, which she launched during the Covid19 pandemic. She is the author of two books: *Single Lives* and *Woman: An Island*, which is out now in hardback, published by HarperCollins in the UK and Penguin Random House in the US. She was included in the Top 10 Women to Watch on the Internet by *Forbes* in 2020. She is represented by Jaime Fagan at The Fagan Agency. She lives in London with her ginger cat, Bisous.

Since I've blocked Dom on all my social channels, her Instagram feed has become my go-to scroll before I go to sleep. She's posted something new this morning, though, and I go and check it out.

She's uploaded five pictures from a recent trip to Porto, where she took herself on a series of 'solo dates'. I scroll through the pictures and read the comments from her fans:

issaboo
i love you naz!!! I just got back from the hospital, going through chemo atm but am going to have a naz inspired self-care evening tonite :) Single life for the win :)

elephantpants
I'm with my five best friends from school just chatting about how much we love u – we have a WhatsApp group dedicated to you!!! NAZ's GALS :)

deliad
you are the voice of your generation! Don't ever forget that! Voice.of.a.gen!

Under the guise of 'research', I look up photos of Naz on Google Images. I find it strangely soothing. Endless, perfectly posed photos, some professionally taken, some on Getty, some of her at home on the sofa, at events, in cafés, in long coats, in expensive shoes, in bars, in restaurants, at launch parties, with different-shaped Champagne flutes in her hand. I zoom in on one of them, looking at her face, her smile, up close. Signature red lipstick, teeth showing, eyes creased, tongue poking out. Is this the face of somebody who actually has it all figured out?

I can't pull away. I am fascinated by her – fascinated by the apparent ease with which she navigates the world. She seems to think anyone can change their life in an instant.

Could I do it? Could I write the piece for Elaine? Could I meet her, get under her skin, and write a provocative piece about two opposite lives? Would I have to lie about still being in a couple with Dom?

I think of Elaine, her prominence in the industry and how good it would be to start writing properly again, not just churning out content about products people don't need. I think about how it would feel to reignite my old career and get that full-body buzz of chasing a good story, of writing up a profile piece that is both hooky and true, specific and universal.

That night, for the first time since that awful evening at Zetter, I fall immediately into a deep and dreamless sleep.

The next morning I wake early, seven a.m., and pad down the corridor towards the kitchen. I feel fired up. I realize that this article could be something to distract me from my inward misery, even if it is a slight obsession with a woman ten years my junior. At least it would stop me from the temptation of stealing Carla's phone and doomscrolling through Dom's Instagram. I make myself a coffee, and I'm about to head into the She-Shed to do more research and email Elaine back, when Elaine's name pops up on the phone, calling me.

'Doll. Are you going to write my "Opposites Attract" piece or not?'

'Yes! Sorry for the delay. I've been thinking and researching. Of course, I'd love to take this on.'

'*Fabulous.*'

'I also think I've found a great person to interview for it.'

'Ooh! Who?'

'There's this young influencer woman called Naz – people are calling her the Gen Z poster girl for a single life.'

I do not tell Elaine about my horrendous break-up with Dom.

'Naz who?'

'Naz Chopra. She has over 2 million followers on Instagram.'

'Right. What intrigues you the most about her?' I can hear Elaine scribbling on a notepad. 'And what level of Gen Z are we talking? Is she on TikTok? Does she have ADHD? That generation have all got it these days from watching too many three-second videos, those poor guys.'

'Well, I don't know about that, but she's very different to me and my friends.' Suddenly, I have a surge of energy that I haven't felt in weeks. I go into pitch mode. 'Nothing seems to trouble her. She said on a recent TV interview that women my age pretend to be confident, independent and into wild sex and everything, but actually they just tick all the same boring boxes. We *say* us Millennials are different and rebellious and want to change the world, but in fact we all want the standard white wedding, the conventional office career, the 2.4 kids. Whereas *she* really isn't interested in marriage, kids, or following any rules. She rejects all of it. She thinks my generation are completely bland and boring.'

'I LOVE it! You think she's spicy. She thinks you're bland. Perfect. You're an Old Millennial smug almost-married; she's the Gen Z singleton.'

I blink to myself, trying desperately to look past the phrase 'Old Millennial' and the fact that I am not in any way 'smug married' to Dom.

'Yeah.' I continue my pitch: 'She's sort of turning the old Bridget Jones paradigm on its head. She's not interested in a man, only interested in self-love. She's not weighing herself; she's body-positive. She's not drinking booze; she's probably having a vitamin smoothie.'

'This is GREAT content.' I can hear Elaine typing in the background now, probably Googling Naz.

'You know what: I actually think this could be a big piece, outside of the series. I think this should actually be a profile piece on Naz Chopra. She's obviously a bit of a character,' Elaine says, sounding interested.

I sigh with relief. If it's not part of the series, I won't have to overly pretend I'm still in a couple. 'That's a great idea. I'd love to put all the focus on her – I really don't think anyone wants to read about my boring old life anyway!'

'Doll, you know the best journos put themselves in all their pieces. I still want you in there, too! Find out what she actually does all day, and go and do it with her. And tell her about your situation. Argue with her if you can. Does she think marriage is for losers? Does she make you think differently? What does she think of you and your life in a stable hetero relationship? Is it all a PR trick, and she's secretly miserable, sat at home with her cat? "Spill the tea" as my daughter says!'

I settle into one of the deep wicker chairs in the She-Shed, the one that has a faint view of the grey-blue sea, and make a start on things right away. I'll decide how to handle my own newly single status in the piece later.

First, I reach out to Naz's team. Elaine's emailed me a login to a big media database, and I find the contact details for Naz's PR and talent manager, Jaime Fagan. I go on Jaime's website, and there are testimonials from actors and musicians singing her praises and a black-and-white photo of her sat on a wooden chair with tons of dark eyeliner.

Jaime's bio is impressive: she used to work with Take That in the Nineties and Coldplay in the Noughties, and now she's pivoted from managing musicians to managing influencers and 'online activists'. I craft an email pitching the new *Z Life* magazine, telling her how many readers it will reach with its massive advertising spend and marketing campaign. I reel off Elaine's credentials so that Jaime knows it's legit. I explain that the focus will be on Naz, but the hook is a clash of the generations: *Millennial journalist meets Gen Z influencer*. I don't mention the single vs coupled angle. *Send*.

I feel a great whoosh of adrenaline – and immediately get an out-of-office from her, saying she's away for a week on a silent meditation retreat. The autoreply is signed off: *blessings*.

But then, I get a reply almost straight away:

willow
    hello
    gr8 to hear from you
    new magazine sounds super cool
    gonna be quick as currently on meditation retreat and not meant to be emailing
    i know that naz would love to do this
    she likes doing press
    when is good for you
    she can do next week
    she likes to meet at blue legume in islington for meetings
    thnx
    blessings

Even though nobody's around to see it, I do a little fist punch. I'm going to start writing again! And I'm finally going to meet the woman I've been obsessively Googling ever since I heard of her. I'm kind of nervous; I wonder what she'll actually be like.

14

THEN

August 2013

A decade ago, Pen and I were living together in a poky little ground floor flat in Stoke Newington. We would spend Sunday nights together no matter what; it was our night in the calendar. We'd moved to London together after we'd graduated, and luckily the rent was super cheap. This rich old lady owned it, and for some reason, she liked Pen and me. She charged us peanuts and gave us her old expensive clothes and designer bags instead of giving them to charity shops. We couldn't believe our luck. £400 a month each, and the occasional freebie of vintage Gucci. We really couldn't complain.

We spent most evenings pissed on cheap Co-op wine in our kitchen, either watching *Girls* or flicking through trashy magazines, and tonight was no exception. I was wearing fluffy socks and lying on the sofa, reading some Royals issue of *Hello!* magazine. Pen had just started as a midwife at the

Chelsea and Westminster Hospital. I was doing well at *The D-Low* with Elaine Jefferson as my boss – a notoriously terrifying editor who used to work at big magazines like *Lucky* and *Vogue* in the US before she came to the UK.

'Look, I'm pretending to be Jamie Oliver. This is what he does,' Pen said, emptying pretty much a whole bottle of red wine into the already liquidy mixture and stirring with a wooden spoon. 'Jamie never measures anything out, just glugs it all in.' She added a huge splash of oil. 'Glug, glug, glug.'

I laughed at her from the sofa, shaking my head.

'Woops!' she said, spilling oil all over the countertop.

'Any gossip at your work? I feel like I have no boy chat because the office is full of women,' I said.

'Well, funny you ask. There's this junior doctor at work, and I don't want to be mean, but I've noticed she's got zero personality, and she totally changes depending on who she is dating.'

'Go on,' I said, pouring us more wine.

'Well, I've only ever spoken to her in between shifts, but when I first met her, she was dating this guy in a band, and I spotted her wearing his band T-shirt. Then she was dating this French guy, so she came to a work party recently wearing a *beret*. Then, the other week, she brought along this nice guy who works at a local church, and then the other day, I saw THE BIBLE in her bag. I mean, don't you think that's nuts?'

'Yes!' I said. 'Definitely.'

'Promise me you'll never change your identity for a man? Like, can we promise we'll just stay being *ourselves* when we meet someone? We won't lose all the bits that make us *us*.'

'I promise,' I said, putting my hand on my heart.

I opened the little wooden door that led out onto a small terrace where we had a second-hand bistro table and two chairs, currently covered in bird poo and really in need of a wash. It was too cold to eat outside, but I needed to air out Pen's potent garlicky cooking smells so that the fire alarm didn't go off.

Pen turned up the radio and the song 'Do It Like a Dude' by Jessie J came on. Pen was wearing baggy pyjama bottoms and singing along, quite horribly out of pitch.

'It must be amazing being a man,' she said, turning down the little red Roberts radio. 'Going around grabbing your crotch and just not giving a shit.'

'Is that what you think men do?' I laughed, reaching my hands up to the ceiling. 'We're doing pretty good. Look at us. We're living in London; I'm living with you. Life is good.'

'Agreed. We're doing it. We're living the life we wanted for ourselves. Remember at school? We couldn't wait to get those shackles off. We're finally free from all those frumps telling us what to do.'

'I feel like the sky is the limit, genuinely.'

'Let's promise each other, we will always put ourselves first. And always bail each other out.'

'I promise,' I said.

'What are you up to next weekend? Shall we go to IKEA? Could get some more bits for the flat.'

'Oh – um – actually, I've got a date.'

'WHAT? Who with? Why don't I know about this?'

'He's called Dom. I met him at Alice's barbecue. I think it was when you were on shift.'

'Wowwwww, OK. Show me pictures.'

She added salt and pepper to the pan. Jessie J continued to sing in the background.

I flicked through his Facebook photos for Pen. 'He's good-looking, isn't he? And you can't tell from the pictures, but he's so confident! He just walked straight up to me and struck up a conversation, and then he outright asked if I'd like to go on a date. Honestly, it was so refreshing, and he loves the cinema, too! We talked about movies for ages. He's more into blockbusters than indie films, to be fair – he's taking me to see *Rise of the Planet of the Apes* next weekend at some rooftop cinema thing.'

She looked at me funnily. 'Ha, it must be true love then. That is not your cup of tea.'

I smiled. 'I mean, who knows where it will lead. But it's exciting to be going on a date with someone I met *in real life*. I have a good feeling about him.'

'You must do, if you're really lowering your cinema standards,' she said, raising an eyebrow while literally and figuratively stirring the pot on the stove.

'And don't worry, I'll stick to The Rule.'

The Rule was that we'd agreed to not bring any guys back to the flat unless we'd been on at least ten dates and/or were getting serious, and we had to discuss it with each other first. We made the flat a no-men zone – a sanctuary just for us two. It was perfect how it was, just how we liked it.

Even so, I was really excited about seeing Dom.

15

NOW

A waitress with pink hair takes me to the table at Lina Stores; I'm a little bit late. I can see Pen, Lola, and Alice chatting away at the back of the restaurant. Lola is gesturing dramatically, showing them something, possibly the new green silk scarf she's just taken off her neck.

'There she is!' Pen says, giving me a massive bear hug.

I sink into her embrace, inhaling the familiar smell of L'Occitane body oil that she douses herself in regularly. Today, it's underscored with something else – cedar or wood smoke, something masculine, and I wonder if she's just come from a date with Mike. I feel a spike of annoyance (or envy?) – it's been ages since I last saw or spoke to her – but it's hard to be cross when she's enfolding me in her arms.

She pulls out the chair next to her for me and rubs my arm. 'How are you?'

'You know, just one foot in front of the other,' I say, shrugging.

'So good to see you,' Lola says.

'Your hair looks nice!' Alice says sweetly.

Pen puts her arm around me again. 'Sorry it's been so shit.'

A waiter comes over, and we order a bottle of white wine.

'It's OK. How's Mike?' I ask. I don't say I'm sad that she hasn't rung me up to spill the juicy details of her new relationship. I expect she's held back for fear of rubbing my nose in her coupledom after my break-up. Still, it makes me feel unusually distant from her.

'He's good – thank you! I just came from his, actually. We've got the same day off for once. We're usually on shift at the same time.'

I wonder whether she's annoyed that my lunch has got in the way of a potential romantic day together.

There's a pause, but then the wine arrives, and Lola pours everyone a cold glass.

'How long has it been now, Pen?'

'Only a few weeks. It's a bit intense after my decade-long drought, but we're trying to keep things casual for now.'

'So you've been spending a lot of time together?' I ask, not meaning to sound so direct.

'Yes, we have.' She reaches for my arm again, but I pretend not to notice and pull it away to grab the water jug.

I'm happy for her – I really am – but I can't quite bear her pity.

Pen chats a bit more about Mike and about how similar they are – neither of them want children; both work in the hospital; both really value their freedom; they're both vegan (important); he'd rather eat his own toenails than eat a dead animal – but it feels awkward, and I can tell she doesn't want to gush too much about him in front of me.

After our glasses have been filled, Lola hands me a big bunch of flowers and a voucher for Cowshed. 'Look, just a little something from the three of us. Go and pamper yourself.'

'Thank you,' I say, my throat thick with emotion. It's thoughtful of them, but it also shifts the already strange mood around the table. Now it feels like a 'leaving' party – for a life I didn't choose to leave.

I just don't think any of them get it. I can't just slather on some Cowshed creams and move on as if everything's fine. All I want to do is wallow at home in self-pity, comb through my 'Dom' folder on my phone and cry, ideally while rewatching *A Star Is Born*.

I take a deep breath and confess that I'm not doing so well. 'I've been writing letters to Dom on my typewriter. Is that really sad?' I don't say some of the letters turned into ones to my mum.

'No . . . of course not,' Alice says, gently touching my shoulder.

'I just feel like I need to talk to him, even though I can't speak to him or follow what he's doing,' I say. 'It's so weird to just have someone there one minute and gone the next. He's got this big new exciting life in New York already. I'm back in my childhood bedroom, in bloody Eastbourne.' I can feel tears gathering, a scratching at the back of my throat.

'We can't speed up the process for you, Willow, but we

can eat our body weight in cacio e pepe with you,' Lola says, picking up the menu.

'I'm so sorry. It must be like he has died,' Alice says, looking at me sympathetically.

'If anything, it would be easier if he was actually dead,' I say, 'because then at least I'd know what he was up to . . . i.e., lying in a coffin.'

'Jeez,' Pen says.

'What?'

'Isn't that a bit overdramatic? Look, I know it's probably too soon for you to see this, but I'm excited for you. It's a fresh start. A new you. An element of freedom that you haven't had for *years*,' Pen says. 'Think of how much Dom held you back.'

There is an awkward pause.

I look at her, cheeks flaming, trying not to take it the wrong way.

Held me back?

Alice tries to change the subject, asking me where my jeans are from.

I look at Pen again. She seems different, lighter. She's full of beans instead of her usual snark. Her skin looks great; her cheeks are lightly flushed. It's like she can't contain her newfound vibrancy, and it's bouncing around the room.

Pen continues, topping up her wine glass: 'Honestly, it's quite fun being single, and once you get used to it, you attract better people into your life. I think we should be celebrating, not commiserating.'

'Let's not get into it, now,' Lola says. 'It's too soon to think that far ahead. I think Pen is just saying she feels positively for you, Willow. A new chapter.'

'You don't even need to look far ahead, though. I'm talking about things you can do right now, like watching whatever you want to watch on TV. Eating what you want for dinner. Peace and quiet in the evenings. Star-fishing the bed. No dirty dishes in the sink or crusty shirts to iron. There are some upsides!' Pen says.

'I'm not quite ready to look at the positives,' I say bluntly.

Lola and Alice watch us like a tennis match.

Over the years, as the single one in the group, Pen was always available to book tickets on the Glasto website or organize a girls' trip away. Always happy to tag along with couples things, too, seemingly never worried about being the gooseberry. She was the friend who would take you on a night out and make you do karaoke if you were sad, and that's why her lack of support is really noticeable. I can tell she is trying to be present, but she also keeps looking at her phone every five minutes.

A plate of oily focaccia bread arrives, and I tear it with my fingers. Even though Pen's being insensitive, I know she's kind of right. There are some positive things about starting a new chapter. Like the article I'm doing for *Z Life*.

'I have actually taken on something new,' I say. 'It's a writing project from my old boss Elaine.'

'Oh, that's *great*,' Alice says.

'That's really good news,' Pen adds.

'No way!' Lola says. 'Mad Elaine from the *D-Low* days! Tell us more?'

I tell them about the original 'Opposites Attract' series and the bigger profile piece Elaine wants me to do. For some reason, I keep it vague about who my subject is. I'm not ready for them to know about Naz and her whole 'be your own life partner' ethos. Instead, I tell them about being called an 'Old Millennial' by Elaine.

'Oh man. I guess we are old now,' Alice says.

'Yep,' says Lola. 'You know that bizarre client of mine – the one who wants the insane paintings at the wedding? She's only twenty-two. A baby!'

'It's just what young people do in the suburbs. They get married as soon as they can to someone they met at school,' Pen says, with her mouth full.

I sigh. How did thirty-five creep up on us so fast? One minute, you're making a big song and dance about turning thirty in a silver dress, and then bam: you're in your mid-thirties and time has just flown and you're looking forty square in the eye.

'What have you been up to lately, Alice?' I ask, happy to change the subject, as plates piled high with pasta arrive.

'Manifesting, mainly. Is that sad? While Luke's been running Mystery Road, I've been making a vision board with a load of baby stuff on it. I have faith it will happen.'

I realise in that moment that, since breaking up with Dom, I've not thought about babies at all. Poor Alice, cutting and pasting pictures of prams out of magazines. I let the thought of a baby hover and then float away, like a helium balloon. I close my eyes for a moment and make a wish for Alice.

The girls settle the bill, kindly paying for my meal. I give them all a big hug and promise I'll come back up to London soon. I can tell by the way Pen hugs me quickly that there is a slight tension between us.

We all go our separate ways. Alice has a yoga class, Lola is off to a meeting with one of her bridezillas, and Pen says she's going home, but I bet she's off to see Mike. I leave the restaurant, relieved to be on my own again. I put my AirPods in; Spotify has made a 'Reflective Mix' for me, with some Stevie Nicks, Michael Kiwanuka, and José Gonzalez. I walk to the Tube so I can get to Victoria station for my train back to Eastbourne, back to Carla's. The clouds, the buildings, cranes, St Paul's Cathedral, the skyscrapers, the telephone poles feel so big, and I am so small.

I feel like I need some sugar, so on the way to the station, I duck into Starbucks. Big familiar chains soothe me. Like service stations – places that are so neutral, so bland, and therefore safe. I place my order for a frappé with a hazelnut shot and watch as they write *WALLOW* on my cup.

I glance around the coffee shop and have a flash of recognition at the woman sat in the window, wearing a green silk scarf. Lola! I walk over and touch her arm.

'Oh, hi again!' she says, surprised to see me.

'Hey! I fancied a calorific drink,' I say, holding up my venti.

'How funny. I'm doing my meeting here!' she says, putting her phone away, looking very much caught off-guard.

'Thank you so much for lunch – it was so lovely.'

She moves her coffee cup to make room for me to sit down, and then I see it. Flashing at me. A ring. A big diamond. A very big sparkling diamond.

I stare at the ring; I can't help it.

'Err – what? Congratulations!?' I say, nodding towards it.

'Ah. Yes,' Lola stutters. 'Look Willow, I . . . I wanted to tell you earlier – but I didn't want to make the lunch about me.'

'You took the ring off?' I ask, thinking back to her gesturing her hand towards the girls just before I'd got to the table.

'Yeah,' she says, looking sheepish.

'Why! I would have wanted to hear this news.'

'I didn't want to distract. It was meant to be a lunch to cheer you up.'

'It's lovely,' I say, reaching out for her finger. I pause. 'When did it happen?'

'A couple of days ago. Fred got it made at a special jeweller in Amsterdam. He proposed on the beach in Devon. I was going to tell you. I just . . . Oh, Willow, I've been so worried about you. And I also felt *terrible*, with everything that happened with Dom. The fact that I egged you on, thinking it would happen because of Lisa getting involved and everything. Then with Pen and her new bloke . . . and Alice trying to get pregnant. I had no idea Fred was going to do it now, and it just feels like bad timing. I didn't want to make things worse.'

'It's not bad timing, Lola. It's your life.'

'Sorry. I was overthinking it.' Her phone beeps. 'Ah. There she is. My current *nightmare* client. The twenty-two-year-old leaving me thirty-one-minute voice notes. Each one is a bloody podcast. Can you believe it?'

A woman with dark hair in a low ponytail with menacing eyebrows walks through the double doors.

'Wish me luck,' Lola whispers.

'Hope the meeting goes well.'

'Love you.' Lola gets up and kisses me on the cheek.

I walk out of Starbucks into the bright street, wondering why everyone else's lives but mine are suddenly hurtling forward.

I trudge towards the station and pull out my phone to see if Carla has replied to my text asking if she wants me to pick up any dinner on the way home, and see I've got an email from Jaime:

naz is so looking forward to meeting you!
just a reminder, next thursday 1 p.m. blue legume.
any probs let me know, my number is 077888929210
love & blessings

I sigh and stand motionless in the hustle and bustle of the city, trying not to let it swallow me.

16

THEN

September 2012

One of my very first assignments from Elaine was over ten years ago. She sent me off to do a piece about London Zoo – specifically about Butterfly Paradise, where you can immerse yourself in a world of butterflies and caterpillars. She was trialling a new 'Millennials in Nature' column, where we learned something new about nature within cities. I was itching to get going, to interview someone, write it up, get my own words out there after weeks of doing the dogsbody jobs. My toolbox consisted of: a scribbly notepad, a phone charger, a Dictaphone with a cracked screen, and three broken pens.

    I arrived at Butterfly Paradise with my bright blue nails, nose piercing, and big Dr Martens boots (I was in my 'grunge' phase), and a very enthusiastic man called Brian met me at the entrance. His hair was turning white in places, and he was wearing a dark green gilet, a cream polo shirt, and brown trousers. He had dirt under his fingernails, and his hands were in desperate need of moisturizer, but on the whole, he seemed friendly enough.

He led me through a massive walkway in the shape of a caterpillar. We reached quite a large space, a dome-shaped enclosure with netting keeping the butterflies in. It was heated to 27°C, allowing all the different fluttering species to fly around and feel like they were in their natural habitat. Then we sat down on two stools outside his office, which was basically a little wooden hut. He made me a cup of weak tea with a very old kettle and poured it into a polystyrene cup. He was pleasant and calm, though clearly very excited to talk about his favourite subject. We strolled back towards the butterfly enclosure.

'I couldn't believe it when I saw the email – it makes my heart happy to hear that young people want to learn more about what we're doing here at the zoo.' He straightened out his shirt and cleared his throat. 'Is it a live interview, or will it be edited after?'

'It will be transcribed and edited down.' I smiled. 'It'll be online and in print.'

He made small talk while I fiddled about, making sure I had the right batteries in my Dictaphone.

'Wonderful. You know, this one time, there was a family here, and one of the kids pointed at the biggest butterfly and said, "what kind of bird is that?"' He slapped his thigh. 'She must have been about twelve.' He howled with laughter.

I smiled along, getting ready to interview him properly. I hoped I'd be able to get some decent material out of this guy.

'This is why education matters – do you know what I mean? People don't know the bloody difference between a bird and a butterfly. Young people have never been more disconnected from nature. I'm laughing, but it's sad, really. Sorry, here's me being rude about young people to a young person!'

'Right, shall we get started?' I said, smiling, trying to sound like a serious journalist, even though it was the first interview I was doing myself and I had just walked through a big fake caterpillar tunnel. 'Can you first tell me a bit more about yourself and your job here at the zoo?'

Three butterflies landed on him, one on his head, two on his shoulder.

'Well, when I was a small boy, I became so utterly fascinated with the caterpillar-to-butterfly transition. Meltdowns. Metamorphosis in fact – oh hello,' he said, as another butterfly came and landed on his hand. 'This is a classic monarch, which are easy to recognize by their striking orange, black, and white markings.' He looked up at the sky for a moment. 'Also, not only are butterflies obviously *incredible* to look at, but their fossils date back 56 million years. They've been around for such a long time. There are over 20,000 species – and they only live a few weeks. And they taste with their feet!'

'Quite a short life span then.'

'Oh, but a very bright and special one,' he added. 'Quality not quantity is the key, really. There's actually nothing wrong with a short life span – it's just us humans who make that into a bad thing, because we are a rather self-obsessed species.'

A butterfly fluttered down and landed on my shoulder.

'Oh look – you've found yourself a friend. A purple emperor.'

I stayed very still, so the butterfly stayed put. I could just see its purple wing out of the corner of my eye.

'So I guess it's very important that people donate to the zoo? Can you explain more?'

'Oh, gosh, for *so* many reasons! The opportunity to learn more about life cycles, biodiversity and climate change for starters – but you're young: I'm sure you don't need me to prattle on about climate change. But also! The caterpillar-to-butterfly cycle is not only miraculous but an important symbol of greater life in general. All of us go through huge transitions, and it might be frightening, but we do come out of the other side as a butterfly. Did you know that caterpillars have twelve eyes but terrible vision? And they're colour-blind, too. So, if you ever feel like a caterpillar – slow-moving, myopic, directionless – remember that you will become a butterfly afterwards. You must keep the faith.'

I looked again at the butterfly on my shoulder, its wings rising and falling. It really was quite beautiful. 'What is it about the cycle that you find "miraculous"?' I asked, really listening to him now. The purple butterfly took flight.

Brian got very excited and took me over to a big drawing in a corner of the enclosure – the kind of thing you would see at school in the biology classroom.

'When the caterpillar is inside the chrysalis, it has something called imaginal cells. The caterpillar becomes bug soup. It literally melts down and then builds back up again. Hence the phrase "meltdown" whenever we are going through internal hell. I call it bug soup because you *literally* melt down into liquid gloop before the cells rebuild. After my partner of thirty years left me, for example, I was gloop for a long while . . . but . . . anyway—' He coughed and drank some tea before continuing: 'These cells hold the blueprint for the future – it's like the cells know it's going to be a butterfly, but the caterpillar doesn't. They go on to multiply, form clusters, push back and forth and resonate at the new frequency of the emerging butterfly. Isn't that something? Every one of us has infinite potential – we are full of imaginal cells, cells that carry a hidden map of who we will later become. Inside, we already *know* who we'll be. Isn't that incredible?'

My breath caught momentarily. Who knew Brian was such a philosopher?

The purple butterfly landed on me again. It stayed there, gently for a while. I felt comforted by its presence.

'They're attracted to the salt in your sweat,' he said, and I felt a bit less comforted. 'And, now, this is a little bit more *out there*, shall we say, but butterflies are often said to be a deceased ancestor visiting you. Many cultures believe they are a "sign" that someone is watching you and supporting you. Usually someone very close.'

I looked around. The butterflies were so colourful, so bright, so in charge of their own life force and destinations.

Brian continued: 'I'm not sure if you've ever been through any big changes in your life—'

I shook my head. I did not want to start telling him the story of my mum leaving. Sometimes I found it hard to know if I'd ever processed it or whether I processed it over and over every single day.

'There's one more thing that's important to know about the butterfly process of metamorphosis. If the caterpillar is helped out of the cocoon (by a human for example) – it dies. They must transform on their own. Another little detail for you: the more they struggle, the stronger they become. So, Willow, if you are ever struggling, just think of the caterpillar. The struggle might be hard and painful, but you will come out the other side stronger, with better vision and with beautiful thick wings, I promise you. It's very profound to be surrounded by God's creatures.'

'I don't believe in God.'

As if dismayed by my sacrilege, the purple butterfly flew away off my shoulder.

'But you believe in butterflies?' said Brian. 'Same thing, really.'

17

NOW

I scroll, click and read until my eyes hurt and my brain aches. It's the night before the interview with Naz. I stay up super late in Lola's spare bedroom, where I'm crashing for a few days, filling my brain with more and more information off Google:

- She gave a TEDx talk in 2022, based on an article she wrote for *ELLE* magazine: *'It's Time for Women to Embrace Time on Their Own'*.
- I listen to a speech she made at the Oxford Union, 'debating' the negative impact of the word 'spinster'.
- She loves statistics. All the stats about divorce within her articles show that single women are able to earn more, travel more, live longer, and this increases yet more if you are a single, child-free woman. She argues that surveys and data suggest that loneliness is not the same as being alone. That everyone's lifestyle is a choice. That almost half of all marriages in the UK end in divorce.

- I read a think-piece about how dumbing yourself down as a woman is dumb. How dumping someone is empowering. An image of Britney Spears wearing the *DUMP HIM* T-shirt accompanies the piece.
- I read a blog piece called 'Life Is Long', all about how many of us could live until we are a hundred, questioning how we will love the same person for decades on end when we grow and change and shape-shift so much over the course of our lives.
- I listen to a podcast interview called 'Naz Chopra: On How Marriage Is Soon to Be Dead'. She speaks about how we are always finding new versions of ourselves, how our relationship with ourselves really is the most important thing we have.

At three a.m., I put my laptop on the floor by the futon, and I fall into an exhausted, fitful sleep.

12.50 p.m. I walk inside The Blue Legume ready to meet Naz. I've been careful to arrive slightly early for our meeting at one o'clock. I have sweaty palms and a slightly moist lower back from walking quickly from the Tube. My heart still aches, like I've pulled a muscle, but I have put on a tiny bit of blusher today to give my pale face more colour. I am wearing black trousers and a white T-shirt. I'd planned to wear something a bit more stylish, a patterned Zara dress, but I couldn't reach the zip at the back on my own.

While a waitress with electric blue fingernails looks on her iPad for my booking, I see that Naz is early, too, already sat at a window seat with her back to me, tapping on her phone. I'm surprised. For some reason, I thought she'd be late, too cool for school.

'Oh, I can see her, actually,' I say.

'Cool,' the waitress says, 'go ahead.'

Naz looks round as I approach. 'Hi! Willow, is it?'

'Yes, hi!'

'It's *so* nice to meet you,' Naz says. 'I recognize you from your LinkedIn pic. I must confess I Googled you last night.' She laughs lightly.

And I Googled you. A lot.

'Good to meet you, too.' I sit down, and she starts pouring me some water from the jug on the table. I get out my notepad, pen, iPad, and phone and place them on the table. 'Thanks for agreeing to do this.' I feel a small rush of excitement to be doing this job again.

'Of course. The new magazine sounds great. I don't meet journalists very often.'

'Journalist is a big word.' I snort. 'I don't exactly cover politics or fly to war-torn countries—'

She cocks her head very slightly to one side, bemused at how quickly I've attempted to put myself down.

She has narrow shoulders and seems smaller sat before me than the woman in all the Instagram videos or even my memory from the fitting room. I'm relieved that she doesn't remember me. She's not wearing a scrap of make-up and appears more gentle than her online persona. A bit more tired looking, but still fresh-faced.

'So my editor wants us to spend a few days together, as

it'll be a proper profile piece in the magazine and online. The aim is to get a flavour of your life and job, so today is just us settling in a bit and getting to know each other.'

I get out my Dictaphone and place it on the table.

'Happy to. Mainstream magazines hardly ever want to interview me.'

'Really?'

'Yeah, I'm just some random Internet woman to them. No one thinks people like me actually have any talent. But it's no accident that I have a thriving business.' She takes a sip from her water glass, smiling.

The waiter comes over. We both order flat whites.

'So,' she says, 'my agent tells me you have a pretty settled life – ten years with the same man. Do you guys live around here?'

I swallow. I don't want to lie to her, but I don't want to derail the interview either. I settle on a lie. 'I'm in Brockley,' I cough. 'What about you?'

'Hampstead.'

Oh, *very nice*, I think to myself.

'Shall we start?'

I'm eager to get going; I'm not good at small talk at the best of times, and I dread her asking me anything specific about my relationship with Dom.

'Sure,' she says, sounding relaxed, leaning back in her chair.

'So! Your brand is "Single Naz". I would love to dig into that a bit more. I've been in one relationship most of my adult life, so I've never really been single for any stretch of time—'

Until now.

'Obviously, you speak to your community of thousands online about the benefits of being single. How did this turn into your career?'

'Well, I didn't really mean for it to turn into what it is now. I've always been very outspoken. People were enjoying my blog and what I was posting online, and it sort of snowballed from there. Lots of people my age are waking up to the cultural conditioning that goes on around marriage and heterosexual norms. I think most of us get into relationships because it's the done thing – we don't really ask ourselves if we could live a happy, or happier, life alone.'

'Are you close to your family?'

'No. Don't really speak to my family of origin any more. My parents had an arranged marriage and never questioned it. They don't understand me at all. I don't really want to talk about my family, though.'

'OK. Of course. Do you think you influence other young women into being single or remaining single? A lot of your posts are very inspiring – but a lot of young women might want to copy you? Do you ever wonder if that could be dangerous?'

'Dangerous how? I feel passionate about being yourself and celebrating individual choices. I think people should do what they want. It's not really my responsibility what other people do.' She shrugs.

I scribble down some notes and pause for a moment, thinking of something slightly different to ask, something to soften her slightly. 'Bit of a rogue question, do you have a special talent?'

'Ooh, I like that question.' She pauses and takes a sip of her coffee. 'Yes, I do, actually. I can immediately spot when a woman is miserable in a relationship. Sometimes, I see people on bad dates or a husband being horrible to his wife in Sainsbury's, and I want to go over to the woman and do some sort of sign language to warn her to get out. I see so many women who are bored or trapped in a relationship or give up great opportunities, just because they think being in a relationship is the ultimate goal. Seeing a woman lose her sparkle – ah, it really bothers me.'

'I know you don't want to speak much about your family – but would you say you've always thought this way about relationships, since you were a child?'

'I don't know. My mum and dad don't love each other – that I know for sure. I would actually go as far as saying they kind of hate each other – they're just like two business owners who have learned to get along well enough to do admin and children together. It was pretty grim growing up with that. Why do people need to "join up" so much anyway? "Joint assets". "Joint bank account". *Bleurgh*. Life is too short for that. That's why I do this. Do you actually know anyone who is happily married after ten years? I don't. You get married, you both let yourself go, you both wish you were freer than you are, you both hate your life, and then you divorce. The divorce rate is currently 42 per cent. It's all a big scam.'

I can feel Naz warming up to her theme; she's even more direct than I expected.

'You don't want to fall in love one day?'

'No. I believe in self-love more. That bit in *Sex and the City* where Kim Cattrall tells Richard that she loves him but loves herself more? That's the vibe I'm going after. I have it printed and framed on my desk.'

'You don't like the idea of ever being with someone? Having a life companion? Someone to do life with?'

'Nope. Not interested. I am the main character in my story. It makes people uncomfortable to hear that, but it means I get to be the centre of all my life choices. I am not "on the shelf"; it's a choice. I love my life.'

'What about children?'

'I wouldn't rule it out, but I don't need to be in a couple for that. There are also many happy single child-free people.'

'If you think there is pressure on women to conform and get married, do you also find there's pressure on you to love being single? Do you feel like you have to constantly be this Fun Single Person?' I ask.

'I just think it *is* fun to design your life from scratch and make up all the rules.'

'OK, OK. On paper, it all sounds great. But I think a lot of people would struggle with the life you're describing. Not everyone can afford to live well and have fun if they aren't splitting bills. Some people aren't sociable or find it hard to spend too much time alone. What do you say to that?'

'Well, like with everything in life, it takes practice. And support, which is why I'm passionate about community. Women have been conditioned to always serve someone else. To ignore the idea of putting your needs first or doing exactly what *you* would like to do. Say you had an entire month to yourself, Willow – do you know what you'd do?'

I pause. I glance away. I don't know.

'Sorry – I'm not personally attacking you. It's just the space and the freedom, watching what I want to watch, cooking what I want to eat, having my own schedule, lazy mornings, no one to answer to. I fucking *love* it. And I feel like I have to always sell it or defend myself or tell people at weddings: "No, I don't want to be set up with your random cousin's friend." I do know it's a privilege to live alone, by the way. I am lucky to be paid well for the work I do. I don't know many people who can afford the rent on their own place at my age – not in London, anyway. But I can't sleep with anyone near me or touching me now. Have you seen that Whoopi Goldberg meme where someone asks her why she isn't married and she says she doesn't want anybody in her house. Absolutely *that*.'

'OK. So, do you have any tips for our readers? For women getting back on their feet after heartbreak? Who have ended up single, not out of choice? And who might not be able to afford to live alone?' I ask, trying to remain casual.

'Take time. Be gentle with yourself. Go on walks. Borrow a dog. Drink water. Masturbate. Slowly figure out who you are again,' she says, without blinking. 'When we are in a relationship, we outsource our needs to someone else constantly. It's a slippery slope. One minute, you're asking your partner to open a jam jar; the next, you can't do anything for yourself.'

I scribble some notes down in my pad. My cheeks grow hot. 'So, you *never* get lonely?' I ask.

She pauses. 'Rarely.'

'Really?'

'Well, I don't really view it as an issue, even if I do. I think feeling lonely is a fundamental human condition, because we can never ever feel completely understood. I know countless people who feel lonely in a marriage, lonely when someone is on the sofa next to them or in their bed. "Lonely in a crowded room" is the phrase. Loneliness isn't actually about being single.' She takes a breath and looks at her watch. 'Do you want to go shopping?' she says, drinking the last bit of coffee in her cup.

'What?' I ask, laughing. 'I haven't finished my—'

'Oh, come on, we'll chat as we browse. You said you wanted to accompany me in my daily life. I want to take you to this amazing secret place. I bet you'll love it.'

She grabs her bag off the floor and puts down some money.

'Hang on – I'm meant to pay for this, and my boss will expense it,' I say. The interview process has spun entirely out of my control.

'It's just two coffees.' She laughs. 'Come on.'

I press pause on the Dictaphone, and she barrels out of here like a whirlwind. I grab my bag and try to keep up with her.

Naz links arms with me as we walk down the street. It's probably just a ploy, to get me to like her and write nice things about her; it feels slightly uncomfortable. We walk for ten minutes down Upper Street. She knocks on a black door with no sign on it. It doesn't look like a functioning shop, with blinds closed over the window, no sign on the door or the side of the building. A petite woman with a big bunch of keys unlocks the door once she's seen Naz through a gap in the blinds. The woman is wearing a black cashmere jumper with pearl buttons, her hair in a tight bun.

'Naz! What a *delightful* surprise to see you! I have some amazing new pieces for you to try . . .' She locks the door behind her and pulls the blinds down further. A secret shop.

'Sorry I didn't call to give you a heads-up. This is my friend, Willow. Willow, this is Beatrix.'

Friend?

'No worries! You're always welcome, darling. Come through,' Beatrix says, walking us through a shop floor and then leading us through an orange curtain into a back room full of incredible clothing. 'How have you been?'

'I'm good! Willow here is writing an article about me for a new magazine. Willow, this secret place is called Alice's Wonder Wardrobe.'

'It's invite only, though, so don't put the name or address in any writing please,' Beatrix adds.

'This is one of the best-kept secrets of Islington,' Naz says to me. 'Every piece is iconic, worn by a celebrity in a film or with a gorgeous piece of history to it.' She touches the fabrics with her hand, lovingly, in the same way I saw her touch the clothes in John Lewis. 'Let's try some stuff on.'

I feel weird and uncomfortable being here. I'm dressed in black and white as usual. Now, I am surrounded by colour. Naz grabs a load of clothes from the rails. I haven't 'tried stuff on' since I was tiny with Mum's dressing-up box. It's one of the only memories I have of my mum before she left for good: dressing up together in fancy dress and funny outfits and stupid velvet jester hats. Now, I'm surrounded by feather boas, wigs, hats, sequin jackets, long velvet gowns, fluffy earmuffs, stripy socks, costume jewellery. I've not had fun with my outfits since the days before Dom. It reminds me of Pen, our glittery capes, our festival years.

I look over, and Naz is digging into a treasure trove, loving every minute. I feel awkward and keep scratching at my arm nervously.

'What would you wear these outfits to?' I ask, making conversation, touching some of the clothes on the rail.

'I don't know! At home? To sit at my desk? To get milk? Anywhere! Wearing mad clothes just makes me feel so *alive*.'

'Dopamine dressing,' Beatrix says matter-of-factly. 'Scientifically proven to raise your mood.'

Naz tries on a massive kaftan and swishes around in it.

'By the way, Willow – here. Before I forget.' She fishes around inside her handbag for something. 'A ticket for this night I'm hosting soon called Girls' Night In. Please come. It's meant to be a celebration for my new book, but it's basically a load of women getting together and dancing and having a nice time. No men. Great women. You'll love it. Don't tell your boyfriend,' she laughs.

'Oh, thanks! I'll see if I'm free.' I put the ticket in my bag, knowing I definitely won't go.

'Try this on,' she says, throwing a huge leopard-print fur coat to me. 'And these.' She gives me a pair of large pink sunglasses. 'I swear these were in last year's *Bond* film.'

'I – I don't think so. It's not very me.'

'Go on! It's just a bit of fun.'

I catch a glimpse of myself in the mirror, my plain white T-shirt, faded black trousers, beaten-up Converse.

'I'll stand over here,' I say.

Beatrix stands next to me. 'You should really give it a go and get in the fitting room. These items are full of such good energy – some of these clothes have been worn on stage before 90,000 people at Wembley Stadium, so they are guaranteed to make you feel something when you put them on. I believe clothes hold the electricity of the person. We don't normally let people try everything on. But Naz is a special customer.'

I grab a few items – a long silver dress, glittery boots that belonged to Taylor Swift apparently, some heart-shaped sunglasses, and a cape. I come out of the dressing room and look in the full-length mirror, hoping for a transformation into someone effortlessly cool, confident, and fashion-forward. I burst into laughter. I look like Elton John on acid at Disneyland.

Naz appears from a fitting room wearing a gold Lycra onesie and a big top hat. She gestures for me to zip her up, then turns and looks in the mirror. 'Fucking hell, I've got a massive camel toe in this. It's right up my front bum.'

I laugh again, so hard I actually double over. I realize I haven't laughed like this for ages. I can't remember the last time I did anything on a whim or just let myself enjoy the moment.

I certainly hadn't laughed like that with Dom – or with anyone – for months. No actually, probably years.

18

THEN

September 2007

It was the tail end of a scorching summer, and we arrived at Robin Hill, Isle of Wight, aged nineteen, ready for Bestival, looking the part: me with a leopard-print scarf tied around my head, Pen in her massive wellies, both with electric blue eye glitter, sequin capes, and bumbags. We had a small rucksack each and a huge tent. Excitement rippled through us: that feeling of not knowing what would happen at our first festival, not knowing who we'd meet, what we'd see. The feeling of invincible youth: your body able to drink and digest alcohol and food in a way that doesn't leave you totally comatose the next day, your energy levels topped up to the brim. The festival was a popular one, and the Chemical Brothers were headlining; we couldn't wait.

Outside our tent, Pen lay on the grass on her back, smoking

and flicking ash away, the sun shining on her, thumbing through pixelated photos on her digital camera.

'Showing yourself having fun at a festival is *perfect* online dating fodder. It ticks lots of boxes. Shows you don't take yourself too seriously – tick. Shows that you're able to put up a tent – tick. Shows you're not a boring introvert – tick. And everyone looks sexy in glitter and sequins.'

Pen made sure we got some pictures of us in our matching sequin capes to put on Facebook and potentially woo boys in the future. But right then, it was just about the two of us.

It was my first trip to the Isle of Wight. The night before, we'd stayed with Pen's older cousin, Phil, who lived in a small flat there. We needed a bed to crash on before heading to the musical festival, and Pen's aunt thought it would be nice if Phil offered us his tiny box of a spare room for the night so that we could get to the festival early the next day, beat the rush. It was lovely in theory. Phil was pleasing his mum by saying yes, but clearly Phil did not want us in his flat. He wouldn't look either of us in the eye and played loud video games in his room. He also made a big song and dance about the length of our showers and made us pay to the nearest 1p for his precious water meter.

'Good luck putting that tent up,' Phil scoffed in the kitchen, after noticing the big bag in the hallway, which, to be fair, was insanely heavy.

We left for the festival early the next morning. As we shut the front door, Pen secretly gave Phil the middle finger.

'Those sheets on the blow-up bed did *not* smell clean,' Pen said.

'Argh, don't!'

At festivals or nights out back then, boys weren't really on the agenda. It was just us two, our warm white wine in plastic cups, linking arms, dancing under an open sky and smoking and singing until our voices went husky.

On the last night of the festival, it started to rain while we were in a drum and bass tent. At first, we could hear the pattering of raindrops in the music breaks, and then, the heavens opened. The dance tent was clearly cheap and thin, and it started to rip with the wind and rain, and so we were dancing, getting drenched, opening our mouths and putting out our tongues to taste it.

Bouncers came in, worried about the electrical equipment, so the DJ set got shut down, and some guy gurning on drugs got out his phone and speakers and played his own songs. No one cared about the weak sound. We were all warm and high on drinking countless tinnies; we all carried on dancing and hugging late into the night.

When we left the tent, Pen and I started laughing, shocked at what we saw. The rain had caused the green grass to turn into a muddy swamp. For miles and miles in front of us, there was a deep brown landscape under the night sky, thick and squelchy, with pools of water. Suddenly, we were like characters in a video game, ready to face an obstacle course. It took us hours to get back to our tent. It was the type of mud that was one step forward, two steps back, like you're skating on ice. Pen's ankle got stuck in a boggy bit, then I fell on my arse, and when Pen tried to lift me up, she fell over, too. We were laughing so much our stomachs ached and we couldn't breathe – quick inhales like small dogs.

By the time we made it back to the tent, the sun was rising, the grass was drier, and the mud caked us like thick paint. We fell asleep side by side, holding hands, legs covered in mud, both dribbling slightly on our pillows.

I'd never felt so free in my life.

19

NOW

After I reluctantly return the glittery boots and silver dress to Beatrix, I say goodbye to Naz and hop on the bus back to Lola's flat. Lola and Fred are out for the night with some work colleagues, and she's left me some risotto in the fridge. I've hardly seen Lola around the house; she's either up super early for the gym or out in the evenings, wining and dining her awful bridezilla clients. That night, I stay in my room and watch a film on Netflix on my laptop on the fold-out futon.

When I wake up, I realize I dreamt of Naz, and I write it down on my phone. Another creative prompt I remember receiving from Ms Gower all those years ago.

Naz is in Carla's house, in my room, sat on the end of my bed. She is wearing the same outfit she was wearing on TV. *Come with me,* she says gently. I try not to. I stay sat where I am, but there is an energetic force between us, and it pushes me towards her, like I am on a rollercoaster that is slowly creeping forward. I am not in control; I don't want to be on the ride. There is a trap door in the ground, and she opens it. It's like the scene out of *Alice's Adventures in Wonderland*. I follow Naz through the trap door. I start growing, growing, bigger, bigger, like I must burst. I am a rainbow; I am a spectrum of light. I feel big and bold and – and – then I wake up.

Feeling spent and bleary-eyed, I decide to have an extra-long lie-in. I can hear Lola and Fred arguing in the kitchen, and I don't want to interrupt or make it any more awkward.

'. . . £500 for flowers is fucking ridiculous . . .' I hear Fred saying.

'Are you kidding me? That is the CHEAP END OF THE SPECTRUM!' Lola yells.

'It's the biggest rip-off – these people are scam artists. You could go on a week-long holiday with that. It's a waste!'

'I work in this industry, Fred, and I know who the best suppliers are. For god's sake. Do you want to get married or not?' I hear a pan being thrown in the sink with a loud clatter.

Fred leaves, closing the door loudly, and I hear Lola stomp into her bedroom to get ready for the day. I decide to run a bath and stay out of the way.

I flick through my emails while waiting for the bath to fill. There is one from Lisa and the Scatterbox lawyers, confirming that I am getting a larger-than-expected 'exit payout' because of my involvement in the company, the fact that I was one of the first employees. The documents are all very long and boring, but essentially, I'm getting a lump sum of money that's quadruple my yearly salary (£60k), paid out in four instalments over two years.

I'm not entirely sure how to process so many emotions at once. Of course I'm happy to have money coming in, to not have to worry for a while, but it is such a *final* feeling. Once this goes through, I will have absolutely no link to Dom left. I will never go into the office. The documents make it clear that I am not allowed to contact anyone at the company, or speak about it publicly. It feels very much like a 'take this and please leave forever'. I wish now that I'd insisted on being listed as a co-founder in our first official document. I guess I never thought it would ever really matter. I was with Dom, I trusted him. He and I were building the company, and that was that.

I pick up my phone to text Pen but decide not to. Instead, I get in the bath and ring Carla on loudspeaker. She answers at once.

'Fucking menopause,' Carla says down the phone.

'Hello to you, too!' I say, laughing. 'You OK?'

'I'm hot and bothered Willow. I am sick of those stupid women's magazines advertising it as a bunch of gorgeous older ladies with streaks of grey in their hair laughing over coffee – it's not. It's feeling hotter than the sun, waking up at all hours, losing my bloody mind. And I don't think this hot latte is helping. The menopause is not some amazing "death and rebirth" opportunity – it is sweaty and annoying and hormonal, and I'm sick of everyone trying to make women always be positive about everything. I just feel so *ill* all the time.' She takes a big breath. 'I just don't feel quite right.'

'Have you been to the doctors?'

'I think it's just a woman-of-a-certain-age thing. I'll live.'

I stretch out my legs in Lola's bath, the phone precariously placed on the side. I'm using all of Lola's nice products: luxurious hair conditioner, beeswax body scrub, a moisturizing facemask. She gets loads of free stuff from her wedding planning work (brands and potential suppliers send her things, hoping her clients will buy them or put them in bridesmaid goody bags), so I don't use it sparingly. I squeeze out loads of the stuff into my palms.

Carla tells me she is sitting on a deckchair at the beach, Bubble and Squeak lying patiently by her side. It's cold today, but Carla is hardy, out on the beach in all seasons, usually wearing a swimsuit under her clothes, just in case she fancies a cold dip. She tells me that Eastbourne beach is calm this morning (unlike her, clearly). I can picture it exactly: her deckchair nestled in the sand, her discarded yellow clogs, the lap of the waves in the distance, the beach divided up with little wooden groynes, a latte cup balanced between her knees.

I imagine her shining brightly. You can't miss Carla on the beach. Unlike everyone else in their boring grey or navy anoraks, she will be wearing statement earrings, a loud patterned dress, her clogs, and – if it's raining – a bright orange poncho. The smell of the salty sea always reminds me of my teenage years: going down to the beach with Carla on the weekend, where she would allow me to have my first

Bacardi Breezer on a Friday night with her and her friends. I can imagine it all as the waves crash in the background and the dogs run around barking.

'I'm sorry you're feeling ill,' I say.

'At least I'm in Costa del Eastbourne. Anyway. Missing you. How's your assignment going?' she says, changing the subject.

I look out of the bathroom window. I think of Dom in New York, surrounded by yellow taxis, street food and iconic brownstone buildings. The grey sky of London feels pathetic in comparison to a bigger, brighter city like New York.

'It's going well. It's nice staying with Lola. Naz is an interesting person. Very different to me. Which, I guess, is the point of the article,' I say, lathering some shampoo on my head. 'Also, by the way, I forgot to tell you: Lola got engaged.' I suddenly realize it's purple shampoo – unsure what that will do to my auburn locks.

'Oh really! That's lovely news! Good for her.'

I decide not to tell Carla that it took Lola a while to tell me, that she actually hid her ring, which made me feel like the big green jealous ogre of the group.

'How are the others? How's Pen?'

'Got a new boyfriend. Disappeared off the face of the Earth,' I say, putting some orange scrub on my forehead and cheeks.

'Ah, the classic honeymoon period. We've all been there. Don't you remember it?'

I think back to the weekends before Dom dumped me. Pen trying to get a date in for the cinema. Pen wanting some help with her new flat. Pen asking if I fancied our annual trip to the seaside. I was definitely distant from her, and I wasn't even honeymooning. When I first met Dom, he would bring me a single rose whenever I saw him. He probably got the idea from some cheesy American romcom, but it was sweet at the time. I sigh, wondering if I'll ever have the honeymoon period again. I feel guilty having such negative thoughts about Pen. But I feel so distant from them all suddenly.

We go silent for a bit, me splashing about in the bath, and the background noise of the sea sounds like a meditation app through the phone.

'I know it's going to take a while. But . . . I think a bit of solitude is doing you the world of good. Don't you think?' Carla says.

'Maybe. I'm not really making the most of it, though. Shouldn't I be on a hot holiday or drinking cocktails in a hotel lobby or something?'

'You're just in your cocoon for a bit, that's all. Anything else going on?' Carla asks.

'I got the details through for the "exit fee" that Scatterbox are giving me.'

'Ooh! Good news then?'

'Yeah, it really is. It's an amazing thing to have. I've got enough for a deposit on a very nice flat. But I just feel down.' I sigh. 'It's like it's Dom's guilt money.'

'Oh, honey.'

'UGH . . .'

'What?'

'I've just realized that one of these products I've put on

my face at Lola's has snail jizz in it,' I say, reading the label on the back, translated from Korean.

'Snail jizz. You can't be serious.'

'Snail mucin. Sounds too much like mucus to me. I feel sick.'

I can hear Carla cackle, and my spirits lift a little.

'At least you've still got your sense of humour.'

There's a pause. I feel a bit lighter for talking to Carla. I think about Naz and the secret clothes shop and smile to myself.

I tell Carla I hope she feels better soon and hang up the phone. I get out and scrub the snail jizz off my face, and head to Lola's spare room to dry my hair when my phone pings. It's an email from Jaime.

> hey,
> hope all went well with naz yesterday
> naz is hosting her girls' night in event in a couple of weeks, did she tell you?
> just in case you don't already have a ticket
> i have attached jpeg invite with details, please rsvp to me.
> might be good for you to include in the piece if relevant.
> blessings

I reply and tell her that I'll be there. I didn't think I'd fancy it in my current state, but it's not like I have anything else to do.

Suddenly, I'm flooded with dread at being single at Lola's wedding. I can imagine it all: everyone walking into the ceremony with their partners, who will later sit side by side at the tables. Me, on my own, in the corner. People feeling sorry for me. Making small talk with old school friends who ask me how I'm doing. Someone's weird second-cousin who makes a beeline for me. Someone whispering about Dom or pulling a dramatic sad face at me. A drunk uncle trying to set me up with someone, unsolicited. At previous weddings, I always had Dom to hide behind.

Then I imagine Dom walking down the streets of New York with a new young woman on his arm, and before I know it, I've tapped on the App Store and downloaded Tinder. Lola has told me that loads of her brides met their soon-to-be husbands on Tinder. I was surprised by that, but perhaps the more retro the app, the better: cutting-edge hipsters move on to the latest tech, and the normal people just stay on the original one and hope for the best.

I do some swiping. Man wearing gold chains. Left. Man in tweed. Right? No, left. Man doing topless selfies in the mirror. He's good-looking, but . . . no. I sigh.

Lola knocks on the spare bedroom door; I quickly close the app. She pops her head in. I'm in my underwear.

'Hey. Quick thing, but I just need to confirm. I'm going to try on some wedding dresses with my mum tomorrow. I want a two-piece kind of vibe. If you're up for that, I'd love you to be there and help me pick something.'

'Yes! Of course.'

'OK, great! I'll confirm with them now that you're coming.'

'Sounds like a plan.' I smile at her widely.

'And see you later for dinner? Remember the girls are coming over tonight at seven.'

My smile falls away once she leaves.

Lola is a terrible cook; she's too quick and clumsy, and the kitchen soon smells of burning things as black smoke floods the room, billowing everywhere. She wafts a tea towel to stop the fire alarm going off and opens the back door.

'For *fuck's* sake,' Lola says.

It's 7.10 p.m.; Pen and Alice have just arrived. Pen is wearing a second-hand jumper with a slogan saying *Slow Love*. Alice looks chic in a navy jumpsuit.

'It's OK. We don't love you for your cooking. Thankfully,' Pen says, patting her on the back.

'Do you need any help?' Alice asks, washing her hands under the tap.

'Maybe just prepping the salad, please. There's a bag in the fridge, and onion, tomatoes and avocado.'

'I'm sure it will taste just fine,' I say encouragingly, as Lola takes a very watery-looking lasagne with a burned top out of the oven. I look enviously at Pen's tofu curry ready meal, which Lola is popping in the microwave and which already smells delicious.

Pen and I head to the adjoining living room to get away from the black fumes. Alice continues cutting up an assortment of salad items.

'How are you doing?' Pen says, putting an arm around me as she balances a glass of wine. Her jumper smells of her favourite lemon detergent, and I find it calming.

'I'm OK, I guess. How are you? I haven't seen you for ages,' I say, trying not to sound accusing.

'I went away with Mike for a few days – we went to this new eco-farm getaway thing, absolutely no signal there. We both work such mad hours that we have to be really strategic with time off, especially as we work in the same department – honestly, it's like a military operation whenever we need to get annual leave signed off.'

'Did you have fun? And can we meet him soon?' I ask, as Lola carries the wet, burned lasagne to the table, along with Pen's curry.

'Definitely soon,' Pen says, taking a swig of her wine. 'And yes, it was so nice. Though I have thrush now.' She laughs wickedly, her face lit up. 'I mean, it's been a while since I've had any action, so I'm not surprised. My vagina hadn't completely closed over, luckily. But anyway, how are you all?' Pen asks.

I don't tell her about Naz or my rash decision to download Tinder; I worry that she'll judge me – according to her, I'm supposed to be 'enjoying' my newfound singledom and solitude. I feel there is a widening gap between us now. Even if the weeks of silence are accidental, there's a rift that we're pretending isn't there.

Lola hands me a fistful of cutlery, and I lay the dining room table. I carefully place the white and blue plates and cutlery, while Pen shows Alice photos of the eco-farm in the living room and Lola grabs a water jug from the kitchen.

I have always found it therapeutic arranging a table. When I was younger, Carla put me in charge of laying the table while she cooked. I would solemnly place the napkins, put some flowers in a vase and light her long candles. It was our routine. Then I used to do even more elaborate tablescapes at home for Dom, so that he'd relax after a long day's work. I'd use lavender-scented candles to try and soothe him.

It angers me that something as mundane as laying a table has now been tainted by the memory of him. I can't escape our interwoven life together. It isn't a song or a specific thing that reminds me of us – it's the smallest, stupidest little things that make me the most homesick for our past relationship, my past life. I remember him in corner shops, in the cinema, in the post office. The memories engulf and surround me.

I overhear the others making excited noises.

'No *way*!' Pen says. 'That's *incredible*, Alice!!'

I poke my head around the corner, intrigued.

'What's happened?' I ask.

'Alice and Luke have sold Mystery Road,' Pen says, mouth wide open.

'The deal went through yesterday,' Alice says, beaming. 'Can you *believe* it? And of course, the money will be split four ways with the other founders, but yeah.' Alice breathes out slowly. 'It's *mad*, to be honest. Our life will change – has changed.'

'I can't even *compute* the amount of money you guys will get. Fuck.' Pen perches on the armchair. 'Are you going to live in a palace? A castle? A yacht? Can we move in?'

'Ha, you know what Luke is like. I'm sure nothing on the surface will really change. He'll still wear his faded holey jumpers and old trainers. Doesn't even like upgrading his phone or buying new socks. But of course – we are beyond privileged. He – well, we – will never have to worry again.'

'Secure the bag, as the kids say,' Pen says.

I'm stood in the doorway, frozen. I have a weird impulse, almost a muscle memory, to message Dom and tell him. I have a deep longing to discuss it over dinner with him, in that gossipy way that friends do. This is what Dom wanted – what *we* wanted – to eventually sell Scatterbox. That was our plan, together. Instead, I now have nothing to do with the company or with him. Nothing. The emptiness of my life rings in my head.

'That's amazing, Alice!' I say, my cheeks feeling tight.

We sit down at the table; I spark a match, lighting two long tapered candles in gold holders, and Lola serves up the sloppy lasagne and a nice avocado and tomato salad that Alice has made. Pen tucks into her tofu. Google Home plays music from a Spotify playlist of gentle acoustic songs while we chat.

'So, Alice, what kind of job will you get now that money isn't an issue?' Pen asks, spearing tofu onto her fork. 'Now that you're going to be able to pursue your passion – and have as much childcare as you like!'

I blink back the tears that are pricking my eyes and stare down at my plate. Is Pen not aware that I must find this conversation difficult?

'Well, hopefully I will be pregnant soon, so actually I'd love to just stay at home with the kids, if it happens for us.' She taps the table. 'Touch wood.' She looks at Pen's raised eyebrow. 'I know you think that sounds anti-feminist, and honestly, I used to think that, too. I always judged my mother for staying home with us. I was so weird about it. But now I'm realizing it's actually a pretty radical act. To put your career on hold to raise the next generation. I have so much respect for stay-at-home mums now. It's a fucking hard job, and my mum did it amazingly. Much harder than sitting at a desk tapping out boring emails all day.'

'You're right,' Lola says. 'Screw trying to balance a million plates.'

'Hang on a minute,' says Pen. 'That's all very well, but what about the generations of women who fought for you to have the right to work? I mean . . .'

She trails off, and I sense that they're all looking at me, realizing that I'm not joining in the conversation or even looking any of them in the eye.

'What's going on with you and the Scatterbox stuff, Willow? Sorry I haven't asked,' Alice says kindly.

I look up, relieved that my eyes are still dry, and cough to clear the lump in my throat. 'Oh, well, I'm sure Dom will sell in the future. I've left now though, officially, and I'm getting a settlement. So, just waiting for that to go through.'

'That's good news, surely?' Alice asks, tentatively.

'Yeah, it is,' I say, licking some balsamic vinegar off my thumb.

There's a slight pause in conversation while everyone starts eating.

'Is it a life-changing amount?' Lola asks, wrinkling her eyebrows, which have now returned to her normal shade of dark blonde.

'Not quite like Luke and Alice, but it's enough for a deposit on a flat, so I know I'm really lucky in that respect. I'll be able to move out of Carla's soon,' I reply.

'That's really good, Willow,' Alice says, reaching across the table to touch my hand.

'How's the wedding planning going?' I ask Lola, changing the subject.

'It was going very badly, but we've turned a corner today,' Lola says, using a spatula to lift up a piece of lasagne that is now resembling soup. 'I hate the planning – I think it was triggering me. Fred and I kept arguing. He's been worried we would waste money, but I couldn't bear for my big day to just have the cheapest, shittiest version of everything. Plus, our parents keep trying to expand the guest list and invite all their bloody friends. SO: change of plans. We decided this morning that we're going fully low-key. Registry service, followed by a pub. That's it. A handful of guests. No white dress. No wedding bollocks. I feel like one of those people who worked at a chocolate factory and now feel sick at the sight of chocolate.'

'Good for you,' Pen says.

'And I have a question for you all. Will you be my anti-bridesmaids? I won't make you wear matching ugly pastel dresses, but will you all stay with me the night before?'

'Oh my god, of course.' Alice jumps up from her seat; Pen throws her arms around Lola. I smile across the table.

I'm still being quiet. I can't help it. All I can think is that I'll be The Single Bridesmaid. No one wants to be The Single Bridesmaid. It is the curse of all curses. This was not meant to be my path. I was meant to go to weddings with a tall, handsome Dom on my arm.

'I'm *so* excited,' Alice says, clasping her hands together.

'The four of us are going to have the best time. Let us know if you need help with anything. Which pub are you thinking of?'

'The George. That big one near Finsbury Park. Great food, good beer garden area, room for a big dance floor, nice bar, loads of space for tables. I just want it to be super chilled. It's just about Fred and me. No bells and whistles, just us and our mates with no pressure. And Pen – you're being a bit secretive. Come on – spill the beans, then. Will you bring Mike the mystery man to the wedding?' Lola says, wiggling her eyebrows suggestively.

'Not sure. It's early days, so let's not get our knickers in a twist.'

Lola turns to me. 'I know it'll be weird that Dom won't be there, Willow,' she says, touching my arm. 'Obviously, we aren't going to invite him.'

I feel grateful for her confronting the elephant in the room.

'Hey, at least you don't have to see one of those gilets he used to wear ever again. They were *bad* . . .' Pen says, taking a big sip of wine.

Lola lightly slaps her arm. 'Shh!'

'What! When are we finally allowed to be honest about all the stuff we didn't like about him?' Pen says. 'He was awful to you at times, Willow. I'm glad you're coming on your own to the wedding. He was so bossy, telling you off like a bloody head teacher for having ideas about your life! It was hard to watch. And stingy. He never spent money on you on your birthday. He was selfish with work, *and* you kept telling me the sex was mediocre. I always thought he was quite emotionally stunted. There were no layers to the onion. You are far too good for him, Willow, and if I were you, I'd want someone to tell me the truth about him.'

I'm now looking at the others for support. My mouth is hanging open. Pen drains her wine glass and looks as if she's about to launch into another speech.

'That's enough now, Pen,' Lola says sharply, as though Pen was a small terrier yapping at someone's leg.

'Fine.' She taps the side of her head. 'I'll just keep a list of the things he was an arsehole about in here until you're ready to listen. I promise, in a few months, you'll want to hear all about his faults from our perspective.' She looks around the table and realizes we're not at the drunk-confessional stage of things yet. 'Sorry, I'm slightly pissed – I went for a few drinks with Mike before I came here.'

I look down at the watery lasagne on my plate, the sound of scraping cutlery cutting through the silence.

Later in the evening, with all the plates cleared, we sit in Lola's living room – candles burning, flames dancing, low lit.

Pen and Alice overhear me talking to Lola about the writing I'm doing.

'Oh, that's brilliant, Willow. Back doing what you love,' Alice says.

'Yes,' I say. 'I'm interviewing this interesting Gen Z "single" influencer. Her whole thing is about living life alone and learning to love it.'

I pick up my phone from the table and show them her account, @singlenaz. The phone gets passed around.

'How old is she? Fucking hell – her skin looks great. Surely she hasn't had Botox already,' Pen says, zooming in on the Instagram photo.

'Dunno. Twenty-three, I think.'

'Oh I've heard of her! I think we contacted her about doing some merch with Mystery Road once,' Alice says.

'I remember being that young.' Lola sighs. 'That used to be us, with that taut skin and carefree life. I'd chain-smoke and do shots and still look great the next day.'

'I didn't know anything about life in my twenties – I was an idiot,' Pen says. 'How is she dishing out the advice and to who? Who's listening? Bloody hell – 2.2 million people follow her!'

'Yes,' I say, taking my phone off her. 'I interviewed her yesterday, and I'm seeing her again soon.'

'She looks quite sassy and fun,' Alice says.

'Does she really know anything, though? Those influencers are good at business but bad at life, let's be honest,' Pen says. 'Remember those posers who used to jump on the Extinction Rebellion bandwagon but bring their own security and entourage? They don't have an actual backbone – they just follow trends.'

I smile at the memory. The Instagrammers always looked so out of place on the various marches Pen dragged me on, yet they had always managed to worm their way to the front. Pen took great pleasure in 'accidentally' waving her placard between their selfie sticks and their carefully contoured faces.

Somehow, though, I don't think Naz is like them.

'I dunno, her whole single vibe is very intriguing,' I say. 'If

I can get the right information out of her, I think the piece will be really interesting.'

Pen scrunches up her face and hands me back the phone.

'Why have you got an issue with her?' I ask, my irritation bubbling close to the surface now. What is her problem tonight?

'I don't have an issue with *her*. I've got an issue with where you're getting your information. I was single for literally *years*, but you're not asking me about any of it. Instead, you're following some random Gen Z TikToker and asking her for advice when your best friend is sat right here!'

'Oh really, Pen? You're "right here", are you? You're not, though. You're off shagging Magic Mike! You've been gone for weeks. You've totally disappeared. To be honest, I'm surprised you're even here tonight. You didn't come after Dom dumped me – you didn't even call. You've been silent on WhatsApp!'

Pen's face is frozen, like she's been slapped. Then she puts her wine glass down and raises her hands in a *you caught me* gesture.

'Fine,' Pen says. 'Yes. Maybe I *have* been a bit distant lately, but I am *sorry* for thinking I should be allowed some time with a man who makes me happy after years of playing second fiddle.' She puts her hands down, fidgets with them in her lap. 'You weren't exactly always *available*, Willow.' She looks me in the eye accusingly. 'But the minute Dom disappears, *now* you want to hang out.'

There's a palpable silence while I stare at Pen and will myself not to cry.

I get up and go to leave the room.

'Hey, don't go, Willow,' Lola says, standing up and hovering, unsure whether to follow me.

I get to the door, turn on my heel and take a big breath in: 'It's like you've ALL forgotten what it's like,' I whisper. 'To be *alone*. To feel utterly alone. To have no one to talk to. To go to bed alone every night. To have nobody to make mundane conversation with over a cup of tea at home. To wake up every morning and make all your own decisions. To have nobody to share a joke with in the kitchen. Nobody to stack the dishwasher with. Nobody to text when you get home after walking in the dark, or when the plane touches down to say *Landed!* No one to do up the fucking zip on my dress. No one there to help me do the shopping or take my suitcase upstairs or tell me mundane stuff about their day. There's no one to rub my feet or tell me it's all going to be OK after a shit day at work. There's no one to stop me spiralling when I'm having a moment of self-doubt. You don't understand what it's like to be standing outside the life you thought you had. Dom may not have been perfect, and you may not have liked him even, but he was all those things to me. I'm going to bed. I need to be alone. *Don't* follow me,' I say, my voice thick with tears.

Diatribe over. I walk down the corridor and loudly shut the door to Lola's spare room. I rip off my jeans, then lower myself onto the fold-out futon, pulling the covers over me. I can't be bothered to put on my pyjamas.

Lola slides a note under the door saying: *We love you. Glass of wine waiting for you if you want to come out xxx*, but they leave me be for the rest of the evening.

I can hear them chatting in hushed tones outside and clearing the plates away. I prop myself up with two pillows behind me and go back onto Tinder. I've had a few matches and messages, and though none of them are a patch on Dom, one looks OK: a man called Rich. He's wearing a suit in his profile picture and holding a glass of Champagne. Nice smile. No missing teeth. Has a job. Unlike the other messages, his doesn't describe in graphic detail what he'd like to do to me (ugh) but just says: *Fancy a drink?* I like his straightforwardness, and I need something to distract me. Something to hold onto, to remind me who I am, how to live, how to be. To remind me that I am in this world and that I have choices.

I don't reply right away, but I hug the knowledge close that someone out there wants to be with me, if only for an evening.

20

THEN

December 2006

It was 2006, and I passed my driving test the third time.

I walked into Carla's kitchen, pretending to be gutted. She looked worried, like she'd been on edge all day.

'How did it go?'

Then I waved the sheet at her. 'I passed!'

'YOU DIDN'T!'

'I DID.'

'Third time lucky! You know what – I had a hunch!' She walked over to the fridge and took out a cold bottle of Champagne, then got out two glasses. 'Well done you. How do you feel?' She looked relieved.

It had been a long road to get there: multiple failures and meltdowns at the kitchen table, with Carla rubbing my back and telling me not to give up. It felt like a million multicoloured fireworks going off the moment I passed. A taste of freedom.

'I feel *amazing*. I want to drive to London with Pen and Lola. I want to get some fluffy dice! I feel like the world has opened up a brand-new portal! Would I be able to borrow your car for the weekend?'

'OK, look, I'm super happy for you, darling, but *please* be careful? Those London roads are a nightmare. Mad drivers about. It's not you I don't trust . . . it's them . . .'

'I know, I know, I promise I will.'

I heard a sniffle.

'Wait – Carla, are you . . . crying?'

'Maybe,' she said, grabbing a tissue and turning away from me.

'Why?'

'Because you're a grown-up now. I mean, you'll always be a baby to me, but . . . you're free now, Willow. You are untethered; the world is your oyster. These are happy tears. It sounds stupid, but you know that Virginia Woolf quote, "a woman needs a room of her own"? I think it should be "a woman needs *a car* of her own". It means you can drive off and do whatever the hell you want, be whoever you want. Always remember that, OK? You are free. Always remember you can do whatever you want. OK?'

'OK,' I said, hugging her.

The next day, a present popped through the letter box. A gift from Pen. A wrapped CD of Tracy Chapman's 'Fast Car' single – with a note:

I knew you'd do it. Love you. P xxxx

21

NOW

In the morning, I wake slowly with sleep in my eyes to the sound of Lola cranking up her coffee machine.

I hear footsteps approaching; she knocks lightly on the door. I let her open it and tiptoe in. It's her house, after all.

'Are you OK?' she says gently. 'I've brought you coffee.'

'Thank you,' I croak, sitting up in bed.

'I'm so sorry about last night,' she says. 'I think Pen was a bit worse for wear.'

'Yes, I think so. I'm sorry, too. It all got a bit heated, really.'

'I think we all assumed you were more OK than you are. You're such a tough cookie, and you seemed to be moving on and throwing yourself into work, but I shouldn't have assumed that. This is going to take time. I'm sorry it's so shit,' she says, sitting on the end of the futon.

'It's OK. I just feel really left out at the moment. I don't want to drag everyone else down.'

'You're not. I promise.' There's a pause. 'Willow, I totally understand if you don't want to come wedding dress shopping with me later—'

'No, no,' I interrupt her. 'I want to. I'll get some work done here this morning, and I'll join you and your mum at three p.m. – is that cool?'

She smiles and gives me a big hug. 'Thank you. See you at three.' She squeezes my knee and skips out of the room to get ready for her client meetings.

I can tell how excited she is, and I don't want to burst her bubble, but I wonder how I'm going to get through it. Can I handle a bridal shop when I'm feeling this vulnerable?

I head to the kitchen to make another coffee, and see Fred is putting things away from the dishwasher, clanking the plates against each other loudly. He's very tall, and unlike Lola, he doesn't need the stepstool to reach the top cupboards. I didn't really want to run into him. He is kind and sensitive, but I'm not in the mood for pity.

'Hey, Fred,' I say.

'Oh, hey!'

'Hope you don't mind that I'm staying here for a bit.'

'Not at all. Make yourself at home. Sorry I've been hidden away in the office. Working overtime to pay for the wedding.' He laughs.

'Yes, of course – congratulations! Very exciting.'

'Thanks. It's been a bit stressful – sorry if it's been a bit tense between us. We're just working out some . . . logistics.'

'I get it,' I say.

'How are things with you? Really sorry to hear about Dom . . . Can I get you anything? Tea? Coffee?'

'Thanks. I was going to make a coffee.'

'Let me – you're our guest,' he says, grabbing a mug from the rack. 'I hear you're braving a wedding dress trip with Lola,' he chuckles. 'Any plans afterwards?'

'Just meeting a friend,' I say. Lying.

I actually have a Tinder date, Fred, wish me luck.

I feel embarrassed about my singleness suddenly. Alone with Fred without an anchor. Just me. Like a soft crab without a shell, like something has been removed – something I used to always return home to.

'This is so *fun*,' says Lola's mum, Suzie, beaming like an excited child. Suzie and I are sitting on a chaise longue in a little fashion boutique in Soho, sipping on a glass of disgustingly sweet fizzy wine. Lola has paid for a stylist for a few hours. It's not your standard bridal shop, but it has the same energy. Lola is behind a dark green velvet curtain, getting herself into one of the dresses she's picked for the 'maybe' rail.

Suzie used to be the local GP when we were at school, so she knows way too much about everyone but pretends that she's forgotten it all. She's wearing a white shirt with a necklace of tiny blue and purple beads and the same kind of gladiator sandals that my old Latin teacher used to wear. I've tried to wipe any encounters in her clinic from my memory: conversations about the morning-after pill; the way she would over-pronounce all the S's in 'safe sexual intercourse' and I would want the ground to swallow me up.

I shuffle in my seat; I can't get comfortable. They are taking ages trying to get Lola into one of the dresses. They've put a weird linen bag over her head to stop make-up going on the dress, and now she's got stuck, like an upside-down woodlouse flailing around. While they're attempting not to suffocate the bride, I go over to the rail and look at some of the other options she's chosen: a pink jumpsuit, a polka-dot two-piece, a dark green suit, a red strapless dress. They're all gorgeous, but I flinch at the price tags. Being in love sure costs a lot of money.

I need a breather. I excuse myself to go to the loo while they try and get her head out of the bag. In the bathroom, there is a framed picture of Jade Jagger wearing one of their dresses, and she has signed her name in lipstick.

When I go back, Lola is out of the fitting room and the bag has been removed. She is wearing a big, pink A-line skirt and a red crop top, both pinned in place by a woman wearing lots of bangles, who keeps speaking in a very close-the-sale kind of way.

'Doesn't she look *wonderful?*' the saleswoman says.

'Oh, she does! My gorgeous girl.' Suzie takes a tissue out of her sleeve and dabs her eye.

Lola does look beautiful.

'You look amazing,' I say. 'How do you feel?'

'I feel *great*. I know I'm a bit old for the cropped top but fuck it,' she says, twirling around. 'Bit different, isn't it?'

'Look at your face – you can't stop grinning,' the saleswoman says. 'That is the tell-tale sign that it's the one for you.'

'It's really, really gorgeous,' I say, getting up out of my chair. Suddenly my feet feel heavy, and the lights seem very bright. 'Do either of you fancy a coffee? I'm just going to pop out for a sec,' I say.

'I'm OK, thank you, darling,' Suzie says, smiling, waving her glass of fizz at me.

'Just need a little jolt of caffeine. Back in a sec. This is so fun!' I say, not wanting Lola to worry about me or to distract her from the try-on session.

I go to the coffee place next door and head to the toilets at the back. I needed to get out of that room. I lock the door, sit on the seat, breathe out. Hot tears, proper waterworks, big heavy droplets, stick to my face.

I catch a glimpse of myself in the mirror and am surprised by how unhappy I look. I allow myself to wallow for a moment and dwell on the reasons for my sadness:

1. I'm not going to marry Dom.
2. My mother will never see me try on a wedding dress.
3. I will be single at Lola's wedding.
4. I am unhealthily fixated on a woman from the Internet.

I sit back down on the loo, and I message Rich on Tinder, confirming where we're meeting tonight. I get a message back almost immediately, with a thumbs-up emoji and the address of a restaurant in Lexington Street.

I feel a tiny bit better and slap at my cheeks, trying to bring a bit more colour and life back to them. I need to let off some steam before I go back to the dress shop, and I need to hide the fact that I've just had a crying session. I know they're going to be in there for hours longer, trying different options, knocking back the sweet wine, loving every moment.

I walk out of the café and along a busy main road, wrapping my scarf tightly around my neck, stomping forward. I take a big deep breath in, trying to summon the energy to go back to Lola, her mother, and their joint happiness. Right before I decide to turn back, I see a sign for London Zoo – for Butterfly Paradise, the place I wrote about for one of my first pieces. It feels like a sign: it's time to transform myself, come out of my cocoon and re-enter the world of dating.

By the time I get back to the bridal shop, Lola and Suzie are hugging by the till. The red and pink two-piece is hanging at the back, ready for alteration. Suzie is handing over her credit card and asks if she can whisk me and Lola out for an early evening drink.

'Ah, you bought it!' I say, hugging Lola.

'We're going to go and celebrate,' she says.

'You two go – enjoy.' I smile. 'I'm meeting a friend in Soho later and need to go back and get changed.'

I'm not quite ready to tell Lola that I'm going out on a date.

I put on my navy coat and beret and get the Tube towards the little Italian restaurant on Lexington Street that's known for its romantic, candlelit vibe. I'm surprised at how civilized this all feels – despite what Lola told me about her brides meeting their soulmates on Tinder, I still fundamentally thought it was where people met to shag in alleyways. Maybe the dating landscape really has changed. People don't mess around, it seems; they want to meet you IRL before committing to the back and forth of potentially pointless texts.

I am nervous, but I remind myself of how strongly I feel that I *cannot* be on my own at Lola's wedding. I imagine it again: the drinks and canapés circling; me hanging on like a gooseberry as Luke and Alice chat; me lurking on the edges as everyone joins in the first dance. It gives me the kick I need to plaster a fake smile on my face and walk in looking confident.

He is already there, sitting at a small round table, candles burning in front of him. He's wearing a crisp white shirt and a navy jacket with navy trousers. I wave awkwardly, and he nods.

'*Enchanted* to meet you,' he says, standing up and pulling out my chair for me. 'Care for a drink?'

He's ordered a bottle of Champagne, which already feels a bit full on, and he pours as I sit down.

'I hope Champagne is OK?'

'Yeah, why not!' I say brightly, thinking *is this normal for a date* while wiping my sweaty hands on my jeans. 'Thanks for organizing. I've not been here before.'

'It's one of my favourites. It really has a *je ne sais quoi*.' He takes a sip. 'So, are you new on the apps? Technology is amazing, isn't it? A mere few days ago, both of us were just living our lives, not knowing each other existed. And now, here we are. Poof! Like we have little magic wands in our pockets all day long. Is that a wand in your pocket . . .' He winks at me strangely.

Some bread arrives for the table, and we are handed the full menu to choose from.

'So, how's your day been so far?' he asks.

'Good, thank you.' I mutter something about spending time with a friend and start digging into the bread basket. 'You?'

'I like a girl who likes her carbs,' he says, looking at me up and down. 'I've been on a protein-shake diet for weeks, plus my tight gym regime, so this is my rare "treat day".'

'Right.' I smile at him, tearing off a big bit of bread.

'So whereabouts in London do you live?' he asks.

'I'm actually living outside of London at the moment, so it's nice to be back.'

'Whereabouts?'

'I'm in Eastbourne.'

'Oh shit, really – I've heard it's a bit of a dive.'

Suddenly, I feel defensive. I think of Carla's book-lined She-Shed, with its dangling wind chimes and view of the sea. 'It's lovely, actually. My aunt lives there,' I say, frowning. I take a sneaky look at my watch. Only ten minutes have passed.

'Well, I do love London life, but you know, stress upon stress upon stress. But I've learned to block it all out. It's in one ear and out the other.' He laughs. 'I basically turn myself into a brick wall, and it all bounces off me.'

'What's stressing you?' I ask.

'Oh, my job. Finance. It is suuuuuper stressful,' he says, unbuttoning his shirt's top button and leaning back in his chair. 'But I'm good at distracting myself. Thinking of moving jobs maybe. I have lots of transferable skills.'

I leave politely to go to the ladies. I sit on the loo, breathing hard, I suddenly don't feel right. I want to text Pen, but we're not really talking.

I decide to WhatsApp Lola:

Me: I lied. I'm not actually with a friend, I'm on a date. It's so bad.

Lola: Oh lordy.

Me: I'm in the loo, and I don't want to go back out there. He's reeling off his CV and has his shirt open

Lola: Leave now. Just leave. Come back here, and we can watch the new Black Mirror on Netflix. I'll be home in half an hour

Me: We haven't ordered the mains yet

Lola: nooooo, mains? willow you never ever agree to a full-blown dinner for the first date!!!!!

Me: How should I know that! I've not dated since 2013

Lola: I know the apps are new to you. But seriously, just leave. Next time, you do ONE drink and see how it goes from there. So you don't trap yourself

Me: How do I get out of this?

Lola: Just go back and say you're feeling unwell

I sit back down, and before I can muster up my lie, Rich stares at me intensely.

'So, what are you looking for?' he asks, leaning forward.

'Out of what? Life?'

'Life!' He snorts. 'No. God, that's a bit deep. No, I mean, out of tonight. Dating, romance, etc.'

'I don't know really. I was in a relationship for a long time, and then—'

'Look, I'll cut to the chase. I know I look young for my age, but I'll be forty next year – would you believe it? So, I'm sort of looking to crack on with all of that stuff. Hope you don't mind me being forward. But you know, time is ticking, and I'm keen to get a move on. You seem nice, but I'd need to know if you're interested or not. Whether it's worth my time here.'

'Well.' I nearly choke on some sourdough. 'Definitely good to be honest,' I say, swallowing hard, trying to gather the courage to just skid my chair back and leave. I need to get out of this tiny restaurant and away from this brick wall of a man. 'I'm really sorry, I'm actually not feeling well, at all, and er . . . sorry, I think I need to leave.'

I'm not even lying. It feels like an anxiety attack of some sort. I put £20 down on the table and make a bolt for the door.

He sends me a text five minutes after parting ways.

I would love to see you again.

I block his number and delete the message.
Either he is incredibly desperate, or he is a psychopath.
Abort mission.

When I get back to Lola's, she opens the door and gives me a big hug.

'That was *horrible*,' I say, nestling into her. 'It went very badly, and he wanted to see me again?'

'Oh, mate.'

'I'm trying not to compare, but my early dates with Dom were never this awkward. Everything was so easy – he made me feel good from day one, and this date was just so grimy and made me feel terrible about myself. I can't bear the thought of having to do that over and over again.'

'You don't have to do anything – not until you're ready.'

'I just want to go back to the way things were. I want to go back to the comfort of having someone there. Someone who just knows me, all those little shortcuts we had.'

'I know. I know,' she says, stroking my back. 'I don't know what to say. But I'm here, while you ride it out.'

'I miss feeling like myself.'

'You will again. It will just take time. Promise.'

She makes me a mug of camomile tea to soothe me.

We go into the living room, and Fred is on the sofa in a onesie. I sit between them both. We watch TV together, like I'm their weird adult child, with a massive bag of Kettle Chips and a blanket stretching across the three of us. It's comfortable, but not exactly how I pictured things turning out.

22

THEN

April 2004

On a school trip in 2004, our teacher Ms Gower took us on a hike into the mountains near a small town in Mallorca. We hiked and wrote messages to ourselves on pebbles, the idea being that we'd throw them into the sea when we got down to the beach. We stopped off for some water, perched on rocks. People removed sweaty layers, and someone handed out energy balls from Tupperware containers.

'Well done, girls. Just another two hours to go.'

'My legs ache,' sighed a girl called Mary.

Pen was squirting factor fifty onto her palms and applying it to her pasty legs. Lola was wearing only a sports bra and Adidas shorts, with a huge backpack that made her look like she'd topple over any second.

'So, who here thinks they're bad with directions?' Ms Gower asked. 'Who often loses their way?'

We all went quiet.

'Willow is,' Lola said, elbowing me.

'I am,' I said.

'She is – she is *shite* with directions,' Pen said, half an energy ball in her mouth. 'She forgot the way back to her aunt Carla's from my house just the other day. Which is only a five-minute walk, I might add.'

I stuck my tongue out at Pen.

Lola tapped Pen's arm, lightly. 'Oh, shh, she's not *that* bad.'

'OK, Willow, you're leading the next portion of the hike,' Ms Gower said. 'Here is the map.'

'No, no, I can't. We'll get totally lost. We'll all die. Honestly. I *cannot* read maps.'

'OK, I hear that, but I want you to give it a go. Women, especially young women, are made to feel like this a lot, like they have to wait for someone else to take the lead. To tell them where to go, how to navigate difficult paths. It is something that a lot of us pick up as children through subtle social clues. Women are not especially worse at directions, and yet, it's something I notice in all female groups. When we are given a chance to find our way, we usually do. This is an exercise in trusting yourself.'

I took the map, and my eyes went blurry; none of it really made sense.

'You'll figure it out,' she said. 'Go on – go up ahead.'

'What if we go the wrong way?'

'Have a few minutes to look at the map on your own. I've highlighted the route in red marker: here, look. And we're *here*, currently,' she said, pointing with a tanned finger. 'I'll give you some clues if you need. I won't leave you totally alone. I can re-route you if you go wrong, but I'd like to see you try.'

Ms Gower asked us to walk in silence, believing it was good to have time to contemplate instead of our 'constant yapping'. Twenty minutes into the hike, me at the front, with Ms Gower a little behind me, we came to a fork in the road. All the trees looked the same; the map didn't seem to correspond with the small lanes I could see. There were a few rogue huts and some stray dogs starting to bark, showing their sharp little teeth. All the colours and shapes of the landscape bled together, and I wasn't sure which direction we were facing. I wasn't sure which path to choose. Both paths led downwards, but one would take us to the beach and one would surely take us to a dead-end. My palms were sweating.

'Take your time,' Ms Gower said, while the others enjoyed a welcome pit stop and drank from their water bottles.

I spotted a large statue on my left and matched it up with what was labelled on the map. I noticed that an old farmhouse was no longer there, now just a pile of rubble. I noticed the horizon was in sight now, the faint blue of the water line. I worked out that the path we needed looped back on itself slightly, whereas the other path didn't.

'OK, this way,' I said, with confidence, leading the group.

Ms Gower followed me, not saying anything.

Eventually, we made it down to the beach. Ms Gower handed around apples and ham sandwiches wrapped in tin foil, and we kicked off our hiking boots and stripped off our socks, cooling them in the shallow water.

'You did well today, Willow,' Ms Gower said, taking off

her big rucksack. 'Remember it's always OK to stop and look. You don't need to charge ahead. It's good to doubt yourself every so often, good to slow down, stop, reassess. We need to do a lot of slowing down and reassessing as we go through life. Complacency can often set us off course. Mistakes are often made when we are too rushed.'

'Thank you. I felt a bit under pressure, but I'm glad I figured it out.'

'Would you still say you're bad with directions?'

'Well, I'm still not great with them.'

'You were great today. Be careful about what you label yourself, because a lot of the labels we put on ourselves might not be true. You led us in the right direction. You focused. You weren't just a side passenger; you had to take control. Sadly, a lot of women become side passengers in life. I just don't want that for you girls.'

Ms Gower crossed her arms over her T-shirt and lifted it over her head, then stripped off her hiking trousers to reveal a swimsuit underneath. She ran down to the water's edge and dived in.

I wondered in that moment why she felt so passionately about us taking control of our lives and taking charge at the age of fifteen – and I wondered why she hadn't yet thrown her pebble into the sea. Perhaps she wanted to keep it.

It was sitting on top of her rucksack and said: *You know the way.* I looked over, and saw Lola had written *stay joyful* on hers. Pen wrote: *find a soulmate, if they exist?* I quickly scribbled something on my pebble: *Always follow your own path.*

23

NOW

I get back to Carla's after the hour-long sleepy train journey from Victoria. I drop my bags in the hallway, knackered. I go the kitchen and splash my face under the tap, cold water running into my eyes. It wakes me up slightly. The smell of Carla's bungalow, the very specific flowery laundry detergent that wafts around, brings a huge feeling of comfort and a deep sense of home. I shake my head at Rich, daring to slag off our beloved Eastbourne.

The following week back at Carla's is admin heavy. I spend lots of time in my room, at my desk, tapping away at my laptop in the glow of the little yellow lamp on the desk. I sort out plans with Elaine for the Naz article over email, suggesting ideas of things we can do together (a walk, a gig, her fitness routine, that sort of thing). I get all my expenses signed off by Elaine to spend five days in London in a hotel, which will make it easier to attend the Girls' Night In evening. Carla pops her head round the door every so often, offering me a tea, giving me an uplifting smile. Life looks different now; I can't work out if it's better or worse – it just is, and I'm starting to feel intrigued about where it might lead me.

One morning I rise early and I take the dogs out for a walk; it's cold but that beautiful time of day where the light shines off everyone's faces in an orange hue. I take Carla's quirky leopard-print dog leads and a handful of poo bags, and walk the twenty minutes towards the beach, sniffing the smell of seaweed in the air, taking in the expanse of the clear sky above me. I remember once reading about an artist who believed the weather always mirrored his internal state, not the other way around. The clear sky represents my clear head, and I'm grateful for the respite.

Carla's neighbour, an elderly man whose name I don't know, tips his hat to me like a gent and wishes me a good morning. I smile at the other dog walkers, laughing at Bubble and Squeak sniffing everyone's feet.

When I get back to the house, Carla calls, 'Willow, come here a sec.'

I go to the bathroom, where she has a soap dispenser in the shape of a lighthouse and a bar of soap in the shape of a fish. She's in her bra, looking in the mirror.

'What is this?' She lifts up her arm to expose her armpit.

I look closely and see a raised circular bit of skin. It's a lump.

'I knocked it the other day, and my armpit really hurt – it's what made me look in the first place.'

'It's quite firm to touch,' I say, frowning, concerned.

'Yes, I think so too,' she says, looking in the mirror, turning around. 'Fuck.'

'I'm sure it's nothing,' I say, but suddenly there's a frog in my throat, and I hold onto the wall to steady myself.

'I'm sure you're right,' Carla says, quickly. 'I'll book a doctor's appointment tomorrow, to be on the safe side.' I watch her put on a brave face, and she goes downstairs to start on the stir-fry she's making for lunch. She gets the wok out and puts on the radio and hums along. I hover in the doorway, unsure what to say, but get the sense that she doesn't want to talk about it.

I sit at the kitchen island, reading an old novel to distract myself, trying not to spiral. I welcome any distractions right now: a portal to the outside world, a fantasy land where people don't have mysterious lumps.

I open WhatsApp, expecting a message from Lola or Alice but secretly hoping for Pen.

> I got a new US number while I'm in NYC . . .
>
> I understand if you might not want to, feel free to totally ignore, but I'm going to be back in London next week, and I feel like we should probably see each other again and chat properly. Would be good to catch up, etc.?
>
> Just putting it out there.
>
> D

My heart thumps in my chest. I stare at the message. I freeze, like a rabbit in headlights. I don't know what to make of it. My palms feel sticky and clammy suddenly. My stomach is tied in knots. I put the phone face down on the table, blocking it out.

Carla plates up the stir-fry, and we start picking at the food. I don't know if I should bother her with Dom's decision to text me when she has a much bigger, weightier matter on her mind. But I can't help it – I need her wisdom. I also feel it would be a good distraction. The mood feels extremely heavy all of a sudden.

'I just got a message from Dom – he wants to meet up.'

'Oh, darling, how confusing.'

'I know, I've no idea what prompted it.'

'It does seem strange. What are you going to do?'

I close my eyes for a moment and think of Naz. 'I'm going to tell him no.'

'Door definitely closed?'

'I don't see how meeting would help.'

'It's up to you, of course, darling. You never know – it might give you a sense of closure to see him one last time. You were each other's person for such a long time . . .'

'I think I'm going to leave it for now. Anyway, there are more important things going on,' I say gently.

'Don't worry about me,' she says. 'I'll get an appointment sorted pronto and we'll take things as they come. What are your plans for the week?' Carla asks, changing the subject, adding more salt and pepper to her food.

'I'm meant to be going to London again tomorrow, I have to collect my remaining stuff from the Scatterbox offices. And then I'll actually be there for a few days longer as I've got some Naz-dedicated time for the article.' I sigh. 'I feel bad leaving you. I should be with you. I don't care about anything else.'

'No! Sweetheart, I'm fine. Honestly.'

I forget that Carla is fiercely independent; I know she would actually want to go to any appointment alone. She hates people fussing.

'We don't have any idea what's going on yet. It could be absolutely nothing. In fact, it probably is. I don't want you to feel like you have to hang around here just for me. You have things to do. I promise you, I'll update you once I know more, and you can come back then.' She puts her hands on my shoulders. 'Please, don't be worried. I will be fine.'

She gets up and opens one of her cupboards above the oven. She's moving stuff around, crockery clinking. She does seem slightly on edge.

'What are you doing?' I ask.

'We need something stronger. Where are my martini glasses? We should be celebrating your return to freelance writing.'

'Really? Is this a good idea?'

'I don't care!'

'OK.' I laugh. 'I'm not going to stop you.'

She sets to work with mixing us both a drink and plonks down two martinis on the table.

'Here you go. Vodka, dry vermouth and garnished with an olive.' I take a sip and wince. It's mostly vodka.

'Bloody hell,' I say, my face scrunching as though I've eaten a whole lemon. 'It's strong.'

'Stanley Tucci style. He makes these absolutely lethal cocktails on Instagram – have you seen the videos? Marta keeps sending me the links,' she says. 'Come on, let's take these to the She-Shed.'

We take our lethal drinks outside, and the dogs follow us.

'I need to do some smudging,' Carla says, taking a huge bundle of sage from her shelves and lighting it, wafting the smoke all around. 'I need to keep this space refreshed with good energies. I'm going to need all the help I can get. Will you say a mantra with me?' She lights a few different candles around the She-Shed.

'Of course,' I say, sipping on the petrol-like drink once more.

'I release any and all things that are not in alignment with my natural state of being.'

I repeat, 'I release any and all things that are not in alignment with my natural state of being.'

She closes her eyes. 'Harmony is the natural order of things.'

'Harmony is the natural order of things.'

'I choose to align with peace, love, and abundance.'

'I choose to align with peace, love, and abundance.'

Carla sits in the silence, eyes closed, for a few more minutes and then makes some sounds with her wind chimes.

I feel like she is also smudging away Dom.

'Right – shall we put our cocktails in a flask and finish them on the beach? I am very proud of you for feeling strong enough not to reply to Dom and for this new career you're forging,' she says, blowing out the candles.

'Something, somewhere is giving me strength,' I say, thinking of Naz, thinking of the way she linked her arm with mine.

The next morning, I think about Carla for the whole train journey back to London. I always find it difficult tearing myself away, but this time it felt much worse. I also don't want her to think I'm panicking as though something's wrong. Nothing is technically wrong yet. Plus, she has plenty of helping hands in the neighbourhood. She added me to a local WhatsApp group with a few of her book club friends when I first moved back, so I know there's a good support system.

When I left her, she was lighting candles around the house and playing relaxing music (Enya, her favourite) and making herbal tea. At least she's not tucking into more vodka. She'd managed to get a same-day appointment at the GP, so when she knows more later, she said she'll let me know.

As Elaine is covering the costs of a hotel in Soho, I can spend five days with Naz and gather enough information to finish the article. I couldn't bring myself to ask to stay at Lola's again; it didn't feel right being there while they're preoccupied with wedding planning – *plus*, when Fred snores, it's so loud it's like he could suck up all the furniture.

On the train, I scroll through Instagram, intending to research Naz but really stalking my best friends. Our WhatsApp group has been practically silent since Lola's dinner, and I feel out of touch. Usually, I know what they're all up to outside of work, and it feels so alien to have these tumbleweeds; the chat is usually full of old stupid photos, private jokes, memes, celebrity gossip and aubergine emojis. Pen hasn't written anything for ages. Perhaps the moment is here, the moment we dreaded: our lives all going in different directions.

I spot that Fred has posted something on his Stories, and I immediately wish I hadn't seen it. With a pang, I see that the six of them have all been away for a weekend in the countryside. All wearing fucking wellies. We secretly did this a few years ago without Pen, but it felt different back then, Pen wouldn't have wanted to come. I screenshot the picture and Zoom in on Mike. His hand around Pen's waist. A kind face with laughter lines around his eyes. I feel a sinking sensation in my belly, a disappointment that Pen hasn't introduced him to me yet.

I feel further from them than ever, but I swallow my pride and message Pen, hoping to bridge the distance between us by telling her about Dom's text. I feel like I need a tough-love friend, someone who will keep me off the forbidden path back to him. I also need an excuse to message her, to reinstate our ghostly WhatsApp chain. I can feel her drifting away. I wonder if she'll confess to going away with the others. I'm trying not to mind, but a gut-punch of failure and disappointment is twisting through my stomach nonetheless.

Me: Guess who texted me last night

Pen is typing.

Pen: Adam Driver?

Me: No . . .

Pen: Oh, shame

Me: Dom

Pen: Oh shit. Sorry. I did NOT expect you to say that

Me: I know

Pen: What did he say?

Me: That he's back in London and wants to 'catch up'

Pen: Jesus. Are you going to?

Me: No

Pen: Good. Stay strong Willow

Me: Have you had a good week? Hang out soon?

Pen: YES. Work is so busy. Lots to fill you in on. I'll send you dates. Promise

I sigh and click back to Naz. She's posted another self-affirmation mantra, accompanied by a picture of her about to board a flight:

Remember to fully enjoy yourself when travelling alone! Flight socks, eye mask, good book. No one can love you like you can.
   #Selflove #Solocare #Singlebychoice

I roll my eyes a little, but her positivity is infectious, and undeniably, it's become a place I feel 'seen'. I 'like' the post, then switch my phone to *do not disturb* and spend the rest of the journey immersed in a new novel, trying not to think too hard about all the things that are totally out of my control.

I find myself clicking back into the message from Dom. I can't help myself; I keep reading it again and again.

I put my phone in my bag, out of sight. I close my eyes and think of Naz instead. *No one can love you like you can.* I pray that she's right.

Part Three

24

NOW

I'm outside the Scatterbox offices, my foot tapping nervously. I have to collect a small desk lamp, a plant, and a few other documents, including my passport – which I left in a bloody desk drawer. Lisa said it was best to move everything out soon, because there is a new starter joining who will have my old desk. The last few things I need to gather up before I am completely rid of it all. A bittersweet feeling.

When I walk into the office and cross the parquet flooring, dragging my small navy suitcase with me, it is deathly quiet. Lisa is sat at her desk at the back of the office, tapping away, wearing a black designer hoodie and her signature big tortoiseshell glasses. It's just her, in the big echoey office, with only the office parrot, Pete, for company – making a few repetitive sounds.

'Oh, hey,' Lisa says, looking up from her screen.

My footsteps ricochet throughout the empty space.

'Hey. Very quiet today?'

'Everyone's away at a team building day in Brighton.'

'Oh. I was hoping to say bye to a few people. You didn't go?' I ask.

'Nah, too much to do. Gotta hold down the fort.' She smiles. 'How's things with you?'

'I'm doing OK. Just picking up my final bits and pieces,' I say. 'This will be the last time stepping foot in here. Feels strange.'

I turn around and take one last look at the office. Empty beer bottles are strewn across the sink. One whiteboard says:

NO PRESSURE, NO DIAMONDS
THERE'S NO 'I' IN TEAM, BUT THERE IS IN WIN!

Another whiteboard says:

Song suggestions please! Money-themed karaoke night with new investors!

And people have scribbled down ideas in bad handwriting.

Money, Money, Money – Abba
Got Your Money – Ol' Dirty Bastard
Price Tag – Jessie J

I notice some building work going on in the corner of the office, mini scaffolding and some dust sheets.

'What's going on there?' I ask.

'Oh! We're building a big slide and ball pit.'
'Seriously?'
'For the employees. Dom's idea . . .' Lisa gets up from her seat and sits on the edge of her desk. 'He was inspired by that WeWork guy.'
'Wow.'
There's an awkward silence for a moment.
'I hope this is OK to say . . . but I'm really sorry for everything you've been through, Willow. I don't know the full details, of course, but for what it's worth, I always thought you were kind of too good for this place. You're obviously a creative soul. You have to do what makes you happy.'
I'm surprised by the kindness. I've only ever seen her in her bossy office manager role or sending me anxiety-inducing emails. She takes her chunky glasses off for a moment; her eyes look smaller and kinder, less stern.
'Thanks, Lisa.'
'I mean it. I think you will really spread your wings outside the confines of this place. Good luck.'
She smiles at me, with a sincerity that I've not seen before, and then sits back down at her computer, pulling in her wheelie chair, about to start tapping out more emails.
I take my things from my desk, take in one last scan of the office and leave.

I check into my room at a very fancy new hipster East London hotel, booked by Elaine. My room is called a 'womb', and the bed is actually shaped, with the help of specialist designers, to resemble a literal womb. The womb rooms have soft, soothing lighting and cosy 'nooks' that enhance REM sleep, according to the leaflet on the bed. I'm excited to be staying in the city for a bit; for good coffee and bakeries, the diversity of people on public transport, street style, interesting people-watching – all the things you don't find so much in seaside towns.

The hotel has a restaurant downstairs, and I ask for a table for one. I'm seated at a table booth with banquet seating, and the waiter pours me some sparkly water out of a silver jug. I'm enjoying the view of the open-plan restaurant, the warm lighting, the hum of people chatting around me, the abstract art on the walls. I feel content and powerful to be eating alone, not needing distraction for company, savouring the fizzy sips and taking in the deliciousness offered to me on the menu. I close my eyes for a moment and soak in this moment of peace.

All the menu choices are based on cosy comfort food for children, like peanut butter and jelly sandwiches and milk lollies, with the womb puns continuing: *do you have womb for dessert?* I take a deep relaxing breath in, noticing how different I feel in myself, how much stronger, how much calmer, and how much more capable to deal with some of the life dramas that still surround me. I sit back on my chair, taking in the tall ceiling, the spacious room, and the delicious smells wafting out from the kitchen. How lucky I feel in this moment, to enjoy my food alone. I get out my notebook, start writing ideas for the introduction to my Naz article. This is how it used to feel. The joy of dining alone.

Back upstairs, I unpack my suitcase and steam the outfit

I'm going to wear tonight to Naz's event: a red jumpsuit from COS that ties at the shoulders, with a matching red bag and plain black sandals. I get out a YSL red lipstick, one I've had for years, a freebie from the *D-Low* days – I'm surprised it's still good to use.

I go to message Pen, but I stop myself. I'm still a bit miffed that they all chose to go away without me. I have an urge to tell her about Carla's sinister lump, how worried I am, but I don't feel that I can be honest with her now and that makes me feel sad. I think about how so many things are changing, always changing.

I take a deep breath and call Carla, gripping the phone with white knuckles.

'Hi, darling. I was just about to call you.'

'How is everything?' I say quickly.

'Everything is fine.'

'It is? You went to the GP?'

'Yes. Don't worry. All under control for now.'

'So, it's nothing?'

'Yep, all fine.'

'Phew. What did they say?'

'I won't bore you with the details.'

'What happened?'

'I've been referred to the hospital for scans, but that's all – they don't feel it's anything to worry about at this stage.'

'OK. When will that be?'

'Next Monday.'

'Are you sure you don't want me there?'

'Yes darling. Nothing to report yet. How's the hotel?'

I notice her changing the subject but don't want to press her unnecessarily.

'It's slightly odd but kind of great. Apparently if I don't "sleep like a baby" in my bed, I get my money back. I'll text you a pic of the bed – shaped like a womb. It's wild.'

'Ha. Only in London. Well, good for you!'

'Will be back to see you soon,' I say.

'Don't rush back. Enjoy your work and your time there. You deserve it.'

I hang up and feel my shoulders relax a little, my jaw untenses.

I go to Instagram and notice that Naz has started 'following' me. I feel strangely excited. She has over 2 million followers and only follows thirteen people. Now fourteen, including me – even though I currently have only one blurry photo on my grid after my Dom-deleting spree: Carla on the beach with a mint chocolate ice cream and her two dogs. I feel honoured, and surprised by how much of a boost this gives me.

I open the reminder email from Naz's Girls' Night In team.

From: Naz's Dream Team <naz@girlsnightin.com>
To: Willow <willowjones@hotmail.com>
Subject: Tomorrow! London VIP tickets

We can't wait to see you tomorrow night!
Dress to impress (nobody but yourself).
REMEMBER:

Bring your dancing shoes
You are a wonderful unique human who matters
We can't wait to celebrate you tomorrow with lots of incredible women who want to see you shine bright.
Love always,
Naz and the Girls' Night In team

Then, a new email from Elaine:

How's it all going with the piece? Will you be ready to file in two weeks, three max? The *Mail* want to do a big piece to tie in with our launch of *Z Life*!

    Can you also please interview her management team or at least attend one of her meetings with them? Would love something in there ideally about how much money she earns . . . a look at how many freebies she gets and some of the behind-the-scenes of the business side, something that gets the comment section going, if you know what I mean . . . Thnx doll!

I dash off a quick agreeable reply to Elaine, then I throw my phone aside and sink into the womb bed for a few moments, adrenaline fizzing through my veins.

The password for Naz's event is 'vibrator'. Of course it is. I say this out loud to a large, bulky, serious-looking man in a black suit, who is standing next to a big red door on a busy street. He nods seriously and then tells me that the event is happening in the room called The Apartment, right at the back through the main restaurant. I go through another doorway and hand my coat to a woman wearing a sequinned dress, and I smooth down my red jumpsuit.

'Hi, I'm Destiny,' the woman says. 'I work with Naz's events team. Do you have a ticket?'

'Yes,' I say, digging it out of my bag. 'And I'm press – I'm writing about the event.'

It feels good saying that again.

'Oh great!' Destiny gives me a token for three free drinks: a choice of margarita, Aperol spritz, or negroni. She also pins a badge on me and offers a free tote bag that says *Consciously Coupled (With Myself)*.

'Would you like a free raffle ticket?' She hands me a paper ticket. 'You're entered into a lucky dip to win a solo trip to Tulum.' She then hands me a tiny bit of card saying *#ChooseYourself*. 'Remember to take lots of pictures of your evening, use this hashtag, and tag Naz if you can.'

I enter The Apartment with all my wares and see lots of Gen Z women: wolf haircuts, loud nail polish, tracksuit bottoms, cropped T-shirts. It feels like the Nineties again – we wore this stuff the first-time round. There's a girl wearing Adidas trousers with poppers.

It's a friendly atmosphere; people are chatting enthusiastically, laughing. I feel slightly out of place in my thirty-something-COS-woman outfit, looking accidentally formal, but the energy is welcoming. I spot Naz in the corner. She's wearing her signature bejewelled headband, paired with bright red lipstick and glowing skin. She's chatting, laughing, holding a handbag made of pearls. She's trying to look natural, but I can tell she is working the room, her loud laugh bouncing off the walls.

At one end of the large space, there is a long wooden trestle table with a light pink linen tablecloth. On it are wildflowers in large, rustic jugs, and each of the guests' names are handwritten on little place cards.

A short woman with blonde pixie-cut hair is also looking for her seat, and she says hi to me. 'Isn't she just *amazing*?' She gestures over at Naz, who is signing a copy of her book for someone. 'I'm Bec.'

'Nice to meet you. I'm Willow.'

'So, how did you find out about this event?'

'I'm a writer, actually writing a piece about Naz.'

'Oh, no way. I've been following Naz on Instagram for *years*. Since she started it. You know, I left my husband this year because of her. Felt empowered by her words. He wasn't . . . very kind to me.'

'Oh god, I'm so sorry, if he – was – you know—'

'Oh, he wasn't *abusive* or anything. He was just quite boring.' She takes a casual sip of her lemonade. 'Naz made me realize I could do better. I was settling. I have so many hours in my day back now: no more cleaning his skid marks off the toilet, no more ironing his shirts, no more thankless tasks. I am FREE! It honestly feels amazing. We're lucky that the younger generation can give us the permission slip we needed years ago.' I look at Bec's face more closely and place her in her mid-forties, which surprises me. I had assumed everyone here would be in their twenties. 'Naz really is a breath of fresh air.'

Everyone gets seated at the long table, and mini arancini

arrive on our plates. Oh God, I didn't realize it would be a full-on meal, I've already had my solo dinner at the womb hotel. The dinner menu is in front of me, printed on a thick textured card. It tells us what the young female waiters are serving after our arancini: a mini lobster roll to start, veggie risotto, and for dessert, a chocolate mousse. I still feel full from earlier, but it sounds delicious. There are also little postcards scattered on the table with inspirational quotes and messages from famous single women. I put a handful of the postcards in my bag.

We all turn around as Naz taps the mic and stands on a chair, clearing her throat.

'Hi everyone! Thank you so much for coming. Just a little welcome speech from me . . . we are *so* glad you are here, for our very special one-off event to celebrate my brand-new book, *Woman: An Island*. Welcome! There are signed copies on the table at the back of the room, and I'm happy to personalize it with your name if you come and find me later . . . Firstly, a huge thank you to my publishers for putting on this super special evening!'

She smiles into the mic graciously while people start clapping. She clears her throat delicately. I carefully extract my Dictaphone from my clutch and press 'record'.

'So, I wanted to start off with some FACTS! Are you ready?' (More encouraging claps from the crowd.) 'According to research, single women are healthier, happier, and live longer. Single women have more friends, which adds to their overall sense of wellbeing! We are better at looking after our own money. We are less stressed, more self-sufficient, more creative. We use our initiative more. Being single has personally made me happier, stronger, and made me realize that in the end, the relationship we have with ourselves is the most important one of all. And YET: 50 per cent of women feel they need a partner to protect them or provide for them or support them! But we know that when you back yourself, literally anything is possible. So, on that note, let's celebrate ourselves and each other tonight. Let's raise a glass to all the empowering choices we make! You all look AMAZING, by the way! Tonight, I want you to mingle, make friends, and remember: you are enough, JUST as you are!'

More applause, wolf-whistles, and *yesssss*'s.

'Oh! After dinner, I'll be presenting something! And remember. Always CHOOSE YOURSELF.'

I look around the room at the other women who have come tonight. Smart, interesting, curious women, showcasing their single badge with pride. Many of them are wearing Naz-style red lipstick and have her tote bag slung on the backs of their chairs. I've never been a part of a club, but I like how these other women make me feel. Like I'm part of something, like I'm no longer alone. Like something could fill that horrible void I've had since Dom left. Like there's somewhere else for me to go instead of round a dinner table with my friends who are drifting away from me. I feel like every woman in this room would tell me to throw my phone into the sea and never reply to Dom's message or speak to him ever again.

'Are you enjoying yourself?' Bec asks once our starters have arrived.

'I think so,' I say, between mouthfuls of lobster roll.

'I just moved to London from Sweden. I don't know anyone here or anyone in this city. I love that Naz brings people together.'

'That's very brave of you,' I say.

'Well, I had to start afresh. Embracing my new single life.'

'Me too,' I say and smile at her.

By the time our rich chocolate mousse arrives in cute heart-shaped bowls, Bec and I have covered a lot of ground. We've chatted about solo travel, journalism, feminism, and loneliness in London. I find myself being more frank with her than I've been with my close friends, and it's liberating.

Once most people have finished eating, Naz dings her glass with a spoon and gets up again as we fall silent and turn to watch. This time, she's standing in front of a screen and holding a clicker. She is passed a microphone by a short woman holding a clipboard and says 'Testing, testing' to check it works before speaking to the room.

'Right, you amazing women! Me again. I hope you're having a great time and enjoying this dinner, lovingly prepared by the incredible chefs here. Don't forget to tag your pictures and tag me, and tag the gorgeous venue @theapartment! Now, if you reach under your chairs, you will find an envelope taped there for each of you. I want you to open them up, please.'

There is a sound of rustling as everyone reaches under their chair to extract their paper envelope. Bec and I open ours, intrigued. Inside is a red paper flag stuck onto a wooden handle. We both wave them, slightly confused.

'Each of you have your very own red flag! Now, we

are going to play a little game. On our journey to self-discovery and solo living, we might occasionally fall into the trap of going back into the dating world or meeting someone who we feel might be "different" and worth the hassle. Then we let those little cautious moments slide, and before we know it, we've lowered our standards. So, let's see if we can spot some of the warning signs – a sign that someone is taking us for a ride and offering us so much less than we deserve!'

The screen suddenly comes on, and her first slide lights up. A screenshot of a dating app profile appears. A man called Tom, chest out, taking a selfie in front of the mirror, with a gold chain around his neck.

'A man who spends too long in the bathroom, staring at his own bare chest, and then . . .' She clicks the next slide. 'Messages you constantly and tries to use you as some sort of free therapist for his problems. What is that?'

'RED FLAG,' the crowd shouts, a little tentatively but gathering strength. All the women sat at the end of the table near the stage are frantically waving their makeshift flags.

'Remember: so many people love to use women for their own needs, and they will drain you. They mine us for our emotional resources – they take take take, giving hardly anything in return.

'Next slide. This is Aaron. He is demanding information after a few days. As you can see, he isn't very good at hearing the word "no". He doesn't understand personal space or boundaries.' The screenshot this time shows an exchange where his personality seems to switch the minute he stops getting his own way. 'What is it?' Naz shouts.

'RED FLAG!' everyone chants in unison.

The room erupts into cheering and whistling. I know Elaine told me to stay sceptical, not to trust Naz's snake oil, but I feel so buzzed to be in a room full of happy, single women. Just being near Naz is exciting. I feel like I know her so well. Like we've spent time together, even though it's one-sided.

After her presentation, she walks round to say hi to each person individually, to thank them for coming and supporting the book. She's holding a cold glass of white wine in one hand and is accompanied by Destiny, the woman in the sequin dress from earlier, who is holding a little felt bag full of gifts and asking each person to take one, to say thank you. Several women are crowding around, and it's hard to catch Naz's eye.

They eventually approach me, and I get a waft of Gucci perfume from Naz – the one I have sprayed onto my wrists countless times in airport duty-frees but can never justify buying.

Naz disappears, before I get a chance to say hi.

Destiny holds out the felt bag like it's the start of a magic show. 'Hello again. Thank you for coming. Please pick a gift from Naz.'

I put my hand in and take out a small pink crystal.

'Ah, a rose quartz, one of Naz's faves,' Destiny says. 'It's best known for being the stone of unconditional love. It's believed to emit strong vibrations of love, joy, and emotional healing.'

'Thank you,' I say, craning my neck to see where Naz went, gripping the quartz tightly in my hand.

'Keep it as a reminder,' Destiny says. 'On your desk, in your bathroom, under your pillow even, wherever you like. Single women are constantly made to feel less about themselves, and it's so important that we have reminders of our greatness.'

Once everyone has finished their after-dinner coffees, the tables are cleared away and the room turns into a dance floor. Bec and I do some stupid dancing to Phil Collins's 'Easy Lover', aided by the multiple margaritas we downed at dinner. My top lip becomes slightly sweaty, but I don't feel self-conscious at all.

At about 11.30 p.m., I decide to leave. I scan the room, but still can't see Naz anywhere. I spot Destiny and ask her where she is; I'd love to say goodbye. Her assistant says she left hours ago.

Despite not being able to chat to Naz, I'm floating on air when I stroll out of the red door back into Soho. The whole night has reminded me of something I've not done for ages: just been myself in a room full of women. The playlist made me think of dancing around my old flat with Pen, being total loons and getting told off by the neighbours for playing music too loudly. I forgot how much I enjoyed the carefree evenings where no one knows where you are or what time you're going to bed.

When I get back to the cosy womb hotel, I feel full of adrenaline, not quite ready for sleep. I scroll through Instagram, inhaling photos and hashtags from the Girls' Night

In event. Then I open the Netflix app and realize mine and Dom's account is still in my name, the monthly fee coming out of my direct debit. I cancel it, a smug satisfaction settling as I think of him trying to log in and being at a loose end. A small thing, but little by little, every trace is being removed.

I feel good. I stand up tall and look in the mirror and nod to myself. Being in a lively room with so many interesting, energetic women has been good for me.

I wonder if I can fully trust her, but it's undeniable: the infectious power of Naz Chopra.

25

THEN

August 2001

When we were about thirteen, Pen and I used to join Carla and her mates down at the beach on Friday nights during the summer. It was the early Noughties, and they had a boombox for playing the music they liked: things like 'Brimful of Asha' and The Dandy Warhols' 'Bohemian Like You'. Pen and I couldn't stop singing 'I'm Like a Bird' by Nelly Furtado, which had just come out.

Carla and her friends, mostly single, all worked in Eastbourne, mainly fellow artists from her old studio days, and their Friday nights were for fun and letting their hair down. They would sit on their deckchairs on the beach with a freezer box full of Coronas, cold ales and Bacardi Breezers. They would dance on the beach, skinny-dip, smoke, laugh, and sing into hairbrushes. They would play Madonna songs and get to us join in singing 'Holiday'. They would kick off their shoes and make dents in the sand, and the smell of smoke and wet swimming costumes circled the air.

Pen and I would join in, trying to be cool, trying to appear older than we were, trying to pretend we could stay up late partying on Friday nights, too. Carla would let us have half a Bacardi Breezer each, and usually all the excitement would lead to us falling asleep on the beach, then being carried inside by Carla and her friends.

The next day, Carla would make us egg sandwiches even though she was severely hungover. She'd bring her duvet down to the sofa, and we'd all watch *Hollyoaks* snuggling underneath it. She'd tell us the real details about her friends: one was going through a divorce; another was about to go to rehab; another had lost their job for shagging a well-known artist who was married to someone else.

Pen would always think it was the best house. So much always going on. Her parents were strict and boundaried, never letting her go out after hours, so she'd stay over at my house often, telling her parents she was 'studying'. Carla let us do whatever we wanted, within reason, and never hid anything from us. We always felt safe. She always believed in telling children the truth – in loving them fiercely but involving them in the realities of life. She was my portal to the real world – and a world full of love.

26

NOW

I leave my 'womb' and head off to The Soho Hotel. Naz is having some headshots taken for the piece with *Z Life*'s new photographer, Ben. Elaine has asked me to go along to get some snaps for the social media account. Naz looks natural and beautiful: wavy hair, a light shirt with a big, patterned collar, gold earrings, a good pair of jeans, and silver pumps. She poses with her laptop and a cup of tea and saucer, multiple gold rings on each finger.

'Look up at the camera, please,' Ben says. 'And then, maybe take a sip from the cup?'

Her eyes crinkle, slightly forced, a smile she's done a million times before. I notice her laptop is open on the table next to me and she's typed *ahrhrhhghgghghghgghghg* on the screen.

I tear my eyes away and try not to look nosy.

Once they've finished, Ben puts all his equipment away and Naz sits down, sighing.

'Do I look OK? I'm *very* hungover.' Now she's up close, I notice her eyes are watery and slightly bloodshot.

'You look great,' I say, comforting her by fibbing.

'Were you at the event last night by the way?' she asks, scratching her head. 'I kept looking for you.'

'Yes, I was there! I tried to say hi—'

'God, sorry. I was in such a daze.' She presses her palm to her forehead. 'Plus, I didn't have my contact lenses in. Absolute fail.'

'It's OK. You were busy. Did you have a good evening?'

'I did! I love seeing my followers in person. Such a bunch of cool smart girls, aren't they? Did you have fun?'

'Yeah, I met a really lovely girl, one of your fans, and swapped numbers. It was nice to meet some new people. It's been a while since I've been to anything like that.'

'What elements of the evening did you like?' She twirls her hair, and I make a mental note of it for the article. Does polished Naz have a nervous tic? She keeps scratching her arm. 'I want to try to make it better.'

'No notes! Food was good, lovely atmosphere – it was fun,' I say.

'Oh, that's so nice.' She seems distracted, her eyes darting around. 'I'm having a little gathering at my house tonight, by the way. It might be fun if you're interested?'

An invite to Naz's *house*?

'For the article?' I ask.

She shrugs. 'Just to hang out. Hey, maybe I can finally convince you that the single life really is better than a ten-year relationship!'

I feel a strong desire to tell her that I've joined her single club now, but Elaine's voice in my head reminds me to keep my cards close to my chest. *Build rapport, but keep firm boundaries! Be the authority.*

'Yeah, I could do that,' I say casually.

Whenever someone popular (especially a popular woman) invites you to anything, it's easy to feel like you're back at school: the hairs on the back of your neck and your arms stand on end. You have been chosen; you have been invited into a club; you're able to go behind the scenes of the shiny Instagram photo.

I think of Elaine, who loves a 'scoop', and I write down Naz's address in the Notes app on my phone.

That evening, at 7.30 p.m., I walk across from Hampstead Heath station towards Naz's house with a bottle of wine rolling about in my tote bag. Her flat is on the top floor of a converted house, and I know from her Instagram that it has a stunning view of tall trees and surrounding greenery. She buzzes me in, and I open the heavy front door and walk down a small, carpeted corridor containing a personal postbox for each of the flats. The floor has a faux marble effect and is pristine.

She comes down the stairs to greet me. 'Hey! You made it!' She gives me a hug. 'Come on up!'

We go up the stairs and I hear DJ music coming from the flat next to hers. Someone comes out wearing their pyjamas and a Jamiroquai-style hat. Suddenly, the building has the atmosphere of a fun B&B, more like a party hotel than converted flats. I feel very aware that I'm no longer in my party era.

I take off my shoes and walk into her front room. There is a disco ball attached to the ceiling, spinning and shining, and the smell of weed wafts into my nostrils. There's a big velvet corner sofa, covered with a dark blue throw, and three women are lounging on it. Two young men are sat cross-legged on the floor, both in fishnets and denim, smoking vapes and drinking bottles of beer. There are lava lamps.

'I brought you this.' I hand her the wine out of the tote bag.

'Ooh, organic orange wine! Fancy. Thank you so much,' Naz says. 'Guys! This is Willow. She's a writer – she's doing a piece about me. I invited her to hang out with us tonight. She's practically married, but we won't hold that against her.' She winks at me.

'Hey.' A woman with a wolf haircut, giant boobs, and a halter neck top waves at me warmly. 'I'm Loz.'

'I'm Kay,' says the second woman on the sofa.

'And this is Bean,' Naz says. 'Well, Bethany, but we call her Bean.'

I nod.

Kay has shoulder-length black curly hair and a tongue piercing, and Bean has a shaved head, the very short hairs dyed a turquoise blue.

'And this is Scott and Jon.'

Scott and Jon look very similar: short blond hair with an earring in the same ear. I realize they are twins.

I smile politely; I'm suddenly chronically aware of how boringly I am dressed in comparison. I'm wearing old black jeans and a grey polo neck with a faded dark green cardigan. Loz and Bean are curvy, juicy, with their skin confidently out. Loz is wearing bright blue eye-shadow, and Bean has bright orange, almond-shaped nails. They ooze confidence, moving around the flat freely, in a way that suggests they are proud of their bodies; they aren't bothered about good angles or needing to be small. They are taking up room.

I'm aware of how much of my skin is covered by my clothes, how hot I feel. I'm suddenly overwhelmingly self-conscious about being invited and being so much older. I sit on an armchair next to the sofa, and Naz hands me a margarita on the rocks in a little tumbler with salt on the rim.

'Oh, great, thanks,' I say.

It slips down well, and I immediately feel 20 per cent less awkward just by holding a drink.

'So then, how's the piece going? Has Naz said anything incriminating yet? Is she going to be *cancelled*?' Loz says to me, elbowing Naz jokingly and winking at her.

'Oh shh,' Naz says. 'Can we not talk about work?'

Jon puts on a Spotify playlist of 'retro' songs, and I realize they are from the era in which I was born.

'So, where do you live, Willow?'

'Oh, um – well, I live with my aunt in Eastbourne at the moment. I know Naz said I'm in a relationship, but actually, truth be told,' I take a big breath in and glance at Naz, 'I just went through a big break-up so—'

Oh god, how did that slip out?

'What! No way? Willow, that sucks. I'm sorry!' Naz says, putting her arm around me.

'Bummer,' Bean says, with a sympathetic frown.

'Yeah, we were together for so long. He's just got back in touch, actually,' I say.

I'm not quite sure why I suddenly felt the need to confess to Naz, but I definitely feel lighter for it.

'Is he breadcrumbing you?' Scott asks, taking a drag on his vape.

I look confused.

'When people feed you tiny crumbs just so you follow them and then they end up ghosting you again in the end. Fuckers.'

'Oh, right . . .' I mutter. 'He might be trying to do that, but I think I'm moving on.'

'Good. You're in the best company for that,' Naz says.

'Straight men suuuuuck. Hey, have you ever thought of booking a little cheeky holiday, just for you, get some sun on your face?' Kay says. 'A solo trip always sorts me out.'

'I could do,' I say, not wanting to admit that I'm currently totally broke. Elaine won't pay me for the article until I deliver and she approves it, and my Scatterbox payment could take ages to sort out. But even if I had money, I'm not sure I'd want a holiday on my own. Dinner alone is fine, but a whole week, or two weeks? I loved being a couple on holiday – going down to breakfast together, choosing where to eat that night, having someone to put suncream or aftersun on your back, the joint decisions, the sharing of the load, the late-night chats, the safety of a warm body next to yours . . .

Scott sits next to me. I notice his small hoop earring and

tight T-shirt. He smells like expensive aftershave. 'Can I give you a spruce?'

'A what?'

He picks up a make-up bag from the floor by the sofa. 'I'm a make-up artist – sorry. I can't help it. I love doing people's make-up. I'd love to do a little glam-up just for fun. You have such a neutral look. Blank canvas.'

'Scott! Oh, please leave her alone. Stop trying to do makeovers on everyone!' Naz shouts over the music.

'Well . . . I don't really wear much make-up,' I say.

'You have a gorgeous face. Different. You don't need make-up. I love your freckles. But your pores are a bit oily, and I could put on some products and shape your eyebrows. But you can tell me to fuck off if you like. It's just a bit of fun.'

'I love your hair. You look a bit like Emma Stone. Pale. Big eyes,' Kay is saying, breathing out vape smoke.

I have gulped down two very strong margaritas now and don't feel any need to say no. It's true; apart from the Girls' Night In event, I've barely worn a scrap of make-up in weeks.

'Go on then,' I say. I pull back my hair, realizing it's a bit greasy.

Scott gets out a miniature can of dry shampoo and sprays into the roots, giving my hair some volume. Then he unzips his little velvet bag, and I can tell he's excited about what to do first. Slowly, he puts a wet facial wipe to my face which smells lovely, moving it around very gently under my eyes, round my cheeks and over my lips. It feels refreshing, though it tickles under my eyes. He is concentrating and dabbing at my skin in a gentle way, pouting his lips. Then he lightly plucks at my eyebrows, which hurts only a little, and puts eyebrow gel on me, eyeliner, lip gloss, bold mascara, a tint on my cheeks, and then a red lip which he puts on using a long, thin brush. I feel so relaxed by the way he does it all, like a serious artist at work. He has a sponge wrapped around his wrist, so that the sponge, not his hand, touches my face while he applies the mascara and eyeliner. He puts a delicious-smelling spray in my hair and gives me a head massage. It's so nice to be touched in a platonic way like this.

'*Voilà!*' he says and holds up a little handheld mirror. '*Stunning.*'

'Oh, wow,' I say, surprised by what I see.

I stare at my reflection, and I do actually look really *good*, different, fresh. The bags under my eyes have vanished. I have a pale highlighter on my cheeks, a subtle winged eyeliner and a glossy lip. Scott gives me a tipsy kiss on the cheek, and I feel a warmth I haven't felt in a while. A random act of kindness.

'Everyone deserves a little pampering,' he says.

A few hours into the night, the mood gets more intense. Naz and Loz are holding hands, swaying to the music. Bean offers me some weed gummies, and I decline. They all start sitting very close and talking over each other. They chat nonstop about their hopes and dreams for life. I am happy to be listening. They cover UFO sightings, gender fluidity, the way the world will heal if we heal our collective trauma. I smile at myself, because if I was still with Dom, I'd never in a million years be sat in this living room, with these people, having these conversations.

Then, the pink mics come out and an at-home Lucky Voice karaoke set. Naz starts singing the lyrics to 'Alone' by Celine Dion. She hands me a microphone and puts her arm around me. I still feel like an outsider – after all, I'm much older than them – but I also feel like they're really trying to involve me. It's endearing.

While everyone is singing away, I excuse myself for the bathroom, and on the way back, I notice that Naz's bedroom door is ajar. I want to have a quick look, just a little peek for some more flavour for the article. There's nothing more intimate than a bedroom. I've seen glimpses of her room on Instagram, and it all looked fit for her influencer lifestyle: the big white super-king bed, the scalloped-edge white pillows she was given as a gift, and a coral-coloured chaise longue by a bright bay window.

When I look inside, I am surprised by what I see. I lean in closer. Her bed is stripped, the sheets on the floor, stains all over the bedding and on the bare mattress, too. The chaise longue is there, but it's tattered up close and covered in old takeaway boxes, coffee cups, and rotting banana skins. Two empty bottles of wine have rolled underneath her bed. A candle has been burning too close to a white wall, and there is big dark mark. There's a sick bucket next to the bed. There are boxes of tampons strewn across the floor that have fallen out of their wrappers.

I creep in and peer down into the bucket – it's mercifully empty. I look down at the carpet and it's completely filthy, covered in big specks of dust and fluff and dark clumps of hair.

I go back into the living room, where Naz and Loz are

swaying and still holding hands, sharing the mic to belt out Blondie's 'Heart of Glass'. They are giggling and embracing, hands on each other's hips, and I suddenly feel very much on the periphery. After seeing Naz's bedroom, it doesn't seem like pure, uncomplicated fun any more, and I can't quite make myself join in.

So, I crack a joke about being a geriatric Millennial, and after a round of hugs and a kiss on both cheeks from Scott and Jon, I book myself an Uber back to my 'womb'.

27

NOW

I wake up early, feeling more refreshed than I deserve after my three margaritas. Maybe this weird high-tech womb set-up actually works. I am itching to write my piece, so I set up my laptop by the window and call down to reception for fried eggs, toast and a cafetière. I use a transcription service to type up my interview notes and recordings from my chats with Naz, and I'm just starting to organize them by theme when Elaine calls. My phone flashes up with an old photo of her wearing fancy-dress novelty glasses and a fake moustache from *The D-Low*'s Christmas party, which always gives me a jolt.

'Hey, doll! How's the piece going? How was the Girls' Night In event?'

'All going well. The event was great. I went to her house last night, too.'

'Oh *did you* – that's brilliant. Any juicy intel?'

'Sort of,' I say. 'I'm still working out the best angle.' I feel guilty for peering into her bedroom and realizing that she and her friends are just a bunch of messy twenty-somethings trying out drugs and finding their way like everyone else, albeit from a gorgeous flat in Hampstead. Her behaviour lately has been at odds with her perfectly crafted online persona, and I know I could write a damning exposé if I wanted to. The glimpse into her room suggested she's someone who isn't handling things so well.

'Well, as long as it gets clicks, I'm happy with any angle you choose. But I was thinking, since we're now syndicating to the *Mail*, it would be great to get something snarky. You know, ramp it up, really rolling our eyes at the whole thing. Another young Gen Z type telling the rest of us that we're doing life wrong. I'd love it if your personalities really clash on the page!'

'Yes, of course,' I say, feeling like I'm twenty-four again, back in the *D-Low* offices, offering everything I have up to her on a plate for that little boost of validation that only she can give. That addictive feeling of wanting to get Elaine excited about something. The brownie points that would give you.

I look back over my notes and start piecing together a draft, moving bits around and typing in thoughts and insights that I can edit later – I still have a few more days to spend with Naz, including tomorrow at the park, and we're going to a gig together later in the month, too. I need to please Elaine with my 'fresh' angle, and although she won't say so outright, I know she'd prefer it to be a bit of a hatchet job. She's looking for something that will get shared online, that will get comments on Twitter, get Reddit threads going, something tongue in cheek. I start work on the introductory paragraph and try and add a bit of spice in there – something Elaine would want.

Single influencer Naz Chopra describes herself as having 'Main Character Energy'. She moves through the world with ease. Everything is fun. Everything is easy. Everything is magical. Her friends are gorgeous, young, trendy. She lives in a converted flat in the expensive postcode of Hampstead Heath, an iconic neighbourhood shared with global stars like Harry Styles, a flat she rents off her wealthy uncle who owns a chain of supermarkets. She tells her Gen Z followers that men are the worst, that they're better off single, and that they can be the boss of their own lives. She enjoys reeling off statistics about how self-love improves your life and how single women live longer. But she's missing out the key issue with society today – we are already chronically lonely. We need each other, more than ever. You could even say that her messaging is dangerous.

We are also in a society where women are told they don't need to settle down, only to realize that their biological clock is, in fact, a real thing. It's all very well being a cute twenty-something who is single and ready to mingle, but what if you're in your thirties or forties? Is being single really as glamorous as famous singleton Naz Chopra makes it out to be? What if you don't romanticize eating alone or spending money on solo holidays? Are you then 'failing' at being single?

And with this dangerous message of telling everyone they are better off alone, is she telling young people that they don't need to reach out for help? That it's healthy to live alone with no one to talk to? That if this makes you feel lonely, you are a failure?

Over the last few weeks, I've been living alongside Naz Chopra, getting into her shoes as the poster girl of happy singledom. But I've realized she lives in an individualistic, self-obsessed vacuum. An Instagrammable hall of mirrors where, quite frankly, not everything is as it seems.

I click save and go and run a bath. Carla has posted a blurry selfie on Instagram by the sea. She's carrying one of the dachshunds and positioning his head next to hers, like a best-friend selfie. The sea in the background is green-grey, like her eyes.

She looks content, and I hope that's because she isn't stressing too much about her scans on Monday. I 'like' the post and then send her a quick message reminding her that I could easily travel down to Eastbourne to accompany her. I know she'll tell me not to come, but I want her to know that I'm here for her.

The next morning, I'm due to meet Naz at eleven a.m. in Hampstead Heath. She's giving me a glimpse into how she spends a work-free day, some extra flavour to add to the article. The woodland isn't too busy: dog walkers, people talking on phones, chatting on benches. She's given me directions to meet her by a huge tree in the middle, so I walk there and spread out my coat and sit on it, enjoying the warm spring sunshine. As I wait, I look at my phone. A message from Dom:

Any thoughts on meeting up?

'Hey, how's it going?' Naz has appeared. She's wearing full Lululemon in bright red, the logo emblazoned across all items, bag included. She's swinging two water bottles.

I clearly look shocked, holding my phone, frozen.

'My ex.' I gesture to the phone in my hand. 'Wants to meet up for some reason.'

She lets out an exasperated sigh. 'You're about to dance on the heath with a group of amazing women. And that's none of his business. He can bore off.'

I throw my phone back into my bag, feeling under Naz's spell again, shaking off the tension in my body. I keep having to remind myself that for the sake of the article, I'm not supposed to like Naz, but she really has made me feel better about my life lately.

I hear Elaine's voice: *Remember, being nice doesn't make a good headline.*

I get my Dictaphone out and press record. I ask Naz to explain where we are and why we're here.

'I have a self-care routine outside of the public-facing stuff. I go for a swim in the Parliament Hill lido or the bathing ponds and then go to this exercise class, which is full of mostly older ladies. No one ever recognizes me, and I enjoy it so much. I'm really inspired by older women. They understand that it's all about loving what your body does for you, instead of what it looks like. I love being surrounded by these women, and some of them have become good friends. Most of them are single or divorced and loving life. Also, women in big groups feels threatening to men, and I love that, too.' She grins. 'Right, shall we go for our swim?'

'We?'

Naz checks into the lido and says hi to a curly-haired woman in reception. She's clearly a regular.

'You not coming in?' Naz asks me.

'Oh! No. I don't have my costume.'

'I have a spare cossie and towel.' Naz taps her card on the machine. 'Done! You're coming in with me!'

I haven't swum in a public pool in years. 'OK then . . .'

We go into the changing room, and I put on a black Adidas swimming costume that is slightly too small.

'Why am I doing this again?' I ask out loud.

'I promise you'll love it. It's cold at first, like a million tiny pinpricks on your skin, but afterwards you feel this little rush of serotonin in your brain. The unheated water is great – it makes you forget everything for a while. Come on, we'll just do a few quick lengths.'

'*Unheated?*'

We walk out of the changing room. I'm seeing Naz in a bikini for the first time, and I can't stop staring at her. Her tattoos are not just on her chest and arms: she is covered. I spotted a small sliver of them that time in the fitting room; now I get to see the full artwork. A swan on her upper arm, the moon on her chest, the stars on the thighs, the palm tree on her ankle. She wiggles her feet. More butterflies on each ankle. She elegantly lifts herself into the shallow end and starts swimming off. She turns around to egg me on: 'Come on! Just don't think about it!'

I am teetering on the edge, dipping a toe in, and it's *freezing*.

'Say one, two, three to yourself! You can do it!'

I do it. I count to three, and I half-jump, half-step in. The water comes halfway up my chest. There it is: the million tiny pinpricks.

'Just breathe slowly – don't panic.'

I breathe in and out, then lift my feet off the floor, spread out my arms, and float on my back. I look up at the clouds, the birds flying over my head, the trees swaying, the sun peeking through from behind a cloud. *Breathe, breathe, breathe.*

Then, suddenly, I feel amazing. Light, breezy, calm. A buoy bobbing at sea. I have nothing else to focus on but the sensations in my body and my chest going up and down.

After we've each swum five lengths, we have a blessedly hot shower and get changed. It's now nearly midday, and Naz hustles us out of the lido at top speed so that we won't be late for her Beyoncé-themed Zumba class.

'Keep moving to stay warm,' Naz says, jumping up and down in her designer leggings, dodging puddles on the pathway as we walk back to the huge tree where we met earlier. She hands me a spare woolly hat.

The trees are all enormous, dwarfing the people walking their little hipster dogs wearing little coats, and I have the sense of being a tiny speck on the face of the world. It's quite a liberating feeling.

'This is really your standard day off?' I ask. I'm usually in bed rewatching *Motherland*, eating a jacket potato.

Maybe she does have her life together after all? Maybe her dirty bedroom and frantic party energy was just a bad week.

'Yes! I love it. It's me-time, but I'm around others – I don't have to talk to anyone if I don't want to. And it's so good to move your body, isn't it? Will you do the class with me?'

'No, I'm good, thanks.' I laugh. 'I've already gone into that freezing pool.'

'Oh, *come on*, you might as well. Come on.'

She physically pulls me into the group, which has gathered under the massive oak tree. There's a woman with grey hair at the front with a long plait snaking down her back, holding a large boombox. There are other women chatting in groups, and Naz says hi to a few of them.

'Carmen, this is Willow – she's my guest today.'

'Marvellous! Hi, Willow. We're always happy when someone tells a friend about the class.'

I think Naz can tell that I feel insecure about moving around in my leggings, jiggling my body. We stand at the back, Naz ditching her normal spot and standing in solidarity with me. The instructor puts on some loud Beyoncé music ('Beautiful Liar') and greets us warmly.

'Hello, everyone. For those who are new,' she says, looking directly at me, 'I'm Carmen.' She claps her hands together. 'Thank you for showing up for yourselves today! Remember, you aren't here for me or for anyone else – you're here to move your bodies, feel good about yourselves, and enjoy the music! Now, move along with me!' She moves herself forwards and backwards, then swings her hips from side to side.

'Keep your posture upright, ladies! Let's get a bit of a sweat on!'

I look around, and Naz and I are the youngest by miles. There are women of so many different shapes and sizes. They are all smiling, wiggling and wobbling and looking joyful. I let myself get into the rhythm of the dancing for a little bit, and it feels good moving together in unison.

After half an hour, Carmen lets us have a little break. I'm sweating a lot now and breathing heavily, bending over slightly. I would never, ever have agreed to this if I'd known.

'Quick hydration break! Before we ramp it up a little!' Carmen says.

Naz looks over at me and smiles, cheeks pink. She presses her face with a mini-towel and grins at me. 'Fun, isn't it?'

Another woman comes over to Naz and gives her a hug.

'Hi, darling,' the woman says to me afterwards, mopping her neck.

'This is Willow – Willow, this is Mimi.'

Before I register anything, Mimi is hugging me too, and I'm pressed up against her big bosomy chest. She looks around sixty-five: short grey hair, gold earrings, matching aubergine workout gear. 'So lovely to meet you. Wow, I *love* your red hair.'

For a moment, I let myself take in these kind words from a stranger.

'How's everything been with you?' Naz asks, adjusting her sports sock that's fallen down into her shoe.

'Oh, yes – good news! My divorce papers have gone through,' she says, beaming, teeth resting over her bottom lip.

'Oh YES!' Naz cheers.

'I'm ecstatic! Never have to see the bastard again. Good riddance. And I've got a casual date tonight – some chap I met walking the dog is taking me out for some fizz. Oh, I feel fantastic. I feel *so free*!'

'Google: *Nicole Kidman when she divorced Tom Cruise.* That's you, right now.' Naz laughs. 'Iconic.'

Carmen pipes up again, clapping her hands. 'Right, it's time for some freestyle dancing. Please grab a hip scarf from the box up the front here.'

Destiny's Child's 'Bootylicious' blasts out of Carmen's boombox.

'*No. No. No,*' I mouth to Naz and shake my head. A *hip scarf*? A scarf to tie around my hips? Absolutely not.

Naz goes up and passes me a tie-dye sarong with small bells, and she wraps a blue one around her waist. 'This is your moment to let go, Willow. Nothing matters. Just enjoy yourself.'

'Now, ladies, remember to plant your feet in line with your hips! Bend your knees slightly! Shoulders back. One step forward, move your hips – that's it!'

We follow her through some basic steps and hip movements to warm up, and then we start to move slightly faster. I feel my body heating up, all my muscles getting a workout.

'Now – for the final fifteen minutes, freestyle with a partner! All the rules out of the window. Do whatever you want with your bodies! Free yourself! *Move! Enjoy!*'

I panic for a moment. I watch all the women move to the music by themselves, so unselfconsciously, literally dancing like no one is watching. A remix of 'Bootylicious' kicks in, and all the women start going mad, bending down, whooping, cheering, laughing. Naz is jumping up and down. She grabs my hands and twirls me around.

'Tonight,' says Carmen, 'I want you to write a letter of apology to your bodies. We drag them around and take them for granted, but every day your body regenerates and heals and grows and gets you out of bed. Right now, your hearts are pumping over one hundred beats per minute! Our bodies are MIRACLES!'

I look at Mimi, twirling around at the front of the class, and she is in her element. She's free. She's happy. Single. Joyful. I close my eyes and shake my body, and I feel like something is being released. I want to be cynical about this, and I want to deliver a good article full of irony and conflict. But I can't help it – I feel a strange, deep fondness for this whole thing.

When I say goodbye to Naz, she gives me a hug and I tell her I'll see her tomorrow at the meeting at her agent's office. I look up at the pale blue sky and smile.

Inspired by Carmen, Mimi, and Naz, I don't reply to

Dom. Instead, I delete his message and delete his number. I surprise myself by this, but suddenly I have no desire to engage at all.

Half an hour or so later, I'm still walking in the heath. I didn't want to leave. It's a nice bright day, and I'm listening to an audiobook, taking my time.

On the next lap round, I notice Naz, sat by a tree. She's smoking a Marlboro Gold, and she looks as though she's been crying. It's such a contrast to the early scenes of us laughing and dancing in the park. I freeze when I see her and squint. Is that really her?

She puts out the cigarette and then immediately lights another. What happened to her healthy, active me-time? What happened to all those endorphins we just experienced together?

I don't know whether to go over to her or not. Maybe she should be left in private – after all, our magazine 'date' is over. But I hear Elaine's voice in my ear. *Where's the friction? Where's the controversy? That's where you'll find the heart of the story. Go over – find out what's going on.*

'. . . Naz?' I say sheepishly.

'Oh, Willow!' She jumps, quickly extinguishing her cigarette behind her. 'I didn't see you there.'

'I was just walking around, enjoying the weather,' I say, taking out both AirPods. 'That was really fun, earlier.'

'Yeah, it was,' she says, trying to smile and cover up her state. She rubs her eyes; her mascara is now smudged.

'Are you OK? Sorry. I'm not trying to intrude.'

'Yeah, yeah, I'm OK – just some stuff going on in my

personal life. No big drama. Thanks, though. I appreciate it.' She sounds very sad.

I smile and nod and take it as a cue not to pry any further.

'OK, well, have a good rest of the day, OK?'

'You too.'

I feel dirty for interfering, but I also feel confused. Who is the happy-go-lucky single girl, and who is the real Naz Chopra? What is she trying to hide?

28

THEN

August 1999

Carla took me on so many trips to London when I was younger. One of my favourites was just before I started secondary school: she knew I was nervous, so she took me shopping for new notebooks and stationery. Then she took me to Daunt Books in Holland Park for the first time and bought me an anniversary edition of *Matilda*. When we got to the till, I spotted a quill with an ink pot in a box, sold as a set. The bookseller, who had pink spiky hair, saw me eyeing it up and asked if I wanted to test it out, then went and got a spare piece of paper. The quill scratched the page, and ink spilled onto my fingers; I loved the smell.

'It's so fun,' I said, dipping the nib into the ink countless times. 'I feel like a ye olden person.'

'We'll take it,' Carla said.

I turned to her, amazed. 'Carla! Really?'

'Yes! I think we should also get you a normal pen to use at school, though, eh? Don't want you getting bullied. They might think you're one of those kids who pretend you're in a different era, wearing a top hat to school.'

'Are you sure?'

'Yes, go on – late birthday present.'

Carla did this sometimes: splurged randomly on me, whenever I took an interest in anything to do with writing or reading. She didn't always buy me everything, and she usually had a rule that if I wanted something, I had to put it on my birthday list. But every so often, when she saw my eyes light up, she would buy it for me there and then and watch me carry it around in a bag, swinging it with joy.

We made visits to Daunt a tradition every time we went to London, and afterwards, we'd always go to Holland Park, weighed down by shopping bags. We'd spend the afternoon with ice creams, lying in the shade under a tree, our sandals in a pile next to us.

'Write me something with your new pen,' Carla said, lying back, her elbows bent outwards to create a pillow, looking up at the clouds.

She handed me an old newspaper from her bag and I found a blank space to write on.

I precariously balanced the dark blue ink pot on the grass and made scratchy sounds with the quill. I loved getting lost in my imagination, crafting a poem with my words – and mine alone. Once I was done, I read it out loud to Carla while she closed her eyes. The park squirrels darted around us, as though they wanted to listen in.

29

NOW

When I walk into the reception area, there's a neon sign that says: *Good Vibes Only*. Underneath it, a woman with a massive doughnut for hair looks at me blankly. Elaine has made it clear that I must meet Naz's management team to get a sense of the business side before I file my piece. They're based in a gorgeous townhouse just off Soho Square.

'I've got a meeting with Naz Chopra and Jaime Fagan,' I say.

'OK, here's a badge,' she says, sighing, giving me a generic-looking pass. 'Just go up in the lift to floor three. Careful of the dog.'

When I get there, it's an empty floor with one big meeting room and a few desks scattered around. I hear barking and a huge Alsatian runs up to me, making me jump.

'Buster! Come back here.' A giant man stomps out wearing heavy boots. He grabs the dog and pulls him back a bit. I'm normally good with dogs, but this one is terrifying – salivating like a hungry lion hunting down a naive zebra (me).

'You must be Willow,' the giant man says, shaking my hand with his huge bear paw. 'Naz has told me so much about you. I'm Kris – I'm the co-founder of the business. Along with Jaime, we look after everything to do with Naz's career.'

'Oh, hi! Good to meet you.'

I look around, and it's mostly Naz plastered all over the walls. Naz's book cover in a frame. Naz doing her Tedx Talk. Naz at an Instagram HQ panel event. A poster of Naz at a London Fashion Week photoshoot in some mad clothes – trousers made of feathers and a big yellow poncho. It's a weird shrine to Naz. Surely she's not their only client, but clearly she's their current favourite. I think about taking a quick picture and sending it to Pen or putting it on the WhatsApp group, but I decide not to risk it.

'We're really looking forward to reading the piece,' Kris says, making an uncomfortable amount of eye contact with me. The dog tries to jump forward again. 'It's Naz's first big press piece for a while.'

'It's been a fun one to work on,' I say, nerves boiling up in my belly. Little do they know what the first draft looks like.

'I bet. Naz is so great, isn't she?' he says, still staring right into me. 'We're actually about to have a meeting with her, so why don't you sit in on that for a bit?'

'Sounds good,' I say, following his lead. 'Hopefully I'm not intruding.'

I pop into the loo – and when I come out of one cubicle, Naz comes out of the other. We both smile at each other in the mirror and go to wash our hands.

'Hello,' she says, squirting some soap onto her palm.

'Excited to join your fancy meeting,' I say.

She laughs. 'It's not that fancy.'

'I saw a woman bringing in pains au chocolat and croissants!'

I notice that her mascara is smudged again around her eyes slightly, like she's wiped her eyes (badly) with loo roll.

We walk into the meeting room, which is covered with more photos of Naz with trophies at industry awards. Kris is acting very friendly, but there's a strange energy to him that I can't put my finger on. He kicks off the meeting, opening up his sleek silver MacBook Air. There are seven people sat around a large table, with takeaway coffees and notepads strewn everywhere.

'Right, thanks for being here, everyone. This meeting is about the new book tour. We're expanding the Girls' Night In event we did the other evening, running them in other London venues, then cities all over the UK and Europe.'

I notice Jaime at the end of the table, chewing on her pen. I recognize her from her website. She is very pale and has long thin hair, long enough to sit on; she is wearing a denim jumpsuit with black sandals. She has that fragile look about her that makes you want to feed her vitamins. Next to Jaime is a young-looking girl, clearly the assistant or intern. She has *Billie* written on her laptop.

'Right, shall we crack on?' Kris says. 'We need to really keep the pedal to the metal on this one, yeah? So, Naz, the tour. How many venues do you want to do? We were thinking Liverpool, Bristol, Bath, Glasgow, and Edinburgh? As a starter? Then Lisbon, Brussels, Vienna, Paris . . .'

'Sure, sounds good,' Naz says, doodling in her notepad.

'Great. Note all this down please, Billie. Naz, any details we need to be across? Your rider?'

Billie types away frantically, and Naz looks up from her pad where she's been doodling.

'I've been thinking, I'd love a day off in between events. In the past, doing them back-to-back has really tired me out,' Naz says, fiddling with her hair.

'Let's circle back to that once we've nailed down the venues. What do you think Jaime?'

I notice Naz picking at a scab on her arm.

'Well, it's good to do some back-to-back because it keeps momentum and means we don't pay too much out on hotel room costs,' Jaime says, writing something onto her propped iPad with a digital pen. 'I know the producers for the event, and lighting, sound and stage designers will also want to do them close together as they'll be joining us on the tour and won't want to be away from their families for too long.'

'It'll be a very busy few weeks, but you can book some holiday afterwards,' Kris says. 'We'll get one of your brand partnerships to give you a free stay somewhere. Billie, can you make a note of that? Maybe get in touch with Kimpton Resorts again? Then Naz can have time off after to relax.'

'Thanks,' Naz says, looking up at the ceiling.

'Great! Billie will block out the dates in your diary, and we'll start reaching out to some brands who might want to sponsor. Then we can set up the website and ticket allocations and send you a social media schedule for you to post and sell out the tickets. We'll drip-feed them, so it looks like they're sold out to create scarcity and to make people want them more,' Jaime says matter-of-factly.

I find myself looking up at the ceiling, too, looking at the cracks. Naz, the woman of independence, of self-love and putting yourself first, seems to be shrinking in her chair as these two business owners tell her what to do. They continue discussing Naz's tour plans, and she is scratching more – scratching her arms, her elbows, her head. They discuss the fashion line that might be in development soon. Naz's own gin brand. A 'Secret Escapes' partnership. 'The sky's the limit here, Naz.'

By the end of the meeting, Naz has covered two A4 sheets of paper with lots of circles that look like black holes.

After the meeting, Naz suggests we go to the Pret next door for a quick coffee. It's quiet, only a few people sat in the window seats. They're wearing headphones and sipping coffee and doodling in journals.

We order two cappuccinos and sit at a table near the back. I don't mention her palpable dip in confidence in the meeting; it doesn't feel like my place to say anything to her, even though I know I'll need to explore it in my piece if I want the article to really sing. Naz looks very young, suddenly, and lost. It doesn't feel right to bring it up.

'So, you're nearly finished with the article now?' she asks, running her thumb over the lid of her coffee cup.

'Yep, it's getting there,' I say.

I feel bad, suddenly, because the article isn't going to be wholly positive. It's snarking about her lifestyle, this performance of persona as a career. But she's smart enough, I reason, to understand the demands of journalism, and right now, more than ever, it's about driving clicks. Surely she doesn't expect it will just be a puff piece?

'And we've got one last hang next week – the concert at Hyde Park, right?' she says. 'It's going to be epic.'

We're off to see Celine Dion. A nostalgic watch for me (Carla used to play her *Best Ballads* whenever she drove me to school and netball lessons) and a new discovery for Naz, who only came across her recently via TikTok memes and vaguely remembers the *Titanic* theme song.

'Yes – it'll be a great addition to the piece. Elaine wants me to film you for some behind-the-scenes content on my phone. Hope you're OK with that?'

'Yeah, yeah, fine!' Naz says. I notice her leg is bopping up and down under the table. 'You know, you've spent all this time seeing what I get up to – I want to know how *you* spend your time.'

'What do you mean?'

'Well, what do you love doing in London?'

I think for a moment. Every weekend used to be spent with Dom. Watching him play football. Watching films chosen mainly by Dom. A trip to IKEA for the house. Dom's parents visiting. Afternoon tea. Barbecues with his friends. And lately, I've been spending all my time at Carla's. I used to do loads of cultural stuff with Pen: trips to the V&A, rooftop cinema, cocktail masterclasses.

'Ummmm, it's hard to think,' I say.

'Go on. Your favourite ever London day out?'

'I haven't done it for ages.'

'Tell me?'

'Well, it sounds silly, but a visit to Daunt Books. Browsing the shelves, buying one of the classic clothbound books, and then a walk around Holland Park – they have this part of the park where you can see peacocks, and the Kyoto Garden is really pretty. I always feel super relaxed there. My aunt Carla and I used to go there a lot whenever we visited London when I was a kid.'

'Let's go then.'

'What?'

'Let's go and do that now.'

'I have to go back and work on the article,' I say.

'Oh, come on. You can spare a couple of hours.' She leans across the table and pinches me playfully, it feels intimate, as though we've known each other for years. 'Aren't breaks meant to be good for creativity?'

'OK, I suppose you're right. Let's do it,' I say. 'I've got a couple of hours.'

We catch the Tube from Tottenham Court Road and get off at Holland Park. The sun emerges out from behind a big cloud, and I feel the warmth on my face.

'Don't the Beckhams live round here?' she says.

'Do they?'

'Yeah, in one of those massive white houses. Imagine that. Those high ceilings and big staircases in London.'

'I wonder what they look like inside,' I say, looking at the multiple floors, the huge white columns, the perfectly manicured gardens.

'Do you think they're happy?' Naz asks.

I shrug. 'Who knows.'

'With all that money and fame. Hard to tell with some people, isn't it?' she says.

We go into Daunt's and browse the sea of books. There's one lonesome copy of *Woman: An Island* on a back table. The bookshop either hasn't been championing her books, or they've just sold out. Hard to tell. We wander around, and I touch some of the clothbound books, running my fingers over them. Then we walk across the road towards the park. The minute we enter into the expanse of greenery, surrounded by dogs being walked and people on benches reading and chatting, all the other stresses disappear for a moment. It's a space of tranquillity in a busy city.

'I often think the squirrels are trying to be my friends by following me around, but really they just want food,' I say.

'They are so rodenty. I can't find them cute.' She breathes in and lies down on a patch of grass. 'I know what you mean about feeling relaxed here. These trees are so tall. You forget London has all this green space.' She pauses, looking up. 'Do you think I seem different now, to when you first researched me?' she asks.

'What do you mean?'

'I don't know – did you have preconceptions of me, from seeing my social media beforehand?'

'Oh – yeah, I did.'

'Were you sceptical? I think most people are.'

'A little bit. Your life looked pretty perfect online. Why do you ask?'

'I don't know.' She stares at the sky. 'I've been having more complicated feelings about it all lately. Not about my life or my community of single women, but I guess . . . how I package up my life and sell it.' She pauses and holds her breath before putting her palm over her eyes. 'I'm not sure I want to go on tour. I'm so, so exhausted.'

'Surely you don't have to?'

'I signed a contract.'

'Can it be wriggled out of?'

'I don't think so. Money has been spent, and I signed up to a year of touring, minimum.'

Naz looks away, and she quickly wipes her eyes with her sleeve.

I remember what Lisa said to me in the office, and I repeat it to Naz. 'I know this sounds simple, but you have to do what makes you happy.'

On the way back to the Tube, we stop off at Gail's bakery and get a pastry each – a spinach sausage roll – and sit outside.

'I got you something from the bookshop.'

'What?'

Naz hands me a paper bag, and I open it. A clothbound

book. A dark brown hardback copy of *Little Women* with small pink scissors all over it.

'I think it's about a woman who's a writer – right?' Naz says.

I swallow hard, a lump forming in my throat. 'Thank you, Naz. That is really, really thoughtful of you.'

30

THEN

September 1998

One morning, when I was about ten, Carla read mine, Lola, and Pen's palms over the kitchen table in Eastbourne. Carla trained as a 'palmist' and reflexologist, but she's also just someone who's always had a spooky level of intuition. She was known to predict big life events and, later, when I was a teenager, she'd always know where I was in my menstrual cycle depending on my mood.

Carla had a few friends in Eastbourne that I always thought were a bit kooky growing up, like her fellow artist friend, Shirin, who was also a medium, and had to take a three-hour nap following any session. People couldn't get enough of it; once they felt connected with a loved one 'beyond the veil' as she called it, they were desperate to keep the session going; they didn't want to say goodbye again, which was understandable but draining. Shirin always used the phrases

'Earth Side' and 'not Earth Side' for talking about the living and the deceased. It became a strange part of my ten-year-old vocabulary.

'I told my friends at school that you do these palm readings, and they didn't believe me,' I said to Carla. 'One friend said you were a witch.'

Carla winked. 'Maybe I am.'

'I like witches,' Pen said.

'I'm scared,' Lola said.

'Why?' asked Carla.

'I don't want to know anything bad or scary,' she said, wincing.

'Darling, I won't tell you anything like that. My readings are only about the future in terms of positive things. I share only what will be useful or helpful for you.'

'OK, OK,' Lola said, laying out her young supple hands, palms up to the sky.

Carla scanned her hands, glasses propped on her head. 'Right, let me see Lola, darling. Right, well, you have a long life ahead of you, with lots of friends and loyalty. You will live by the water at some point – maybe a lake.'

'Ooh OK,' Lola said, looking quite pleased. 'I like the sound of that.'

Next, Pen laid her hands out.

'Again, a long life ahead of you, darling. You'll have a beautiful relationship one day with a very tall man. You'll defy convention slightly in your later life at times. Your job in life will be about birth and rebirth.'

'Really?'

'That's all I've got right now,' Carla said, putting her glasses on her head.

'Now me,' I said, laying down my open hands on the table.

Carla held my wrists delicately and pulled her glasses down again. She paused. 'I see travel for you one day – somewhere very far away. Alone.'

'What? Really? Where will I travel?'

She closed her eyes. 'I'm seeing you travelling to the other side of the world, and you're alone.'

'Why alone?'

'Unsure. But your head line is strong – you'll always have good ideas. The only thing to watch here is your heart line – it's showing communication problems later down the line.' Carla sighed and rubbed her temples.

'Can you tell me anything else?' I pleaded.

'There may come a time when you feel really lost, even when big emotions sweep you off your feet. When it feels like everyone has abandoned you. Please remember, no matter what happens, I'll always be looking out for you. Always, even when you can't physically see me.'

'OK,' I said, holding her hand, pretending to trace a line on her palm.

31

NOW

When I make it back to Eastbourne to see Carla, she's not in the house. I go into every room, expecting to see her pottering around. I notice the back doors are open, a chill drifting into the kitchen. I spot her sitting out in the garden with a cup of tea, the dogs at her feet.

'Hi, sweetheart,' she says softly. She has a blanket over her lap and her favourite furry slippers on, her hands clasped together, gold rings on every finger.

I lean down and give her a kiss on the cheek. Her energy feels calm and serene.

'How are you?' I ask, bending down to pet Bubble and Squeak.

'Do you want to grab a chair?' She is speaking slowly and calmly.

I bring over a garden chair, nerves creeping into my stomach. 'What is it?'

'I didn't want to tell you on the phone, because I wasn't

really sure what was going on. I got the results of my scans this morning, and it's not great news.'

'What?' My voice goes funny, an octave higher. 'Why didn't you tell me?'

'I only got the results through this morning, darling. You were on your way back already. It's still sinking in for me, too.'

'What is?'

I look at her. She seems different, in a way I don't understand. Things feel too still all of a sudden, a feeling of time slowing down.

'It's cancer, darling.'

My eyes start to fill with tears.

'I'm so sorry,' she says, reaching for my hand.

'No, no. What?' I go silent. 'There are treatments, though?' I can hear the desperation in my voice.

'It's stage four. It's spread – that's the problem.'

'What does that mean? There are treatments, right?' I can hear myself repeating words.

'Treatments, darling, but no cure. Things have moved quickly. It's OK.'

'It's not OK.'

I swallow down a big lump in my throat. I can't speak for a moment. What is there to say? I turn away, wiping my eyes with my sleeves.

'My last mammogram didn't pick it up. I don't know why. And I didn't notice anything wrong until I found the lump. It's just one of those things.'

'It's not just one of those things!' I say. I feel a burning sensation spreading over my face suddenly. I stare into space, looking through her, looking through everything. She puts her hand on my shoulder.

'There are treatments to help me extend my life, but these are the facts, and I am sorry to have to tell you this. We'll do whatever we can do.'

'I'm sorry,' I say, holding her hand.

'It's going to be OK.'

I feel a stab of guilt that Carla is comforting me, when it surely should be the other way round.

How is it going to be OK?

She puts half her blanket over me, and rests her head on my shoulder. A moment of long, stretched-out silence between us follows.

I stay in Eastbourne for the rest of the week. I take care of Carla for a change, cooking for her, dusting her ornaments, making endless cups of peppermint tea, and helping her light candles and incense round the bungalow every evening. I lay the table beautifully for all our suppers, though I notice already that she isn't eating very much.

I also accompany Carla to the follow-up meeting with her oncologist. Dr Robertson is good-looking, looks to be in his fifties, and has a kind, calm energy. He confirms that Carla's cancer has very sadly spread, metastasized from the breast to other areas of her body. He keeps saying that 'more people are living longer' and that there are more treatments than ever 'to improve your quality of life'. As Carla said, even though there is no cure, she can be treated, and we leave feeling slightly more positive than before, but still shellshocked by the severity, and injustice, of it all.

Afterwards, we sit in silence in the garden in the same chairs as before. We listen to the seagulls and the whisper of the trees and a Bob Marley song coming from the neighbours' house down the road. I put a blanket over Carla's knees, and she stretches out her feet in her clogs, and tilts her face towards the spring sun.

'I want us to focus on the positive. I like the way Dr Robertson spoke. I can live alongside this. I can be helped as best as possible. It's not going to be easy, but I want to live each day and take it from there. OK?'

I nod, holding her hand. 'I liked him too and what he said. I'm right here, OK?'

'I know, darling.'

'Cup of tea?'

'Better grab the Hobnobs, too.'

Our world might be shifting, unrecognizable to how it was even a week before, but we both still need a cup of tea and a biscuit.

32

THEN

July 1997

Two old-fashioned single beds were side by side, with a sick bucket in the middle, and an old lamp. There was one solitary window, with a blind blowing in the breeze, making a rattling sound. The bedding was thin and an ironic sickly-beige colour – maybe so that any sickness just blended in with the general interior of the room. The walls were cream, and the wallpaper was peeling slightly. There was a small washbasin to the left, and on the back of the door, a sign read: *In case of emergencies, please ring Ms Parsons on 01323 150689.* What was my emergency? I was lying still on the bed, staring at the ceiling.

The old clock on the wall ticked loudly. I didn't feel tired; I felt wired. But there was nothing to do in this room but wait.

Forty-five minutes later, I heard some voices behind the door, most prominently Carla's: 'So sorry, got here as fast as I could – traffic was a nightmare. Thank you, yes. I'll go in and see her.'

There was a little knock at the door, and Carla emerged, looking slightly dishevelled, a big canvas tote bag swinging over her shoulder.

'Oh, Willow, you poor thing.' She put her tote bag on the other bed and sat next to me. She stroked my hair. 'So sorry you feel unwell, darling.'

I closed my eyes, feeling immediately soothed by her presence. 'Sorry to mess up your day,' I said, trying to sound more croaky and ill than I really was. Really, I was fine.

'Don't be silly. Slow day at the studio anyway. Are you OK?' she said, placing her palm on my forehead. 'I can't feel a temperature – that's a positive.'

'I just don't feel . . . very good,' I said, putting my head on her lap.

She looked at me, taking in the colour on my cheeks and my ability to sit up very easily. She got a thermometer out of her handbag and put it under my tongue. She read my temperature: it was fine. She put it away and didn't say anything.

'I'm sorry you don't feel good, sweetheart. Anything in particular?'

'Don't want to be here at school today,' I muttered. 'I can't do it.'

'I understand.'

'The teacher said I had to go back to the classroom unless

I was physically being sick. I told her to call you. She nearly didn't.'

'Well, that's ridiculous. If you don't feel OK, then you don't feel OK. After everything you've been through.' She stroked my forehead, gently.

It had only been a year since Mum left. Carla knew – she could tell instantly – that I wasn't sick, but I was deeply heartsick.

'Tell you what.' Carla lowered her voice to a whisper. 'Let me tell the teachers you're too ill to go into school for the rest of this week – and instead, we'll get some ice cream, watch your favourite films, and if you're feeling better, we could even go to the cinema tomorrow.'

She wrapped her arms around me. I felt so relieved to be reunited with her, the only place I wanted to be. She knew exactly what to say, and do. She made me feel instantly better.

33

NOW

I told Carla about the growing distance between me and Pen, so she forced me to send her a message, asking to meet. Life is too short.

So now, here I am in London, walking into a pub, feeling strangely nervous. I have pins and needles in my hands; it's like I'm about to go on a date with someone I want to impress.

We're meeting at The Star, an old pub we used to go to when we lived together, and when I breathe in the familiar smell of sticky beer from the bar and salty chips from the kitchen, I feel more at ease.

Pen is sitting at our old regular table for two, with a carafe of red wine and two glasses. We haven't spoken properly for weeks. She's typing on her phone, concentrating, but when she looks up to see me, she smiles broadly and puts her phone face down.

'Hey!' I say, pulling out the seat and sitting opposite her.

'Hey,' she says.

'Busy, isn't it? This place got popular, used to be a bit of a shit-hole,' I say, laughing, trying to make light conversation, taking in all the full tables, the loud music, the chitter-chatter. I pull my chair in closer to her, so that I can hear better.

'I'm sure all the creepy after-work businessmen will be joining us soon, too,' she says. 'They usually come here after their meetings to order endless pints and get really loud and annoying.'

There's a palpable change in energy between us. I've known Pen practically all my life, but for the first time, it kind of feels awkward.

Where have you been? I want to say to her. She looks different. Shorter hair. No black nail varnish. Darker eyebrows.

'You OK?' she says, pouring me a drink, not looking at me.

'I'm . . . OK. Lots of change,' I say.

There's a pause. I open my mouth, and I forget to filter myself. 'I saw you went away with the girls on some sort of couples thing?'

'Yeah . . . It was quite expensive for what it was, and it only works if you split a room with someone. Sorry, that's the only reason we didn't say anything.'

'It's fine. Just sometimes, it's nice to be invited even if we all know I won't come.'

'I know. I don't know why the boys posted pictures.'

'It's fine.'

She pours some more wine and then puts down the carafe.

'I'm sorry if I've been a bit distant,' she says. 'It's been quite a wild time. I want to apologize, but I also don't feel like I should have to apologize for feeling happy at the moment.

I've enjoyed being in a cocoon with Mike for a bit,' she says. 'I feel like I've deserved some time getting to know someone, you know?'

Butterfly Paradise, the cocoons, the chrysalis.

She continues: 'I know it's so hard when you're experiencing wildly different things. I'm sorry if I made you feel shit at all.'

'I've just felt so far away from you all. It's hard to know how to ask you for help, when you're so visibly happy and busy.'

'I have been thinking of you, Willow. I really have. I just needed space.'

'Space from me?'

'No, space in general,' Pen says. 'We're all trying to build our lives here.'

'Yeah, I know.'

'I do want to be here for you. I *am* here for you. I've just found it hard lately. It felt like I was always in trouble. Treading on eggshells. It's why I've hardly been on the WhatsApp group.'

'OK. To me, it just felt like you disappeared and couldn't even let me know why.'

'I know, and I'm sorry I got wasted at Lola's and was insensitive. I clearly had stuff bottled up, and it came out in all the wrong ways. It's just, for so long, I've been the third wheel to literally all my friends, always being free at the drop of a hat, always being the available one, always the one to message first on the group, always the one to suggest plans – and for once, it felt so liberating to be the one who was suddenly busy again. Then the minute I had my own life going on, I felt like you were scolding me for it.'

A waitress with white-blonde hair comes over and asks if we want to order any food, and we say we haven't looked yet.

'But I'm really sorry if I've not been there for you,' Pen says. She fiddles with a beer mat. 'That bothers me.'

'Well, I'm also sorry if I lost myself to Dom over the years.'

'I was being too harsh. I just wanted you to understand how amazing you are, just as you. You deserved better.'

'Thank you. It's been hard to see it lately.'

Someone's fluffy dog walks over to our table, and I pet its head. A softening. A light relief.

'We never got our date in to go to the seaside,' Pen says.

'Well, shall we soon?'

'I'll make sure of it.'

'That'll be nice. We'll write some mantras that we can fling into the fire. Or we could write our resolutions on pebbles, like Ms Gower taught us.'

'It's good to see you looking so yourself again, Willow. It's like you've re-emerged with wings.'

'I do feel different. Like my brain has somehow rewired itself. You know that bit in *Runaway Bride*, where the Julia Roberts character doesn't know what eggs she actually likes because she always copies the egg preferences of the men she's with? I think I was like that. I think I know what eggs I like now,' I say.

'What's the verdict?'

'Scrambled, with a dash of Dijon mustard.'

I take a big breath in, pause, and then breathe out. 'I do have some sad news, though.'

'Oh?'

'I wasn't sure when to tell you. Carla is ill. She . . . has quite serious cancer, Pen. It's all been really hard and shocking.'

Pen's face crumples. 'I'm so sorry. That's so awful.'

'It really has been. Carla is a trooper, though. And we're going to keep putting one foot in front of the other. "Turtle steps", she calls it.'

'Is she going to be OK?' she asks, nervously.

'I don't know.'

Pen comes round to my side of the table and gives me a massive hug. I start crying suddenly; she starts crying too. We sit down again, dabbing our eyes in silence, looking at each other.

'Is there anything I can do?' she asks.

'Not really.'

'I'm really so sorry. And let's not argue again.'

I want to change the subject. 'I had a weird dream about Dom the other night. We met up in the Hackney Marshes on a cold day, and I looked down and he was wearing flip-flops. And his feet looked really, really gross.'

'Noooo.' She gasps and covers her mouth with her hand.

We burst out laughing. I'm grateful for the relief our laughter brings. The quick distraction from wanting to cry most of the time.

'Oh, *amazing*, you've got the ick!! Now you can move on.'

'Yes. God bless the ick,' I say.

'That is the universe sending you on your merry way.

How's everything else? How's the piece about Naz? I'm sorry I was mean about her. She's clearly just very young and cool, and I was being an unnecessary bitch,' Pen says, taking a sip from her glass.

'She's an interesting person. And it's been a good experience. I've got one more hang out with her, then I'm filing the article next week. Bit nervous about it, but you know, I've written what Elaine wanted, and it's a job after all. Also, Elaine gave me a gift from one of her sponsors.' I pull two pieces of paper out of my bag. 'Free tickets to next year's Glasto! Will you be my date?'

Pen squeals. 'WHAT! Of course!'

I pull something else out from my bag and give it to her a bit sheepishly. 'This is maybe a bit silly, but, um, I also got you a bumbag. It matches this one.' I gesture at mine, looped over the chair.

Pen grins knowingly. I bet Lola told her about me planning to give it to Dom when he proposed. She thanks me, then tops up my glass again.

She leans across the table and holds my hand. 'Let's be there for each other from now on, though, OK? Let's just make sure we go and get a pint next time we feel annoyed with each other and not leave it to build up silence and resentment.'

'Agreed.'

'I really am so sorry about Carla. I don't know what to say, but I will be here for you throughout all of this. OK?'

In this moment, I'm reminded of the safety and security of an old friend. Something strange is happening with Naz,

Carla's health is starting to feel like it's spinning out of control, but Pen is here.

No matter what gets in between us, she knows my family, my history, my heart, and that will always mean something special. We weave in and out like an old tattered friendship bracelet that just won't break, no matter what direction we're being pulled in.

My last hang with Naz: the Celine Dion concert. Naz received free tickets from some contacts at HBO to this exclusive gig, and Elaine wants me to get video footage of her dancing, drinking, celebrating music from a different era to her own. I think about a caption I can sell to Elaine: *It's easy to always do fun things when you get given them for free. Is Naz's life really something anyone can attain?*

Even though I feel closer to Naz, I still feel it's my duty to take the sheen off her sparkling public persona. She doesn't really have to think about anything. She doesn't have money worries. Yes, she looks tired and anxious sometimes, but that might just be because she's partying too much. Cars are always booked for her; her managers deal with all her admin; she gets sent free clothes; everything is organized for her. She's selling a lifestyle we would all love to have, but she's the only one who can live it. I also feel like there's something she's not telling me – and I'm determined to find out what it is.

It's the kind of Friday afternoon that makes London feel like the best city in the world. The air is warm. There's more laughter and music in the streets than usual. A woman is selling bright tulips on the corner by the Tube. People are walking with iced coffees. And even men in suits are smiling behind their Ray-Ban sunglasses.

I meet Naz near Hyde Park. She's wearing a short purple dress with stars on it, navy Converse shoes, and fishnet tights. She links my arm through hers like she always does. We walk through the majestic Wellington Arch and I breathe in the smells of the park, the flowerbeds and trees boosting my mood. Deeper into the park, groups of young people are sat around wearing jumpsuits, hats and sequins. There's a van selling hotdogs and pretzels that smell delicious, and most people are drinking from supermarket tinnies, chatting closely. The grass is dry; it hasn't rained for a while.

Suddenly, a middle-aged woman with curly hair runs up to Naz, panting. 'Oh my god. Sorry. Are you Naz Chopra?'

Before Naz can open her mouth—

'Oh my god. I had to say something. My friend over there didn't think it was you,' she says. 'I wanted to say thank you. I love following you – I think you're amazing. You've really influenced me over the years.'

'Thank you—'

'I have two kids and I'm pushing fifty, so I'm not your target audience or anything, but you made me realize I wasn't prioritizing myself at all, and so I basically booked myself onto a wellness retreat for two weeks, told my husband he just had to deal with it! Of course, he had help from his parents – anyway, sorry, I'm waffling, but basically, you are the reason I actually like my life again. Eventually, I got out of the relationship. I put myself first now, and it makes me a better mum.' She tears up. 'Sorry, it's just quite emotional seeing you in person.'

'I love to hear these stories! Thank you.'

'It's the reason I'm here with my old mate from school, having gin in a tin. I would *never* have done this before. I would never have got a babysitter, let alone go to a concert.'

Apparently Naz's energy makes grown women turn into babbling fangirls. Watching the smile on that woman's face, I feel a little niggle of guilt about my article. There is definitely a different angle that could have been written, all about the positivity she brings into people's lives.

'Drink?' Naz says to me, grinning, adjusting her shiny gold cross-body bag and taking out her American Express.

'Sure,' I say.

I check my phone and see a text from Carla:

Have fun! Am playing Celine in the kitchen in your honour! Hope you girls enjoy. Love you!

When Naz returns, she's beaming, holding a cold, novelty-sized magnum of rosé and two paper cups.

'The guy behind the bar gave it to me for free! Said his girlfriend is a fan and asked for a selfie.'

I smile. Of course he did.

Just another day in the life of Naz Chopra – a woman who manifests literally anything she likes. It's like moving through the world with a magician.

We make our way into the VIP area, where we are given

wristbands and really great seats. A woman called Meera who works at Sky is there to greet us:

'Naz! We are so glad you could come!'

'Thanks for having us. This is my friend Willow,' Naz says, introducing me.

'Well, have a great time. Here are some vouchers for some free drinks. Although I can see you've already got some!' Meera says.

Naz is holding her giant bottle of rosé under her arm.

'There's a separate VIP bar over there, so you don't have to miss any of the performance if you want a top-up.'

When Celine comes onto the stage, the crowd roars. She looks tall and strong, wearing an electric blue jumpsuit, matching blue eye-shadow, and high heels encrusted with diamonds. Her energy and her power fill the park. She pushes her chest out as she sings. Her arms are toned, strongly gripping the microphone as though it's a sword to slay people with.

We sing along at the top of our voices ('Flying on My Own'), smiling, swaying, waving our hands in the air. Someone beside me accidentally spills his beer all over my left shoulder, and I don't care. For the first time in ages, I'm not thinking about what Dom is doing, and I don't wish to be anywhere else.

I notice that Naz is liberally knocking back the rosé. Her eyes look slightly glazed over, and she's starting to slur her words as she sings along. I'm still on my first drink, taking small sips; after all, I'm still on the job.

After a raucous hour and a half, Celine leaves the stage, takes her bow.

We leave via a VIP exit. It's fairly dark now, and people are in high spirits, throwing their finished cans into park bins, and calling cabs or looking up train times.

'God, she was *amazing*,' Naz says. 'I don't want to go home. Can we go somewhere else now? Karaoke?'

'I have to get back,' I say. 'I've got a deadline, sorry.'

'Pleeeeease,' she says, tugging at me. 'Go on, please.'

I nod along so that she'll walk next to me, but I'm already scanning for black cabs and working out how to persuade her to climb into one and get home safe.

'Wait, I need a pee,' Naz slurs, and she gives me her crossbody bag. 'Can you hold this please? Don't want it to fall off when I crouch down. Weeing outside is actually called a wild wee! Actually, can you come and stand by me, on watch? I don't want anyone seeing.'

I stand next to Naz's naked bum, holding her Prada bag as she crouches down behind a tree. I'm trying to hide her as much as possible with my body. A group of lads pass by and shout 'Oi oi!' but then move quickly on. She hollers 'Wild weeeeeee!' at them.

'Thanksss you,' she says, pulling her pants back up, trying to put her bag back on but struggling.

'Are you OK there?' I ask.

She fiddles with her bag and rearranges her dress. Then, she lets out a big cry and sits abruptly on the floor, like a toddler who's fallen over. She lands in the muddy patch under the tree, and starts sobbing. Tears stream down her face.

Oh god.

'Naz, what's up?' I say, crouching down next to her.

'Look at me! I'm a mess,' she says. Head in her hands. Sitting in her own pee.

'Are you OK?' I ask again, putting my hand on her shoulder.

'You think I'm so *free* – well, I'm actually very much *trapped*.'

'What do you mean?'

I offer her a tissue.

'Nnnothing is real.' She is really slurring now; I can barely make out the words.

All this time, I've almost *wanted* to see Naz unravel; I wanted to see the bugs and dirt underneath the rock, and now I'm finally seeing it, I feel terrible for her. I feel bad about the whole thing.

I try to lift her up, she goes limp. I put her arm around my shoulders and try to support her weight, but she slumps in my lap. Her eyes are closed. Has she fallen asleep? I start panicking, wondering if she has passed out and if she's so drunk that she risks choking on her own vomit. I look around for some help.

'Are you OK there?' Luckily, a kind-looking man in a high-vis jacket comes over, holding a torch. He has *Hyde Park volunteer* written on his badge.

'She's had a bit too much,' I say. 'But we're fine. Naz – Naz, come on,' I say, gently tapping her cheek with my palm. 'Come on.'

'I'll help you,' the man says. 'Fun night, then, was it?' he asks, sitting her up. Her head keeps lolling to one side while she tries to regain focus.

'I guess you could call it that,' I say.

The man lifts Naz to her feet and we both support her weight, hobbling towards the park gates together in the dark.

'Thank you,' I say.

'No worries,' he says. 'It's my job to make sure people get home safely.'

Naz opens her eyes slightly now, squinting in the light of the harsh streetlamps. I realize that I can't just put her into a cab; I have to take her home myself. I open her bag and take her keys to keep them safe. We hobble to the Tube, and she rests her head on my shoulder for the duration.

When we get to her Hampstead flat, I unlock her front door and take her straight to her bedroom. I'm happy to see it isn't in such a squalid state as it was last time, but it's still not great. There's a wine glass on her dressing table with a little puddle of red wine in it, and the bed isn't made, but the sheets look clean, and the bin is no longer overflowing.

I carefully take off her shoes, tights, dress, and I put her in her pyjamas. I tuck her into bed and look at the time: one a.m. I go onto the Uber app, but no cabs accept me. Too late, or too far to Lola's, maybe. There's clearly no way I'm going home now.

I go into Naz's bathroom and use one of her fancy face wipes. I go into her kitchen for a glass of water and spot cartons of Chinese takeaway boxes all around the sink. Eaten and half-eaten. I put it all in the bin, it's starting to smell. I crack open a window, then tie up the bin bag and take it out.

Finally, my body aching with tiredness, I lie down next to

Naz; she's under the covers, and I'm on top. I notice she has a soft stuffed toy by the bed. I put it next to her.

It doesn't take me long to fall asleep.

I get back to Lola's early the next morning. I wanted to get out of Naz's flat early, so I woke her up gently and left her some paracetamol and water by her bed.

I open the door to Lola's using my spare key, and I can hear her and Fred having breakfast together, cutlery clanking. I go into the spare room, shut the door quietly, and leave them to it. I put on my striped, pink pyjamas, remove the remains of my winged eyeliner (inspired by my make-up session at Naz's) with cleanser, and put on a hydrating moisturizer.

I look in the mirror and take a deep breath. It was a long night, but I can't deny I feel good in myself. A whole area of my brain seems freed up now the sadness has lessened. I'm worried about Carla, and that takes up most of my waking thoughts, but I don't feel sad about being single. I feel good – and free. For the first time in months, I don't feel bloated; I don't have backache; I don't have cold sores. I feel secure in my friendships with Pen, Lola, and Alice.

I get into the futon bed, pull the covers over me, and nap for a few hours. When I wake, I grab my laptop and get to work. I need to add the finishing touches to my article and then send it off to Elaine.

I go onto Naz's Instagram page and click on the photo I took of her at the Celine Dion concert, which she posted last night with a caption including *#ad @hbo*, tongue out, peace signs.

I scroll down and read some of the comments:

Scam artist bitch.
   I can't believe I ever bought one of your tickets – you're a liar
   I still LOVE you princess
   Omg are you besties with celine d now?
   We've seen the photos. Your whole brand is fake
   SINGLE NAZ? Lol what else are you lying about
   How do you sleep at night?
   You are a lying c*nt

I stare at my laptop screen, shellshocked by the amount of horrible comments. Of course, she has her fair share of trolls like every influencer, but this is not the usual ratio. Normally, the comments are full of positive affirmations and over-enthusiastic heart emojis from hardcore fans, and perhaps one weirdo asking to see a picture of her feet.

I type Naz's name into Google, and I find a new snark Reddit thread with thousands of replies. I click the link and find the source of the commotion. Some YouTuber guy has been flying a drone over Instagram celebrities' houses to make videos about where they live, which is questionable enough.

When filming Naz's flat, he got footage of her in the building's shared garden, kissing someone, looking extremely intimate and loved-up. I keep scrolling and find out it's Loz, the girl I met at Naz's house. He flew over enough times to establish that their relationship was more than just casual.

Not only did he publish a video but also topless pictures of Naz and Loz sunbathing. He's potentially exposed that Naz has been hiding a secret relationship. Maybe it's 'Single Naz' no more?

I refresh Google and see a story has been published by the *Daily Mail*: 'Do Influencers Lie To Us For Money?' It's been circulated by lots of smaller blogs, and the comment sections are full of vitriol. I sink down on the futon, feeling like I've been covered in toxic slime.

34

THEN

August 1996

One of my most vivid memories is from when Carla and I went to collect Mum from the airport when I was eight years old. We'd spent the morning making a banner. Carla had laid out a big white roll of paper, and we wrote *WELCOME HOME, MUMMY* in bubble writing, and we coloured it in with felt-tip pens and glitter. The glitter had gone everywhere, and I had glue up my arms. My mouth was so dry on the drive there, it hurt to swallow. Even Carla, usually so calm, had been pacing the house, drinking multiple coffees.

At Gatwick Airport, Carla and I stood there with the banner, and I felt my stomach pinch with nervousness as we waited. Everyone was piling out of arrivals, but I was too small. I couldn't see who was coming out of the crowd.

Then I saw her, my dear old mum, with her thin hair and strappy top and tattoos and tattered leather satchel. She was here; she'd come back. My reflex was to pull back, something stopping me from going forward.

'Look, it's OK, there she is, that's your mum,' Carla said, rubbing my back.

Mum stood there for a moment, just looking at us both. I didn't know what to do. Then she crouched down slowly to hug me, and her hair smelled of stale smoke. It took me a while to relax, I couldn't let myself get completely lost in her familiar smells again. Before Mum put her black cardigan on, I saw the scratches on her arms. I could see duty-free vodka in her bag. I could see dark circles under her eyes.

In the car, Carla was making all the conversation: 'How was your trip? Willow and I are so happy to see you.'

Mum was staring out of the window.

'How are you?' Carla repeated.

'Good, can we turn the heating up?' Mum said, trying to press some of the car buttons.

'Yes, of course. What do you fancy for dinner?' Carla asked. 'Willow and I thought we could get fish and chips, as it's a special occasion and we're so happy to see you.'

'OK,' she said. She looked out of the window. 'England is so cold.'

When I went up to bed later that evening, I hugged Carla, and when I hugged my mum, I noticed she didn't move her arms; she barely responded. Carla filled in the gap and gave me a big squeeze. Mum seemed flat, empty, void of something that I'm not even sure was ever there before.

The next morning, Carla couldn't find her house keys. She

looked everywhere for them; I watched her look under bins, empty all her handbags, go back to the car, pull out the sofa cushions.

That night, she sat on the end of my bed. 'Sweetheart.' She stroked my head. 'It's OK if you took them.'

I shook my head at her.

'It's OK if you have. You can tell me,' she said again.

We sat in silence for a moment. Then, I slowly got up from the bed, pulled out one of my pink drawers where I kept my stickers and Beanie Babies, and handed her the keys. 'It's OK, sweetheart.'

I thought if the door couldn't be unlocked, then she couldn't leave again.

35

NOW

From: "Jaime" <Jaime@TheFaganAgency.com>
To: Willow <willowjones@hotmail.com>
Subject: urgent

pls call me asap
thanks,
jaime

I grab my coat and go for a walk. I need to go outside and get some fresh air before I speak to Jaime. I sit on a picnic bench next to one of my favourite ponds, where lots of different birds gather: swans, mallards, and moorhens walk around and fight over their territory.

I need to figure out what's going on before I send my finished piece to Elaine. I go onto Naz's Instagram page again, and see it's been disabled. Then I notice I have three missed calls and another text from Jaime.

I call Naz's number, but it goes to voicemail. I want to speak to her before ringing Jaime, wanting to check on her myself.

I dash off a quick email.

From: Willow <willowjones@hotmail.com>
To: Naz <naz@nazchopra.co.uk>

Is everything OK? xo

I receive an out-of-office response immediately:

Hi, it's Naz! I'm away from my desk right now and won't be able to reply any time soon. Please bear with! Sending sunshine always.

I ring Jaime, a nervousness bubbling in my belly. Suddenly, something feels very wrong.

'Hey, everything OK?'

'Hi.' She sounds sombre. 'Naz is very unwell right now, and we need to protect her mental health. We need your article to be pulled. It cannot go live. We don't want any further attention around her right now.'

'I'm so sorry to hear. Is this to do with the Instagram comments and the YouTube video I saw?'

'I can't really elaborate right now.'

'Of course. I'll have to get in touch with my editor to explain.'

'OK – it's really important that it doesn't go live during

such a vulnerable time for her. If you care about her at all, you will pull the piece.'

'I totally understand. Is she OK?'

'She's . . .' Jaime clears her throat. 'Can you cc me in with your editor? Naz went into hospital a few hours ago. Homerton.'

I feel sick. I left her half-asleep only this morning. Should I have told Jaime about Naz at the concert last night? The empty takeaway boxes? The squalid bedroom? The amount she was drinking?

Jamie won't give me any more details, so I hang up and think about what to do. A family of four are feeding bread to the ducks, right next to a sign that says *do not feed the ducks*.

I take a deep breath and call Elaine.

'Doll! So glad you're calling. I need your piece asap – we're mocking up the homepage as we speak! Such great news about her whole fake singledom thing – just saw – couldn't be a better time to publish! The *Daily Mail* are salivating and ready to syndicate it for Monday a.m.'

'Elaine, sorry, but there's been a delay. Naz isn't well.'

'What do you mean?'

'It's some kind of mental health situation, I think,' I say. 'Her agent told me she's in hospital at the moment.'

'Are you going to visit her?'

'I'd like to.'

'Great. Go today and get some quotes. Maybe even pictures?'

'What?'

'Come on, Willow. *Think*. We should *include* this in the piece. Interview her on her sickbed. Get the juicy details.'

'Um, no, I don't think we can do that . . . her agent asked us to pull the piece, or at least postpone it. Naz is in a really fragile state.'

Elaine lets out a big sigh. 'Oh, Willow. Of course, her *agent* would say that. Even though it's usually the agents who drive these people into a mental hole in the first place . . . Come on, this gives us even *more* reason to publish. It'll get a lot of clicks. Imagine the headline: "Faking Your Life Online Might Even Nearly Kill You!" Naz being in hospital is quite the ending to the story. You can have a short extension to allow time to get those quotes – shall we say you'll deliver the piece at eight p.m. tonight? Make sure you include the gory details. It is our job as journalists to expose the truth.'

'But this is her private life.'

Elaine lets out an exasperated sigh. She lowers her voice, and when she speaks, it contains a venom I've not heard before. 'This is why your journalism career got stuck, Willow. I gave you this chance to prove yourself, and you're not delivering. If you won't send me the article, we can't pay your fee, and you'll need to pay back the hotel costs, too. And we certainly won't be able to have you as one of our staff writers if you're not cut out for it.'

There is a long, painful silence while I gather some words. 'I think you're right,' I say, close to tears.

I think of Naz, and then I think of my mum. I feel a swelling of sadness, but most of all, I feel a strong duty to protect the women I love, even the idea of them – women with complexities, with scars, who find life difficult and need help.

'I won't do it.'

Then the dial tone goes dead.

Part Four

36

NOW

Carla sits on a small wooden stool in the She-Shed, painting a white mirror she found in Oxfam, colouring it in with pastel colours around the edges with a small brush.

'Painting helps,' she says.

'Shall I make us another pot of tea?' I ask. It feels like making endless tea is the only thing we can do.

I've been staying here ever since I hung the phone up on Elaine. I'm still waiting on my payout from Scatterbox, so Carla helped me pay Elaine back for the hotel room costs and said she was so proud of me for refusing to use Naz's misery to further my career.

I tried to visit Naz in hospital twice, but once she was out cold, and the other time, Loz was visiting, and I didn't want to intrude. Other than that, I haven't been in touch with her for weeks. Her Instagram account was deleted as soon as everything started going viral, and my increasingly worried emails were all getting a standard out-of-office reply.

Eventually, I emailed Jaime, who told me that Naz is taking a break from her online career and is no longer a client. She said that Naz is now staying with her uncle in Birmingham and is being looked after, so that's something, I suppose. I don't want to pester or intrude, so I've backed off. I hope Naz will reach out when she's ready, and besides, I'm giving a lot of my attention to Carla at the moment.

When I bring in a pot of tea on a tray with two floral mugs, Carla is rummaging around in a cupboard.

'I've been following these online cancer diaries of people my age "vlogging" their situation. At first, I found it a bit cringey, but now, I feel very grateful. It's helped me feel less alone, hearing from people who have gone through similar things. I left a comment, and lots of people left me comments back, and it was rather lovely actually. It helps ease the nerves about all the treatment coming up. A sign that people can be rather nice on the Internet, sometimes. Not the sort of community I was expecting to join, but a community all the same.'

'It makes perfect sense to want to connect to people going through a similar thing,' I say.

'By the way, I found something for you.'

'What is it?'

'Over there.'

I go over and pick up a medium-sized brown box. A box I've never seen before. I place it on the coffee table in front of me and open it up.

'I found it the other day. I was going through my things, and quite honestly, I had no idea I had it. When I realized, I knew I had to show you.'

Inside is an old photo album. I lift it out gently.

'You don't have to look through it if you don't want to, but I thought you might want to see some old photos of me and your mum. I know she hurt us, and we miss her, but I wondered if you'd like to see some memories from the past.'

I swallow down a lump in my throat. 'Yes, I want to.'

I stroke the rectangle-shaped book made of soft material, sit down on the floor of the shed and place it on my lap.

'It's an album from when your mum and I went on a holiday for the first time,' Carla says, settling next to me on a rug. 'Must be mid-Eighties. She was going through a tough time, a break-up with someone, but we managed to scrape together some money to go somewhere hot together. Portugal, I think it was. We had such fun.'

I open the first page of the album, and I see my mother on a beach, smiling into the camera, wearing a pair of white shorts and a striped T-shirt.

'After our dad, your grandpa, died, she promised herself this holiday. We paid for a boat trip and everything. I had no idea she took these photos, and I had no idea I had this album – it must have been buried amongst some other things. She was lots of different versions. She was many different people.'

I leaf through the photos slowly.

There's one of her in the sea on a white sandy beach, laughing, holding a bottle of cold beer. A photo of her sunbathing with giant sunglasses on and a straw hat, smiling, oily from suntan lotion.

'She looks happy,' I say.

'She was, for a short period of time.'

'Did I make her unhappy?'

Carla puts both arms around me suddenly.

'No. Gosh, *no*. *No*, Willow. You don't think that, do you?'

'It's an easy explanation that I sometimes have in my head.'

'I know. I must admit, there are so many times when I find myself so angry at her. Resentful. I really wish she could have been different – but that's like wishing it was sunny when it's raining. It just doesn't work.'

She takes a big breath in, then crosses her arms. 'But, my darling, anger aside, it was never, ever you. She loved you. She did. She still does; she always will. Whenever she came home and felt triggered again, it was abundantly clear that she was just not going to be able to do it. Motherhood, I mean. She always struggled. She simply wasn't able to be a mother, Willow. She only truly felt comfortable alone.'

I let the idea settle for a moment, that she loves us. That the love can be disembodied, that it can still float through the air and loudspeakers and rivers and old photos and find us anyway.

Then, I see the last photo: a picture of her smiling, doing a 'peace' sign with two fingers in a V-shape, posing next to a red Mini.

Cross-legged, I put my head in my hands, half-smiling, half-winded.

'Is that her car?' I say, stroking the page.

I hear Pen's voice in my head: *you have a thing for Minis, too.*

'Yes. She loved that car. She bought it second-hand off this random old man for basically a handful of beans. It broke down eventually, but she absolutely loved it.'

'I don't know if I can ever fully forgive her for leaving,' I say, closing the album.

'I know, honey. Me neither. But life is very, very hard for some people, and when it's invisible, it can be hard to understand. The greatest act of love is for us to somehow accept that. I'm so sorry she wasn't able to be there for you.'

'Do you feel like you want to tell my mum about your illness?'

'I don't think so, sweetheart. And I wouldn't know how to reach her.'

I hold Carla's hand. Our bond strengthening over and over again.

When she gets up from the rug in the shed, I lead her inside the house, pour her a glass of water and help her to bed. The two of us, always in it together.

Later that night, I'm in the bath researching second-hand cars on Gumtree on my phone. There's only so much cleaning and cooking I can do while Carla's resting, and I'm thinking I'll use some of my Scatterbox money to buy a car and get some refresher lessons while I'm here. I'm just clicking through photos of a sweet yellow Mini when a notification comes in.

I have a new email, and I don't immediately recognize the address it's come from. I sit up, hunching over, and squint at the screen.

From: Unknown <nc_personal@gmail.com>
To: Willow <willowjones@hotmail.com>
Subject: hi x

Willow, I'm sorry I never got in touch after everything happened. Dr Patel said 'a serious-looking woman with red hair' came to visit me in the hospital. And I knew it was you! Thank you for visiting me. Obviously everything came to a head and I was in a scary place. But I'm OK.

I smile, relieved to hear from her.
I reply straight away:

From: Willow <willowjones@hotmail.com>
To: Unknown <nc_personal@gmail.com>
Subject: Re: hi x

It's so good to hear from you. I was just talking about you with my aunt Carla today. I'm so sorry you've been through such hell. I was worried about you. I'm sorry for what you're going through xxx

From: Unknown <nc_personal@gmail.com>
To: Willow <willowjones@hotmail.com>
Subject: Re: hi x

Thank you. It all got too much. My management pushing me to do the Girls' Night In tour that I was really against. I've been dating Loz for a while, which was eating away at me, living a lie, but my agents told me to keep it secret. They didn't want my personal life to 'harm my brand'. Everyone online is now saying I lied for years about being single for money and for my business. I've never felt so lonely, so violated, so awful, and I feel like I was putting on such a performance for you, for everyone. I feel so exhausted by it all. I feel like I need to sleep for a hundred years. I don't know what's happened to me.

Anyway, I think I will be OK, but right now, I'm really not. I'm doing a lot of lying in bed, going for walks. Weirdly, I end up walking around a lot of graveyards. Anyway, I did enjoy us hanging out together, and I'm sorry the article never happened.

PS I hope you didn't meet up with your ex??

From: Willow <willowjones@hotmail.com>
To: Unknown <nc_personal@gmail.com>
Subject: Re: hi x

Please take it easy. My aunt calls it 'turtle steps'. Just a tiny movement forward is all that's ever needed.

I didn't meet with him. I didn't need to. You have helped me so much during this weird time in my life. You strengthened and distracted me during a time when I felt completely lost. I'm so, so glad our paths crossed when they did. I know you're stepping away from social media – but your posts were helpful for people; please know that.

I started out being really sceptical about everything. I wasn't going to mention it, but I saw you once in the fitting room at John Lewis, and you made a comment about me. I was buying a matching bumbag for my boyfriend – I don't know if you remember. It was like you saw straight into my soul – I was unhappy and trapped. I just didn't know it yet.

    I feel like a totally different woman having spent time with you, Naz. You're a really special person, and I believe you will glue yourself back together again better than ever. But please know that you do make a difference and that the energy you put into living a fun, free life on your own terms really does rub off on people.

From: Unknown <nc_personal@gmail.com>
To: Willow <willowjones@hotmail.com>
Subject: Re: hi x

Omg . . . I do remember that moment in the fitting room. I'm so sorry . . . That was you? I know I can be a bit extra sometimes. I was always so out of it – I was taking a load of caffeine pills to stay awake. That was inappropriate of me for sure. Sorry. Who am I to judge anyone else's lifestyle? Even if I was right ;)

    Once I'm better, let's go for a coffee. It would be nice to see you. I'm in the middle of a horrible situation with my management team. I have to pay back loads of money for all the cancelled tours. I'd built this incredible thing, and yet, I felt like I needed them, like I couldn't do anything without them. The ultimate co-dependency. The very thing I used to warn my fans about with relationships. The irony . . .

Anyway, I'm going to go offline for a while now. Take care xxx

PS Turtle steps! Love that!

From: Willow <willowjones@hotmail.com>
To: Unknown <nc_personal@gmail.com>

Oh and also! I just wanted to throw it out there. If you fancied a seaside escape, just know that me and Carla would love to have you here. In general, I have always found that the sea air does the world of good. Zero pressure. Offer is always there. x

I sink into the bubbles, my body relaxing into the warm bath water. Any remaining doubts about my decision to pull the Naz article melt away completely.

37

NOW

Alice: see you tonight!

Pen: cannot waitttttt

Lola: ME TOO

Me: :)

A few weeks later, I'm back in London as Lola and Fred are hosting an engagement party in Soho at a booked-out restaurant. I wear a sea-green sequin top with black trousers and a light trench. I feel like a new person these days. My skin is clear; my cheeks are naturally blushed pink; my eyes are sparkling; my hair looks voluminous and healthy. Life isn't perfect, but I like what I see: my old, lively self returning. I recognize her – me – again.

When I arrive, there's a man in a blazer who welcomes

me and leads me to the cloakroom. 'It's a lovely coat. Don't worry, I'll look after it,' he says, winking.

Is he flirting with me? It's been such a long time since that last happened.

I walk in, and everyone is milling about. I spot Alice passing around glasses of Champagne.

'You look *fantastic*,' she says, touching my arm. 'I love that colour on you. Pen is just in the loo. How are you? How is Carla?'

'She's OK. She's stable. She's just dealing with it all amazingly, obviously, as she always does. Thanks for asking.'

'Of course. I've been thinking about her so much lately.'

I notice a brown-haired man with laughter lines, nodding along to something Luke has said. *Mike*.

'Everything OK with you?'

'I'm good, actually,' I say, meaning it. 'I'm living with Carla and walking the dogs on the beach every morning. I finally got my Scatterbox money, and I've treated myself to a second-hand Mini.' I picture my cute yellow car parked outside Carla's house. 'I'm loving the freedom it brings me.'

'Oh my *god*, that is so exciting,' Alice says. 'You're like a whole new person. I'm glad Carla is doing OK. As well as she can be.'

'Well, I'm trying to keep her feeling upbeat and I'm so glad I can be there for her. How are you?'

'I'm good. I don't want to steal the limelight today, so that's why I'm wearing a baggy dress, but . . .' She leans in and whispers, 'I'm pregnant.'

I squeeze Alice's wrist, but before I can say anything, Pen comes over.

'Hey,' she says, in her husky voice. 'Good to see you.' She kisses me on the cheek. 'You look *great*.'

'Thank you!'

Mike comes over and puts his hands around Pen's waist.

'So . . . this is Mike,' Pen says, beaming.

'Ah! Finally!' I say, going in for a hug. He is very handsome. Tall, bearded, wearing a dark green cable-knit cardigan.

'So good to meet you, Willow. I've heard so many great things. I'm a little nervous, if I'm honest. Pen's favourite people.'

I grin. A proper smile sweeping across my face that feels warm and golden and real.

'Where's our party girl?' Alice asks.

'She's up there. Wait, why is she standing on a chair?' I say.

Lola gently taps a fork against her glass, getting her footing right on the chair.

'Speech!' someone shouts in the crowd, and we all turn to look at her.

'Hi everyone.' Lola clears her throat. She looks beautiful. She's in the red and pink two-piece she bought when I went shopping with her and her mum, her cheeks are shimmering, and her hair is held in a gorgeous chignon by a glittering gold hair clip. I thought she'd save the two-piece for the wedding itself, but maybe she's got something even more outlandish for the big day. Fred stands up next to her, and they hold hands. 'Can everyone hear me at the back?' Lola asks. 'Firstly, thank you so much for coming tonight. We are so happy you're here on this rainy London evening. We have a bit of an announcement to make, and we wanted you all to be the first to hear it.'

'Surely she's not preggers,' Pen whispers in my ear. 'She's had at least three glasses of fizz tonight already . . .'

'Shh,' I say playfully, as we continue listening.

'This may come as a little bit of a surprise, but Fred and I have actually decided to call off the wedding.'

There is a slight gasp from someone who probably didn't want it to be so audible.

'*No way*,' Pen whispers.

'*What?*' Alice whispers back.

'But *please* don't worry,' Lola says. 'We are still very much in love – more than ever before, in fact. We are more than fine. We just decided recently that marriage isn't really for us.'

'Not blaming Lola's job, *but* . . .' Fred adds.

There is a titter of laughter from the crowd.

'When we started planning everything, it didn't feel right. It didn't feel like something we actually wanted, it was something we just thought we should do. So, we're going to use the money for a deposit for a house instead – turns out weddings are that expensive!'

Laughter emits from the small crowd of people gazing up at her.

'So, tonight, we can all have some drinks and celebrate our relationship but without needing the big song-and-dance wedding. This is our celebration of love – but the wedding is off.'

Fred clears his throat. 'Thanks everyone. What she said. I couldn't be happier to spend my life with you, Lola. But we are promising to show each other our love in small ways daily instead of one big day. Let's raise our glasses to Lola and to celebrating love in a way that suits you!'

I raise my glass.

Celebrate love in a way that suits you.

The next day, we all meet at Lina Stores and sit at our favourite table at the back. The waiter is tall and handsome and fills our glasses with cold water out of a jug. Except for Alice, we're all slightly hungover.

'That was one good party, Lola,' Pen says. 'People should *not* get married more often.'

Lola laughs. 'It was a gorgeous night, and so much love in the room. What more could I want?'

'It was definitely memorable,' I say. 'Proud of you, for doing what feels right.'

'Ha. I do feel relieved. Although I wonder how I'll feel when I call Fred "my boyfriend" when we're both seventy.'

The attention turns to me and Carla.

'How is she doing then, Willow?'

'She's OK. Everything is as steady as it can be. Her oncologist has got her on a treatment plan of drug therapies to try and manage it. We're just taking every day as it comes.'

We all raise our glasses to Carla.

'Can I share some good news?' Alice says, smiling gently my way. I nod. She puts her hands on her belly.

'I knew it!' Pen says excitedly.

'Yup.' Alice is wearing a slightly more fitted dress this time and a small bump is just starting to show.

I smile at her. 'The best news.'

'Luke and I have been keeping it close to our chests for a little while, I just wanted to be as sure as I could be before I shared the news. As you know, it's been quite the journey to get here. I'm so glad I get to tell you now. This baby is going to be so lucky to have you three in their life,' Alice says, beaming.

We order three Aperol spritzes and one alcohol-free version. All four orange drinks arrive, bright and glowing, and that's how the future feels in that moment.

'And how's the driving going, Willow?' Pen asks.

I was telling Pen last night about the refresher lessons I've been taking in the Mini, and now I go into more detail. I tell them about my instructor, Jay, who is six foot with a beard and strawberry-blond hair. He looks a bit like Domhnall Gleeson, and sounds like him, too, with a soothing Irish lilt. I tell them that on our last lesson, he asked me out for a drink. I was caught totally off-guard. I had assumed the whole time that Jay had a girlfriend – he has that kind of settled energy, and driving and chatting with him felt easy and relaxed.

'That's great, Willow! When's the date? He sounds hot!' Lola says.

'Um – I actually said no! But I felt really good about it. I told him that I probably would have said yes a few months ago but that, right now, I'm just enjoying where I'm at. I told him that the whole driving thing is part of a bigger mission to get back to myself, and I'm just not looking for anything at the moment.'

'And what did he say?'

'He just smiled and gave me a big hug, said it was cool, but he would have kicked himself if he hadn't asked. It was totally non-awkward, and maybe we'll hang out as friends one day. But it's made me realize how happy I am to be alone just now.'

Pen grins. 'You and me have done a real switcheroo. Can you believe it's my three-month anniversary with Mike next week? Which feels quite significant after a ten-year drought. But I do have a plot twist . . .'

'You do?' Lola asks.

'We've decided to be in an open relationship.'

'*What!*' Lola says, mouth open, loving it.

'But you were in such a loved-up cocoon?' I say.

'I know, I know. It sounds strange, but hear me out: we think we are each other's *person*. But before we properly settle down and do the full-blown commitment thing, and kids and whatever, we have agreed to let each other have fun in other ways. We have to be honest with each other – that's our only rule.'

'That sounds extremely mature and modern,' Lola says.

'Thank you,' Pen says, flicking her hair behind her shoulder.

'What does it mean, like, logistically?' Alice asks, her Type-A brain whirring.

'Well, it's not for everyone – but we have decided to be boyfriend and girlfriend and do the coupley "thing" together – Sunday nights on the sofa and ordering pizza and being each other's date to things. But we're also not really putting a hard line on it. We both miss the unboundaried freedom of singleness. We both want to shag other people still, basically.'

'Oh my god, I've gone bright red.' Alice laughs, hands on her cheeks. 'I'm such a prude.'

'Wow, I am genuinely impressed!' I say. 'Good for you.'

'Thanks, guys. I've honestly never been happier. I feel supported and adored by Mike, but I also feel like we both have access to the "unknown" and "what ifs", at the same time. We have all these boundaries and values we must uphold, too – and always be transparent and safe with it all. But yeah. It might change, and I'll keep you posted. But that's my announcement.'

'Get you. A girl that can do both,' Lola says, winking.

'I loved meeting him last night,' I say. 'Good vibes, that one.'

'I think people should celebrate *not* doing stuff more often,' Lola says. 'Weirdly, since deciding to not get married, my relationship with Fred has just got better and better. I am obsessed with him again.'

'Not getting married is the new getting married,' Pen says.

'Being in an open relationship is the new norm,' Lola says.

'Being single is the new being loved-up,' I say.

'You are all mad, but I love you,' Alice says, laughing, rubbing her belly.

38

THEN

September 1994

I remember, when I was about six, there was a gold trunk with a ribbon on it waiting in a corner of Carla's living room.

'I got this for you, Willow,' my mum said to me, crouching down to open the clasp. 'Belated birthday present.' Inside were dressing-up trinkets: some lace gloves, a hat with bells on, stripy socks, a vintage ball gown, some old boxing gloves, and a magic wand. To my child self, this was the best gift ever. A portal to a magical made-up land.

I hugged her tightly, hip-height. It felt like every birthday and Christmas rolled into one.

'Look,' she said, frantically taking out the gloves and long socks. 'Nice things to play with, right?'

I laid out all the different things and started pulling on the gown and waving around the wand.

'I love it!' I said, swirling around in the pink gown made of taffeta.

'What have we got here?' Carla said, entering the room with a cup of tea. She put on her new Cher CD (*Greatest Hits 1965–1992*), and I started dancing around the living room, carefree, a child, zero inhibitions, unaware of how I looked or sounded or appeared, lost in the moment.

'What an amazing present your mum got you! Let's have a look!' Carla pulled out a feather boa, and my mum put on the old boxing gloves, laughing as she tried to hug me wearing them. The three of us started twirling around with Carla's feather boa, getting more and more tangled up, dancing and letting ourselves be silly to 'The Shoop Shoop Song'.

Later that night, I crept to the kitchen because I couldn't sleep. The house was quiet; Carla was stacking the dishwasher. I couldn't see Mum. Maybe she was in bed. Everything felt fuzzy, like time was moving slowly, like I was inside a goldfish bowl.

Before I had time to ask where Mum was, Carla made me a hot chocolate and put marshmallows on the top ('Shh, I know you've already brushed your teeth'), and we sat in the garden, wrapped in blankets, watching big colourful fireworks being set off next door by our neighbours celebrating Diwali. A welcome distraction.

I learned early on that Carla was the one responsible for my happy memories. It was always Carla. She was behind everything. She'd organized the dressing-up box – I saw a receipt in her handbag the next day.

39

NOW

After five months of living at Carla's, I move into a new duplex near the Olympic Park in London. I wanted to plant my roots in East London, and I found something I could afford. Carla comes to stay for a few days after I get the keys. We order her favourite pineapple pizza for dinner. I eat it on the floor and Carla sits in the one armchair I currently have as the sofa is yet to arrive, her new walking stick resting against it. It brings back a memory of when Dom and I moved into our dream house and we ordered pizza, and I'm surprised to feel warm affection for that moment in my life, rather than the punch in the gut I'd become used to.

Although I have the keys to my new place, I won't be living here full-time straight away. I still want to be near Carla. Nothing else matters. I wanted to delay the move, but Carla put her foot down, and insisted on making the trip here so she could see it and witness me in my new space. Driving her into London in my new yellow Mini felt symbolic. It feels good to have the keys to the flat and for something to feel sorted after so much chaos and lack of control.

Carla moves more slowly now. The soles of her feet hurt, her fingernails are cracked, her mouth is very dry, and her eyes are red and itchy. I try to ignore these things when I look at her.

'I'm so glad you have your own place now. It's important I know you'll be settled when I'm not around,' she says.

'Oh, come on, don't talk like that.'

'Darling, we both know what's coming.'

'I find it hard to talk about.'

'I know. But not talking about it might make it even harder.'

It's nothing I didn't already know. Carla didn't respond well to her last round of chemotherapy, and the sand-timer has appeared above both of our heads.

I go into the kitchen and put slices of lemon cake on two plates. I realize I am crying. I look out of the window into the small garden, a similar size to the one I had with Dom.

I hand Carla a plate, and I lean down to give her a hug; she feels squishy and round and soft.

'You better not be all wearing black to my funeral. I've never worn black in my life. Too depressing.'

'We'll do whatever you want,' I say, wiping away tears, unable to hide them.

She makes a joke that she wants to be carried in a casket while 'I'm Still Standing' by Elton John is playing. I don't find it funny at all, but I can't help choking out a laugh, feeling her gentle warmth and humour as always.

'Also, none of those weird formal funeral parlours. Too corporate. I've seen too many celebrants networking and handing out business cards at funerals. It's not an open-mic night! All I want is a very small gathering on Eastbourne beach, OK? A handful of people, drinks, music. See me off in a fun, less fusty way, please.'

'OK, but we don't have to think about all this yet.'

'All right, but I'm making a playlist whether you like it or not. And it *will* be a groovy one.'

'I've made the bed up for you,' I say, changing the conversation, helping to guide her towards the bedroom. 'Extra-firm pillows, just how you like it.'

She takes my bed, and I sleep in the living room. I still don't have any curtains, but I don't mind. I have a space of my own. I'm waiting on a few deliveries but everything in here is chosen by me: leopard-print cushions that Dom would have never allowed, fun lamps, patterned rugs, ornamental vases, painted plates, new trinkets from Etsy. Carla bought me a neon candle in the shape of someone giving the middle finger. A mid-century table and chairs I found on eBay are arriving tomorrow. I have only a small number of plates, bowls, and cutlery. I have framed pictures of all my favourite independent bookshops in the kitchen, including Daunt's.

Every little corner makes me smile, because it reflects my tastes and inner joy. It's a much smaller space than what I had with Dom, but there is something comforting about that. I have a small writing desk in the corner of my bedroom, and above it, I've stuck up Polaroid pictures of my friends and old photos with Carla and me in the sea, and lots of fun perfume bottles are dotted around. I have space for all my favourite things: inspirational quotes and lyrics, ornaments, crystals, posters, the rose-quartz gift from Naz. I feel like a hopeful teenager again, like I can feng shui my room and my life at any point. Multiple small rooms of my own.

A few weeks later, back in Eastbourne with Carla, I pick Naz up from the train station. I am nervous. It's been so long since I've seen her. She comes out of the station wearing a green shacket, her dark hair is tied up, not as glossy this time, and she's not got any make-up or jewellery on. She looks gentler and softer. She has a large tote bag on one arm, and she carries a hamper with her other hand.

'A selection of goodies for you,' she says, greeting me. Sheet masks, bath salts, sample moisturizers – which is really thoughtful.

'It's so good to see you,' I say, giving her a hug.

'You too. Thank you so much for letting the invitation stand for so long! I'm slowly getting back on my feet. Some fresh sea air is exactly what is needed at this stage.'

'I'm so glad. Also, Naz, just a heads-up,' I say, opening the passenger door of my Mini, 'Carla is using a walking stick now. She's lacking a lot of energy these days.'

'I'm so sorry, Willow.'

'I just have to enjoy every minute with her,' I say, a lump sticking in my throat.

'I'm really honoured that you've invited me, especially with what Carla's going through. It's really very kind.'

'We've been thinking about you.'

I drive the short distance to Carla's and she arrives at the front door, leaning on her stick. She smiles when she sees the hamper that Naz is holding.

'Oh, you sweet girl, thank you,' Carla says, hugging Naz, welcoming her in. 'It's fab to finally meet you – I've heard so much.'

'Likewise – I'm so excited to meet the *iconic* Carla! I'm really sorry to hear about what you're going through.'

'Thank you. You know what's strange? Life feels good, all things considered.'

'Who are these two?' Naz says, kicking off her shoes and getting down on the floor to greet the dogs.

'Bubble and Squeak.'

The two naughty dachshunds run around Naz's feet, sniffing and licking her toes.

'It's such a lovely place you've got here,' Naz says politely, looking around at all the dachshund merch.

'It's felt weird not seeing or speaking to you after spending so much time together,' I say.

'I know! We got so used to hanging out, didn't we? How is *Z Life* doing?' She smirks.

'God knows. Trying not to look too closely. They seem to be doing the weirdest content on their site. "10 Celebrities Who Look Like Pieces of Bread" or whatever. Good riddance.'

'How have you been doing, darling?' Carla asks Naz. 'Come into the kitchen, we'll get you a drink and a snack.'

'I'm on the mend. I feel like a weight has been lifted off my shoulders, but at the same time like I'm in limbo.' I can tell she feels a bit awkward, complaining to Carla of all people, right now.

'Change can be very good, but of course at first it can feel incredibly destabilizing,' Carla says, taking a seat in the kitchen. I get some mugs out for us.

'Have you been OK, day to day?' I ask.

'It's all still a big mess financially, but I'm lucky I have enough savings to tide me over for a bit. I'm off social media and just having a break from everything. I've been journalling. I've been borrowing a friend's dog. I've been watching Disney movies. I feel free for the first time ever! I am a bit worried about what's next. I've decided I just need to get through this stage of recovery by taking baby steps.'

Carla smiles. 'Turtle steps.'

'*Exactly*,' Naz says. 'Turtle steps.'

For lunch, I cook a big red-pepper risotto with garlic bread. We're still sat at Carla's kitchen table, and although it's very mild, she has her slippers on and a blanket over her lap. The back doors are open, and it's a crisp, sunny day. The seagulls are cawing loudly, and we're drinking orange juice out of beakers.

'Do you fancy going down to the beach after lunch?' I ask.

'Yes please,' Naz says.

'I'd love that,' Carla says. Bubble and Squeak run around, clearly keen. 'Shall we drive? I won't be able to walk down there, but it's probably good for me to stretch my legs a little.'

We take a picnic blanket and a basket to the beach. Naz and I strip off down to our bikinis and I get a peek of all her tattoos again. In this vulnerable sunlit moment, she really reminds me of my mum.

'Come on, let's go in,' she says, standing up and dropping her towel on the sand.

'Oh god, it's going to be freezing.'

It's early summer, and the sun is high in the sky, but this is Eastbourne after all.

'You can do it. Remember when we went to the lido together? You were so worried, and then you loved it.'

She's right. I take in a deep lungful of air and start walking towards the water. It's just me, the sea, this moment in time.

I hop on my tiptoes, psyching myself up, and hear Naz laughing further up the beach.

'Go on, I'm right behind you!' she shouts. 'On the count of three, you're going in.'

'OK.'

'Right, one . . . two . . . three . . . !'

I run into the shallows. And as the water hits my feet, I feel a sense of hope, excitement, and thrill for the future. It is piercingly cold, but I take on the challenge, and I keep going, keep wading, until my chest is in, and then I submerge myself, head under, until my whole body feels free and expansive, unsure of its edges, at one with the water, a slight numbness taking over.

'You're IN!' Naz says, laughing, hopping wildly across the pebbles and launching herself in with a shriek.

'Oh my fucking GOD, it's cold,' I say, my arms flailing about.

'We did it!'

When we get out, Carla is on the beach, wrapped up warm in her bright red duffel coat, with a flask of hot coffee and our towels.

'Well done, girls!' she says, handing us the towels. Our biggest fan. 'Better you than me.'

'It's invigorating! I can understand why people get addicted to this feeling,' I say, taking the lid off the flask and blowing on my coffee.

We settle down on the picnic blanket and dry off.

'How's it going with Loz, by the way?' I ask.

'Oh – we broke up,' Naz says quietly.

'Oh, I'm sorry.'

'No, it's fine. It wasn't right. She's a lovely girl though. And I'm not annoyed that it happened either. In a weird way, it was a blessing. I was so trapped in that career I'd made for myself, and I guess my relationship with Loz freed me of it – it's just a shame I fell into such a hole. I was confused about everything: who I am, what I want . . . everything. I felt like I'd let people down. I felt like I'd outed Loz, too. I think she regrets it more than me. We're still friends though. It's OK.'

'People shouldn't have spied on you,' Carla says, blowing on her coffee. 'Very uncouth.'

'With a job like mine, the boundaries are so blurred. I was making money off my life, so people felt like I had no right to privacy. Maybe they had a point.'

'Are you able to have some privacy now?' I ask.

'I think so. I did see a weird paparazzi guy outside my house the other day. But I think they'll get bored soon. I'm looking forward to being a no one.' She smiles.

'No paps in Eastbourne, at least,' Carla says, zipping up her coat. Bubble and Squeak sit patiently on her lap.

That night, Naz and I watch a film on my laptop in bed, *Pretty Woman*, and we relax comfortably in our pyjamas. Then I brush my hair and take off my make-up, while Naz brushes her teeth in the en suite. Instead of going into Carla's office with the pulled-out futon, Naz sleeps in my bed with me. We fall asleep with a blanket on top of us, her hair spread out all over the pillow, her breathing light.

Naz takes up a lot of the bed, so I wake up in the night and can't get back to sleep. I need a bit more space. I smile to myself, pulling the blanket over Naz, so that she's tucked in, all cosy. I go across the landing into Carla's room.

Carla has a massive super-king and, like I have so many times before, I get into bed with her. She doesn't stir. I wrap my arm around her, surprised all over again by the increasing slimness of her frame; as if she's lesser somehow. The dogs are curled up into little doughnuts, sleeping on the end of the bed, and the sun is just about to appear on the horizon.

The next morning, we eat bacon sandwiches outside on the patio. Naz and Carla share a sneaky rollie, bonding over their occasional 'social smoker' behaviour. I take the dirty plates inside, give them a rinse, and then I walk down the corridor for a moment alone. I go into my room, and I brush the dust off the typewriter that sits underneath my desk. I'm always amazed at how heavy it is, how big and brutal. If you dropped it, you'd break your toes. I decided to keep it here at Carla's for now, keeping a little piece of me here, knowing I'll take it to the new flat soon.

I click the buttons and enjoy the satisfying, sturdy sound they make.

NAZ CHOPRA AND ME: HOW I LOST A CAREER AND FOUND A NEW FRIEND

I was supposed to write an article about a woman who lived the opposite life to me. I was commissioned to write the piece by my old boss, a powerful New York editor, and I was excited. I'd just been dumped, and I'd lost contact with myself and my career. This was a way back into writing, to rediscovering myself.

My subject was online influencer Naz Chopra: the Gen Z poster girl, apparently living a big and beautiful single life. I spent a lot of time with her, so that I could get under her skin, tell her story.

I didn't expect to become friends with Naz. A good journalist keeps themselves at a distance. They find the friction, the controversy, and where they can, they puncture their subject. That's what my boss wanted me to do.

I thought online influencers were meaningless – a bit of cultural fluff, a pixellated square we scroll past when hungover in bed or in need of something weightless, moreish, and easy to go down: sickly like candy-floss. What I didn't realize is how much someone online, who you don't even know, can influence your life and bring some sunlight into it during trying times.

During my break-up, I received inspiration from captions and videos and pictures, giving me a sense of the path I could take. When all my friends were busy, and I was feeling lost, one woman on the Internet gave me a boost. Little harmless dopamine hits. A lifestyle. A narrative. An idea of who I could be. A new story. A way out.

Even if the life shown in the pixels doesn't match the reality, it's still OK to be inspired by stories on a screen. We get to befriend the people inside our phones and sometimes figure out who they really are. There's a word for online or 'borderless' friendships: asynchronous friendships. A modern kind of friendship built on voice notes, messages, DMs, WhatsApps, online comment sections, different time zones. These days, we can strike up friendships in so many different ways, in so many different forums, based on so many different interests.

Naz's perfect online persona didn't match up to who she was. Of course it didn't. It's impossible to tell the story of your life via a screen. But our friendship came at the best possible time for me. I needed an injection of youth, hope, optimism – and this is what an Internet friend can give you. A new direction, even if it's part fantasy.

Your friendships don't have to look a certain way. You don't need to hang out with your partner's female friends for the sake of it. You don't need to contort yourself to please others. You don't have to be friends with someone just because you always have. You can reinvent yourself whenever you want. You can embrace new people into your life at any stage. Your family can look different, too – Carla, my wonderful, inspiring aunt, taught me that.

40

AND THEN

On the day she dies, I feel my body vibrate, festering with anger, like a firework trying not to go off in a tiny room. I have so much love for our care team, for the way they made us feel, the safety they created, enabling her to die in relative peace.

I keep thinking of the first book Carla read to me as a kid: *We're Going on a Bear Hunt. We can't go over it. We can't go under it. Oh no! We've got to go through it!* How kids' books are full of things you only understand once you're an adult. I actually saw a young boy reading *We're Going on a Bear Hunt* in the children's cancer ward on the way to see Carla. I remember feeling such a sense of injustice for all of it.

In the final weeks, Carla distracted herself by planning her own funeral. She kept making jokes about it. She called it 'deathmin' and kept asking me what I was going to wear for the big day. Big sunglasses? A sunhat? I would get annoyed with her for making jokes and then get annoyed with myself for policing her emotions and humour.

We have a private cremation and then the funeral happens on the beach, just as she wanted. She picked photos, poems, a mix of songs: 'This Year's Love' by David Gray for when we all sat down; 'You've Got the Love' by Florence and the Machine when we all walked out. She asked me to read 'Poem 133: The Summer Day' by Mary Oliver.

When the day comes, I can't do it, which surprises me. I just can't get the words out; my throat closes over. A deep sadness and stickiness takes over my whole body. Pen reads it for me. She does a brilliant job, and I feel so proud of her and so glad to have her in my life, up there, doing it for me, doing it for Carla. Carla always loved Pen.

A portable projector plays Carla's favourite photos on a slide show. Funny ones of me cross-eyed, Bubble and Squeak wearing little hats on the beach, Carla skinny-dipping, covering her boobs with her hands, Carla on holiday with a massive spliff. That photo of her and Mum wearing feather boas from the fancy dress box.

Her best friend Marta, from the Eastbourne book club, leads the ceremony as a celebrant, with the blue sea behind her, and so everything feels personal. There are so many tears but so much laughter, too, hours of crying and spluttering and so many tissues.

The whole day is the most incredible evidence of love. Carla never had a partner. She had boyfriends before I was born, but in the time I've known her, she's always been a lone ranger. She loved living alone, taking slow walks, enjoying her dogs, her life, her quirky possessions, her own space. She had endless capacity to love, a big open heart that cared for the people close to her.

Afterwards, we go to her favourite pub, The Eagle, and there are more photos everywhere, hundreds of them, lining the walls, the photo album of her life. Carla at her graduation. Carla leading her book club. Countless photos of Carla and me. I need a breather and go outside into the beer garden.

Pen stands in the doorway.

'What do I do now?' I say, looking at her, my eyes stinging.

Pen comes over, and then Lola and Alice appear, all three of them putting their arms tightly around me.

'What do I do now?' I repeat, blinking with confusion.

That night, Lola, Pen, and Alice stay with me at Carla's house. A pregnant Alice sleeps next to me in the bed, and Lola and Pen sleep on a blow-up mattress on the floor.

'Sorry if I wake you by getting up to wee a hundred times in the night,' Alice says, holding her bump with both hands.

'Don't worry. I'm just so grateful that you are here.'

'Good night. I love you,' Pen says, turning out the light.

I wake in the middle of the night and can't get back to sleep. The girls are sleeping, snoring gently, and I quietly open the drawer next to my bed to get some lavender spray, which I hope might help. Inside, my fingers snag on a piece of folded paper tucked right at the back of the drawer. It feels thin and fragile. I gently pull it out and unfold it.

By the light of my phone, I can see it's the poem I wrote to Carla decades ago.

Today, in London, you bought me a quill!
You always look after me when I'm ill.
We are lying down in sunny Holland Park.
You always encourage me to make my mark,
Taking back control after years of sadness.
You make me believe I'm surely not full of badness.
My auntie, my friend, my light.
How lucky I am, when you turn off my lamp to say goodnight.

I put it in my pocket and decide to walk down to the beach, while the others are sleeping. I pull on a long, quilted coat, slide on a pair of wellies. Out of habit I turn to pick up the leads for Bubble and Squeak, then glance at their empty baskets. The dogs have gone to live with Carla's friend, Marta. It pains me, but it's the best thing for them.

I carefully shut the front door behind me and step out into the night. It's so dark, the dim streetlights lining the pavement. I sit on an empty wooden bench and look out to sea. I settle in, listening to the gentle lull of the waves being pulled in and out. *Where are you, Carla? I know you're out there somewhere.* Is she in the clouds? The water? The rock formations? How can someone with so much energy and vibrancy just go? It doesn't make sense.

I think about a conversation I had with Pen on the night Tina Turner died. We were pretty sure that the energy from a person who's so powerful and unique must get transferred onto other living people when they die. Someone else gets a big zap of musical energy. A rotation of atoms and magic. Surely it has to go somewhere.

I wonder whether some of Carla's energy will come to me? I try and breathe her in. I take off my shoes and pad down to the shallow waves.

I let the tears fall and fall and fall.

One Year On

41

Pen: Have the best time. I'm going to missssss yooooou

Alice: Send us a postcard please <3

Lola: please get me one of those lighters with a very tanned man who becomes naked when you turn it upside down. Will miss you loads. See you in a few months, adventurer

Alice: Text us when you land xxxx

The airport is busy. Screaming babies, arguing couples, toddlers running off, nervous flyers spraying Rescue Remedy onto their tongues. I see two young girls holding a sign that says 'Welcome home Mum', and I let the feeling go through me, like a little shard of glass coming out of my skin, hurting a little less each time. Allowing it to pass.

Weighed down by a huge backpack, I walk to one of the many chain outlets and grab a takeaway coffee. The man serving me keeps doing different accents and speaking different languages and making little jokes; he reminds me of a young Robin Williams. I laugh along, while other customers just look totally confused by his charm and odd humour.

I sit and put my bag down, resting my shoulders.

The girls pepper the WhatsApp group with airplane emojis and kisses.

I go into WHSmith, and that's when I see it. It's hard to ignore. I turn around, go to leave, but can't resist getting a proper look. Dom and his two partners are on the front page of a broadsheet newspaper in the top left-hand corner, smiling with their arms folded. The headline reads: 'Best Friend Founders Sell Online Company for £25.5 Million. Read more of the story in the Business section, page 14.'

Did I need to see it?

I knew deep down that Dom would succeed in his business venture; he was so committed to it. I pick the newspaper up, but I don't turn to read the full story on page 14. I don't need to.

I feel a swelling in my chest, a sense of past grief, but I don't feel overwhelmed. I don't feel the need to go elsewhere and cry in private; I don't need to put my bag down; I don't need to call anyone. This is a huge relief. I feel settled in my body. Good for him. Good for Scatterbox. I don't even feel knocked by the huge sum of money. This must mean I am finally free. I am a little goat on top of a mountain.

Me: just saw the Telegraph piece today – have you seen it?

Lola: I have . . . you OK?

Me: I am. I genuinely feel OK

Lola: ♥♥ have an amazing trip, won't you?

I go to text Carla.
That happens a lot.
I walk into the Chanel store, just to look, and the women behind the counter give my feet a strange look. I'm wearing big hiking boots and thick socks, and my legs haven't been shaved for weeks. I smile at them and leave, knowing that there's no point staying in there any longer, and I don't want to, anyway. I may not be rich or have millions like Dom, but I have all the time in the world right now, and I can do anything and go anywhere. It's all up to me.

I have a Substack now, and I write about whatever is on my mind: a perfect solo day out in London; a piece on how difficult it is to stay true to your values if you choose a cut-throat career like journalism. I don't have a huge number of followers, but I have enough to know people are listening. Along with the money from renting out my flat, it should bring in just enough to sustain me on my travels, so long as I stick to the cheaper hostels.

I don't go into any other shops, and instead I go to my gate and sit down, looking up at the screen. The 3.30 p.m. Emirates flight to Vietnam, boarding in twenty minutes. I take a seat in the waiting area, and place my big bag down on the floor, relaxing my shoulders, rotating one of my arms. There's a family of four in front of me, all fighting over the iPad, the mother frantically trying to get her two children to eat some sandwiches. She looks exhausted and hands out grapes from a Tupperware box.

That's when I feel a tap on my shoulder.

'Oh my god – Willow?'

I turn around. The glossy hair, the dewy face.

Naz.

'It *is* you! That could have been embarrassing, I wasn't sure . . .' She opens her arms wide and wants to embrace me, which I let her do. 'I always bump into people in airports. It's a thing that always happens to me. This is wild.'

'Oh my god, hi!'

'How are you?' she asks.

'I'm good! I actually tried to email you recently.'

'Ah, I'm offline. Look, this is my phone right now.'

She pulls a little Nokia 3310 out of her jeans pocket.

'I got it off Etsy.' She starts laughing. 'How are you?'

She's standing next to a woman wearing dungarees, with a tiny bit of grey running through the roots of her hair. 'Oh and this is Steph. My girlfriend.' She squeezes Steph's wrist, and they smile at each other. 'Steph, Willow is a friend of mine.' Steph smiles at me, with soft wrinkles around her eyes, she looks to be mid-thirties.

'Lovely to meet you,' she says.

'How are you, seriously? Where are you off to?' Naz says.

'I'm good. I'm really good! I'm actually off on a travelling adventure for six months. Starting in Vietnam. First big trip I've done alone.' I smile.

'Amazing.'

'And where are you off to?'

'We're going to Thailand to visit some of Steph's family.'

I smile at her. She looks and sounds like a totally different person. Instagram wouldn't have allowed someone to have such a rebrand. She's so far away from Single Naz.

'I need the loo, I'll be back in a mo,' Steph says.

Naz and I are alone, and the energy shifts slightly.

'I'm sorry we lost touch. You were a good friend to me, Willow, during that rocky patch. How is Carla doing?' she says hesitantly.

'Oh, um, she—' A lump in my throat. I can't say it.

'Oh no. Willow . . .'

'Yeah . . .'

'I'm so, so sorry . . .'

'It all happened really quickly.'

'She was absolutely amazing. One in a million.'

'I know,' I say.

She saved me. Over and over again. You saved me, too, is what I want to say.

It feels like we could say so much more. It doesn't feel appropriate to go too deep, right here in this airport lounge. Our lives have practically reversed and swapped over.

There's an announcement to say my gate is open; my flight is boarding now.

Steph comes back and links arms with Naz.

'I've got to go for my flight. I'm rereading this by the way,'

I say, taking the copy of *Little Women* that Naz bought me out of my bag.

'Oh! I'm so glad. Take care of yourself, Willow. Let's stay in touch. I mean it.'

I watch them walk away until they disappear into the lounge of their boarding gate. I grab my bag and take out my passport. I take a big belly breath in, knowing that so much of my life is still ahead, just waiting to be discovered and enjoyed. Wondering if I fell in love with Naz or just fell in love with her attitude of spontaneity, generosity, and warmth. I love who I am right now, the butterfly version of me, flitting from moment to moment, a far cry from that woman in the fitting room.

I walk through the tunnel towards the big plane with the other passengers. I look up at the pale pink sky and think of Carla, trying to find her face up there in the big fluffy clouds I will soon be flying through, and I think to myself: *she would be so proud of me.* Her ashes are with me in my bag. The plan is to take them somewhere beautiful.

As I take my window seat, a young child is kicking the back of it. I turn around.

'This . . . is for you,' she says in her tiny voice, holding out a sticker of a purple butterfly.

After a day of hiking and cold-water swimming, I'm sitting in a café up in the mountains, with my laptop in front of me and a mango smoothie. The group leader on the hike had this idea of writing something we want to 'let go of' onto rocks. I smiled – I've done that before – and thought of Ms Gower as we threw those pebbles into the sea one by one. I remember writing *Always follow your own path* – and I guess I'm doing that now; I don't have much choice.

I'm exhausted but happy. I am getting perspective – a break from the rat race of life. Every morning, I make my bed in my hostel, open the curtains, look out at the vibrancy of the nature surrounding me and the steps down to the clear pool that I've been swimming in each morning, excited for what the day has in store. I think of Naz's constellation of tattoos and the infinite possibilities in an expanding universe.

I spend the day with strangers who now feel like friends, with no small talk, just deep conversation, bonding in a way that feels easy since we'll likely never cross paths again. There is a large age range on this trip; from twenty-one to seventy-five. It makes me excited to grow older, to learn from other women, to say 'yes' more often.

I ride on mopeds and think of the first bike Carla bought me for my twelfth birthday. I knew it was a bike, because she'd wrapped it up but it was still hilariously bike-shaped. It was in the hallway decorated with a bow, because she had nowhere else to store it. When I told her I wanted to cycle to Pen's house, she didn't stop me. She did sit me down and talk to me, though, like I was a small adult. *Don't take random sweets. Ask to use someone's phone in case of emergency. Come home before dark.* The bike was shiny red and had a little basket on the front. I put some chocolate bars in there, one to give to Pen, and I remember feeling such a sense of independence.

I think of Carla every day.

I have factor fifty on my face, and lighter strawberry-blonde streaks are appearing in my red hair from the constant sun. It's 27°C and beautiful, and I sip on my ice-cold mango smoothie in a plastic cup. I feel like I'm seeing the world for the first time, really looking, really taking it all in. The way the trees dance. The way the sun reflects like a jewel on the water. I have nowhere to be and nowhere I need to go. I am happy in the unknown, and time stretches out before me in an expansive way – no longer haunting me. The illusion has been snapped, and now I can't unsee the beauty of the world.

I log onto the Wi-Fi; it's slow, but I just want to check in with my life back home for a moment. My emails take ages to load, but eventually I see one from Alice with some pictures of baby Grace, Lola and Fred at the top of the Eiffel Tower, and Pen and Mike on a retreat in Devon. A marketing email from Nike and one from Netflix. And then, one from Naz.

From: Naz <nc_personal@gmail.com>
To: Willow <willowjones@hotmail.com>

So good (and wild) to bump into you at the airport the other day! I love it when the universe does that.

I'm so, so incredibly sorry about Carla, Willow.

I cannot even compute what a loss this is to you, to the world. She was a powerhouse, and you are just like her. She loved you so, so much. I am thinking of you a lot right now. I feel so lucky that I got to meet her. I will never forget her.

I am here if you need anything.

PS! I can't believe I forgot to send you this. I hope you like it.

I open the attachment, and it takes about ten minutes to load. While it buffers, I peel a banana and eat it slowly, looking out of the window and watching the birds make patterns in the sky. It opens, and I plug my headphones into my laptop so that I can listen. It's a video Naz took on the beach at Eastbourne that I had no idea she'd filmed. It's four minutes long, and it's a series of moments of Carla and me.

The owner of the café goes outside for a cigarette, perfect timing, leaving me alone with the video, with the screen, with Carla. Naz's film-work is shaky; she films me running into the sea and then zooms in on Carla's face as she laughs, her eyes wrinkling, petting the dogs, looking up at the sun, the orange glow on her face.

Carla is holding my sandals for me on the sand, urging me to go in further – *be brave, Willow! Be brave!* – her scarf blowing in the wind, her smile wide and her hair unruly. She is watching me, really watching me, encouraging me to go a little deeper.

From the sea, I paddle my feet in the freezing water, then turn around and wave at her, smiling, blowing her a kiss. She is standing back at a distance, waving her hands to encourage me further.

I close my eyes and remember that moment like a freeze-frame in my mind, feeling as though it was a dream and now I have it captured forever. My eyes hold my tears gently, balancing them before they spill.

Carla: the woman who always encouraged me to be brave, to move forward, to be OK on my own. To love deeply, to see the world, to believe in myself.

I look around the café. At this place far away from home where I've somehow ended up, at this brave version of myself that I've become – or maybe always was. Maybe Naz was right: when we wake up each morning, we get to choose who we want to be. I think of Dom and smile – he was brave enough to tread his own path. And, eventually, so was I.

I open up my laptop and start a fresh Word document with the cursor blinking at me.

Working title: *Table for One.*

Acknowledgements

I tackled the final edits of this book in New York where I spent a month alone in Brooklyn (and yes, many times asking for a 'table for one'). Thank you to my husband Paul, my family, and friends, who understand my deep need for stretches of time alone to write and digest life.

Thank you to Ruby Warrington for the opportunity, Sophia Efthimiatou for your support and kindness, Donna Freitas for the coffee dates (and for reading an early version of this novel when it was originally called *Willow*). Thank you to The Strand bookstore for being a great place to wander around and attend events when you're alone and away from home.

Novels are a labour of love, and this one really was. There were so many wrong turns before I found the way.

Thank you to my wonderful literary agent Viola Hayden

at Curtis Brown. Thank you Ciara Finan for your extra support along the way.

A heartfelt thank you to Charlotte Brabbin, my editor at HarperCollins who walked this long uphill path alongside me and read countless (and I mean countless!) drafts. I'm so proud of where we ended up. I'm glad we got to have a celebratory moment in New York together.

Gratitude to the wider HarperCollins team: Liz Dawson, Maud Davies, Emily Merrill, Katie Lumsden, Frankie Gray and Kate Elton. Thank you Ellie Game for the wonderful jacket.

Thank you to early readers and writer friends. Abigail Bergstrom, for reading an early draft via your brilliant Bergstrom Studio and for being a believing mirror. Lucy Gannon, for a much-needed pep talk when I really needed it. Katy Loftus, for the voice notes and phone calls while we walked and talked. Laura Palmer, for your experienced eye, you really saved the day. Thank you to my dad and Paul for being my last-minute proofreaders.

My friends and teachers: Donna Lancaster, Fiona Arrigo, Julia Cameron, Elizabeth Gilbert, Alice Vincent, Jess Pan, Katherine May, Daisy B, Leyla Kazim, Jenn Romolini, Kim France and Farrah Storr. You all inspire me with your words and friendship.

A shout out to some of my favourite independent bookstores: Daunt Books, Phlox Books, Ink@84, Harbour Books, The Accidental Bookshop, The Edge of the World Bookshop, Books Are Magic, Shakespeare and Company, and Salted Books. Go support your favourite indie bookstore.

Thank you to my Substack community on thehyphen.substack.com, I love you all.